DEATH AT THE OLD HOTEL

OTHER BRIAN MCNULTY MYSTERIES BY CON LEHANE

What Goes Around Comes Around
Beware the Solitary Drinker

DEATH
AT THE OLD HOTEL

CON LEHANE

THOMAS DUNNE BOOKS
ST. MARTIN'S MINOTAUR ⚞ NEW YORK

This is a work of fiction. All of the characters, organizations,
and events portrayed in this novel are either products of the
author's imagination or are used fictitiously.

THOMAS DUNNE BOOKS.
An imprint of St. Martin's Press.

www.thomasdunnebooks.com
www.minotaurbooks.com

ISBN-13: 978-0-312-32300-4
ISBN-10: 0-312-32300-X

10   9   8   7   6   5   4   3   2

To Jim van Etten

Author's Note

The New York City that appears in these pages is filtered through the author's imagination. I've taken liberties with streets and buildings, as well as sections of the city. For example, there are many hotels in Manhattan, but the old Savoy is not one of them. Bainbridge is a section of the north Bronx at the end of the D line, but it is a different place than the one described here: You'll look in vain for the Old Shillelagh, an Irish butcher shop, or Christmas lights. Finally, there is a grand tradition of Irish cops in the NYPD, but none of them ever belonged to the Friendly Sons of Ireland, which as far as I know never existed.

For we knew only too well:
Even the hatred of squalor
Makes the brow grow stern.
Even anger against injustice
Makes the voice grow harsh. Alas, we
Who wished to lay the foundations of kindness
Could not ourselves be kind.

—Bertolt Brecht

"The fooker is spying on us," Barney said.

We were working the stick at the old Savoy Hotel, and the action at the bar was slowing after a busier than usual Thursday night dinner rush. The hotel was almost full, the occupancy rate bolstered by out-of-town Christmas shoppers and the dining room by a couple of holiday parties from neighboring offices. The Savoy Hotel, which is gone now, in those days was located on the far west side of Manhattan, west of Eighth Avenue on 48th Street, and the fooker Barney referred to was the hotel's manager, James MacAlister. The Savoy had seen better days, even then in the early '90s—as had many of us who worked there—but the rooms were clean, the restaurant prices reasonable, and the food better than you'd expect two blocks north of Restaurant Row, thanks to the French chef, Francois DeLouge, who'd bounced around the hotels of New York almost as long as I had.

The establishment boasted a staff of journeymen hoteliers, many of whom had been there since the hotel's heyday. Barney Saunders, my partner behind the bar, a wild young Irishman and a good bartender to boot, had been at the Savoy a year or so before I arrived and had already built a pretty good bar business. There was a growing coterie of regulars, and with some business from the dining room, that's really all a bartender needs to make a living. For the nights later in the week, we had Tiny Waters at the piano. All in all it was as good as many bartending gigs in the city and better than some. The problem was that the pay scale was lower and the benefits fewer than at the other union hotels in the city.

How Barney and I found ourselves in this hotel on the western fringes of Manhattan, too near the coast of New Jersey for comfort, is one of those long stories better told on a rainy night when you're still at the bar because you can't get a cab and don't have anywhere much to go if you could get one. Barney was exiled from the mainstream when he fell out of favor with the bartenders union honchos. He brought me on board at the Savoy when I ran afoul of the new management at the Sheraton. The union was processing a grievance for me but, since I was a malcontent like Barney, wasn't in any hurry to settle anything.

On this night, Barney was trying to talk me into a plan he'd hatched to get rid of MacAlister, whom he suspected of being in cahoots with a crooked business agent from the union. As much a natural-born leader as Napoleon—or in his case, Brian Boru—Barney had taken up the rank-and-file rebellion at the Savoy where he'd left off at his former job, and had dragged me into the battle to reform the union.

My devotion to the cause of the workers of the world—and bartenders in particular—was my birthright, my having been born under the sign of the hammer and sickle, so to speak; that is, my parents were Communists. Barney's background was a bit murkier, having to do with, he told me, being born and reared in County Cavan, a stone's throw—or brick, bottle, or stick of gelignite—from the border of the six counties occupied by the British in the north of Ireland.

"Dere's a deal," Barney had told me soon after I arrived, when he explained about the lousy pay and his plans to change things, "a sweetheart of an arrangement if ever there was one, between Eliot and MacAlister." Eliot was the union business agent, who was bad enough, but MacAlister really got Barney's Irish up.

"A whoore of man," said Barney. "A Scotsman that hates the Irish. The man is dangerous, Brian."

MacAlister was a tall, broad-shouldered, deep-chested, arrogant boss-type. Since I'd been there, he and Barney had had a series of run-ins, the latest over Barney's free-pouring. The night he called him on it, Barney's reaction was sudden and violent, surprising me. We'd been through the free-pour versus use-a-shot-glass wars a dozen times. None of us cared that much. But Barney the cheerful, friend of every man, got his back up with the first words out of MacAlister's mouth. I didn't get it until Barney explained at closing time. "A Scotsman lording over an Irishman, Brian. It's in his voice, his eyes. He'll get me if I don't get him first."

A couple of beers later, I learned that this antagonism between the Irish and a segment of the Scots had its origins in the seventeenth century—when the British sent Scots to colonize the north of Ireland. Both the Scots and the Irish had long memories, it seemed, and battles had been raging ever since. Whatever its cause, the change in Barney was remarkable—the hatred resonating in his voice, the no-quarter-given, no-quarter-asked glare cast in the direction of the departing MacAlister. It was like seeing your old pooch who wagged his tail and licked the hand of whomever he came across suddenly go for the throat of the mailman.

Most of the time, Barney was full of good cheer. When he worked the stick, the long faces of the workaday weary regulars broke into smiles even before they got their first cocktail. With his mop of dark hair and his blue, smiling Irish eyes, he was as handsome as a prince. The waitresses flirted with him unmercifully, but he was as shy around women as an altar boy in a cathouse, so all he'd do was blush and mumble. One of those rare human beings who kept his own troubles to himself but was always willing to heave a shoulder under yours, Barney would do you a favor, as if he were required by law to do it. He had a quick wit and a quicker tongue, the words tumbling over one another, cascading from his mouth, in a verbal blur, so he'd have mumbled three or four things, and if you weren't quick, or if your mother hadn't been from Cavan, like mine, you'd have missed it. The good nature vanished, though, when he talked about MacAlister.

"I've had me eye on him," said Barney, after we'd closed and cleaned and restocked the bar this night. "I'll find out more about

him, to be sure." On top of his hail-fellow-well-met personality, Barney was a derring-do sort of guy, two characteristics missing from my
repertoire. I knew he was up to something, but this was the last I
heard about it until the following Sunday night.

The guy at the bar was small, dark-skinned like a Dominican infielder
with a good tan, and wearing a suit that was, if I remember my son
Kevin's infancy accurately, the color baby shit sometimes gets. He ordered a rum and Coke made with Appleton's—a waste of good liquor,
if you ask me; one of those guys who orders a call brand to let me
know he can afford it. I poured the Appleton's because he was sitting
at the bar watching me. If he'd been at a table, I'd have poured the rail
rum, and with the Coke to mask the flavor, he wouldn't have noticed
if I'd used Sterno.

His eyelids were like hoods, and when he lifted his head to speak,
the hoods came down, so I couldn't see his eyes. On top of this, he
mumbled, and on top of that, he spoke in clumps of words rather
than sentences. Given these impediments to clear communication, it
took some time for me to make sense of what he was saying.

"You're from the union?"

"Smart guy . . . My friends . . ." He waved an arm, gesturing to
take in the small bar and cocktail area. "You could do good." He
drifted off into his own thoughts, after making his point.

"Your friends come in here?" I tried. "I wouldn't know. I'm new."

He nodded a few times, then pursed his lips and changed directions, shaking his head sadly from side to side. "The other guy not so
smart . . . You gotta know better." He raised the hoods for a second, so
I got a good look at the yellowish-white-framed black, expressionless
eyes. "The other guy. Not here?"

"Not now." The other guy was Barney, and he was due to arrive any
minute. I could have told the guy this, but I didn't, since I doubted it
would be to Barney's benefit.

"He listen to you?"

I shrugged my shoulders.

My visitor nodded sadly again. "Busy night."

"Not so busy," I said.

"Busy tonight," he assured me.

Something in the way he said this caught my attention, and those hooded eyes notwithstanding, he didn't miss my epiphany.

"Barney?"

His expression didn't change.

"Did something happen to him?"

This specter, perched like a vulture on the bar stool, drained his drink, shook the glass to rattle the ice cubes, then pushed it toward me. "This a good job?" When I didn't answer: "Am I right? A good job? No trouble?"

"I don't know," I said. "I just started."

The man nodded. "No trouble," he said. This time it was a command.

The call from the hospital came at around eleven o'clock.

chapter two

Barney was in a semiprivate room at NYU Hospital when I went over early the next morning. He'd been moved there from the Bellevue trauma center once the hospital powers ascertained he had health insurance. Fortunately, he'd held on to the union insurance plan he had when he left the mainstream for the Savoy. Without the insurance he'd have been dumped onto one of the wards at Bellevue to be neglected by the overworked and understaffed nursing crew under the direction of a surgical resident who hadn't slept in three days.

Barney's nose had already been flattened a couple of times in Gaelic football matches back in his native Ireland, long before the Local 909 goons got to him, so when the blackened and discolored eyes came around, his face wouldn't have changed much. They did break a couple of ribs and rupture his spleen, but he'd bounce back from that, too. What he wouldn't be able to get along without was the fingers. The sleep-deprived Bellevue trauma team and the hand-surgery fellow had reattached them. Whether they'd hold or not, and consequently whether Barney would ever work the stick again, was, the resident told me, anyone's guess.

To see him lying in the bed, his eyes swollen shut, his brain shut down by the free-flowing Demerol drip running through a tube into his arm, and his hand wrapped in a pillow of gauze and rigidly bound to a board, to see such a robust, hearty guy flat on his back with tubes sticking out of him every which way, his face wan and his eyes fogged in, to see him torn up like this would cause anyone to despair.

When he looked at me, I couldn't read his eyes. He might have been scared or angry; he might have given up hope altogether, as I would have; I didn't know. I don't know what he read in my eyes, either, anger, fear, or pity, except that I stood there not knowing what to say or do.

If it were the movies, I'd say, "You lie there and relax, pal. I'll get the bastards who did this." With that I'd charge out the door, saddle up Old Paint, head out into the hills after the bad guys, catch up to them one at a time, and wreak vengeance, returning in time to see Barney hobble out of bed toward his happy new life, discovering when I arrived that he had an adorable younger sister, who was just so grateful for my having restored her brother's honor that she . . . and so on. In real life, here in Fun City in the early 1990s, if I went after the guys who hammered Barney, I'd end up in a bed alongside him with my own bandages, breaks, and bruises, if not sinking into the mud under the East River wearing a pair of cement shoes. If you've been a New York City bartender as long as Barney and I have, you know how often the good guys win.

So what do you do? Who do you tell it to? The detective in the precinct? "Let me get this down," he says. "Do you know who attacked you?" Well, of course we don't know who beat Barney up, but we know who's behind it. "You do, now, do you? And do you have any evidence?" Of course we don't. "Well, that's too bad. Maybe there's an organized crime unit you can talk to. I'll give you a phone number. A few years down the road they'll get to you. By then, someone will have painted a couple of houses with the both of you. You want my advice? Do your job and leave them alone. You don't bother them; they don't bother you. You want to be a smart guy, you end up like your friend."

When I'm really stumped, even at this late stage in my life, I turn to my father. Pop has been in the labor movement in one way or another since his days at Brooklyn College back in the 1930s. He became a Communist in those days and has been one ever since, though a despondent one since Gorbachev pulled the plug on the Soviet Union. In the past, Pop was a journalist and an organizer for the Newspaper Guild. He helped lead newspaper strikes, joined the army to fight fascism, and came back to become a reporter for *PM*, a left-wing newspaper that had a brief fling in New York at the end of World War II. During the 1950s, he refused to testify about his Communist Party membership. He was willing to testify that he was a Communist but not about who else was or wasn't, so he got himself blacklisted and later went to jail for contempt of something or other—standing by his principles but scaring the shit out of his son, who was afraid his father really was a Soviet spy and would end up executed like the Rosenbergs, leaving his son to be thrust into a foster home or, worse, adopted by his Aunt Maude, his mother's sister, the meanest person he'd ever known. Somehow Pop survived all this, as did his son. Because of the blacklist, Pop went from the newspaper world to the labor movement and eventually retired from the furniture workers union, while his son, in whom he had placed much hope, has spent his adult life in vain pursuit of an acting career and other slow-moving dreams.

After buzzing me in to his Cortelyou Road apartment in Flatbush, Pop returned to his favorite pastime, reading, so I found him sitting at his dining room table with a book open in front of him. The book was *Things Fall Apart* by Chinua Achebe, a novel about the beginnings of the modern era in Nigeria that everyone else had read in the '60s. Pop never went in for trends—he had a habit these days of reading the *Times* a couple of days after it came out—I noticed he'd dug his four-foot-high bent and faded fake Christmas tree out of mothballs in grudging recognition of the season to be jolly, though he'd yet to hang on it decoration number one.

"How's your new job?" Pop asked, and this opened up the floodgates. I told him about what had happened to Barney, about the slimeball who'd been in my bar wising me up, probably at exactly the time his piece-of-shit friends were torturing Barney.

"The worst thing is I don't know what to do. I feel like I should wait for that prick to come back into the bar and then smash him over the head with a Galliano bottle."

Pop dismissed the idea with a wave of his hand. "Sure. Then the boss can fire you and hire a more compliant bartender."

"I hate to tell you this, Pop, but this time it's not just the boss; it's the union, too—and the union's worse." I told Pop about my conversation with Barney a couple of nights before he was attacked. "Barney was trying to find out what was going on between MacAlister and the union business agent for the Savoy. He was trying to get hold of MacAlister's books. They caught him, and smacked him around to tell him to mind his own business."

"You think that's what happened, and maybe so. But you should know how this works yourself. What do you think I was doing all those years?"

Pop had spent years as an internal investigator for one of the garment unions looking for evidence of deals between crooked business agents and even crookeder bosses. Now he headed for his hallway coat closet. "Let's go," he said, reaching for his coat.

I was confused, but Pop was used to that; he'd been confusing me all my life. "What you should have told Barney is that it's a waste of time looking at the boss's books; you want to look in his wastepaper baskets."

What Pop wanted to do was take a look in the trash bins behind the hotel. Here he was in his seventies, and I tagged along as if I were ten years old again. On the way over on the subway, I worried that someone would catch us, like I figured they caught Barney, but it didn't do any good telling Pop.

"Most places don't guard their garbage," he said.

We stopped at a small grocery store on Ninth Avenue, where Pop bought a box of plastic garbage bags and two pairs of rubber kitchen gloves. Then we hoofed it over to the street behind the hotel, where Pop guessed, correctly, we'd find an alley leading to the back of the building. The alley and the walls around it were concrete, something like a handball court. There was a loading dock, with the door closed, and a number of different garbage receptacles of various sizes, mostly Dumpsters. Some of them held kitchen garbage, these immediately recognizable by the stench. Others held whatever crap the maids had hauled out of the sleeping rooms that day—used condoms, sanitary napkins, syringes, bloody and snot-filled tissues. None of this fazed Pop. Wearing the rubber gloves, he poked around in this and that bin, until he came upon a small red Dumpster containing mostly paper— typing paper, computer paper, brochures, letters, envelopes. I followed his lead and began stuffing any likely-looking paper into trash bags.

"We'll have to take a cab," he said when we'd stuffed a half dozen bags.

"You'll have to take a cab. I've gotta go to work," I told him. After a bit of a tussle getting a cab—the first couple of drivers thought Pop, with his collection of garbage bags and wearing his half-a-century-old overcoat, was a homeless person—I helped him load the stuff in.

Before the cab pulled away, he spoke to me out the window. "We've fought these people before. You have to be smart and you have to be careful. But it can be done." His expression was pure defiance.

"You're telling me I should take on the gangsters in the union?"

Pop leaned farther out the cab's window, sizing me up. "These hooligans work in the dark. They're like cockroaches. When you turn on the lights, they scatter for cover."

"This little light of mine, I'm gonna let it shine, eh, Pop?"

"Harrumph!" said Pop.

I went to work.

After visiting Barney in the hospital and Pop in Brooklyn, and spending an hour digging through garbage bins, I was more out of sorts than usual as I set up the bar, until I noticed that tall, blond-haired, blue-eyed, twenty-something Betsy Tierney was the bar waitress for the evening. Seeing her, I cheered up considerably. It makes a difference who the waitress is. A few are pains in the ass; most are okay; some, like Betsy, downright exciting. Besides being a great waitress and lovely to look at, she had, under Barney's tutelage, become part of our rank-and-file insurgency. Brooklyn born and bred, she was the salt-of-the-earth-type New York City woman you don't run across

unless you live and work in the city. She'd grown up in an isolated en-
clave at the far end of Brooklyn where Avenue U meets Sheepshead
Bay. Gerritsen Beach looks like a fishing village, with fishing boats
sliding by in the bay mornings and evenings, the kind of place where
bungalows and two-family houses predominate, and families have
statues of the Virgin Mary in their densely foliaged, tiny front yards,
where married daughters live down the street from their mothers,
grandmothers are not far off, and everyone has a dozen cousins in the
neighborhood. It has as much to do with glitzy and gentrified Manhattan as it does with Mars.

Like too many city girls, even those from Gerritsen Beach, Betsy
grew up too fast and got married too soon, in her case to a guy from
the neighborhood, who became a cop and who later provided her with
a child, still a baby, and a great deal of grief. He'd been in the bar a
few times, watching over her as she worked, and was easy to clock as
possessive, jealous, and dangerous, with that edgy violent streak you
see in some cops when they're starting out and hope they grow out of
before they kill someone. He sat at the bar as cold as ice, putting his
hands on her whenever she came near him—touching her ass or her
breasts, looking at me as if to say, look at what I can do, daring me to
touch her. I didn't care about his threat since I didn't think of Betsy
that way, and even if I did, I'd known men like her husband before
and recognized his kind of perverted possessiveness that passes itself
off as love. I knew from Betsy this guy had a houseful of guns and
that he hadn't come down yet from his recent brief tour of duty in the
desert during the Gulf War. To put it another way, I knew better than
to get involved romantically with Betsy Tierney, even though it was
clear she needed to break with her husband and was looking for a guy
to help her do it.

Barney was either braver or more foolish—or both—than I was. I
saw how he stopped what he was doing to watch each time she
sashayed away from the bar with her tray of drinks, how her lips
brushed his ear when she placed her order above the happy-hour din.
Even though I didn't think it had come to anything yet, I saw where it
was heading and knew I should warn him.

Of course, this night, Betsy wanted to know everything I knew about what happened to Barney. She was hovering around the bar as soon as I got behind it, she and Mary Donohue, one of the dining room waitresses. They had been talking about Barney when I arrived and wanted to hear the latest from me. Mary, Irish, like Barney, was beside herself with worry about him. She was like that, excitable and motherly, trying to take care of everyone in a way that reminded me of my mother, though she was closer to me in age. She'd already been to the hospital to see Barney and make sure the nurses and doctors toed the line in taking care of him. Mary's concern was contagious. When she was worried, she needed everyone else in the hotel to worry along with her, and we did. As far as Barney was concerned, Betsy was certainly holding up her end in the worry department—there were tears in her eyes each time she said his name—so I began to sense that this thing between them might have moved along faster than I'd thought.

"There's something you should know," Betsy said, when Mary had gone to wait on a table. "Someone else should know now after what happened. I'm afraid Barney might get deported if the police look into the attack too closely. He's here in America under a false name."

I shushed her and sent her away after she blurted this out. I figured Barney should know better than to blab about being illegal. He'd told her and already she'd told me. That wasn't much of a secret anymore. What if she got cold feet about him and told her husband? The Irish have a thing about betrayal—they hate an informer—but this didn't mean they didn't get betrayed. I was mad at Betsy telling me and mad at Barney telling her. A secret like this brought you trouble.

When the kitchen closed that night, the bar was slow, so we held a short meeting of the rank-and-file group to talk about Barney and what we could do. Francois the chef, Hector the Ecuadorian sous chef, who didn't speak English and was probably an illegal, and one of the dishwashers, who certainly was an illegal, came, as did a busboy and two dining room waitresses. Without Barney, there was a leadership vacuum, and I got sucked into it, given my tenure with the union and my big mouth. One thing Barney had going for him as a leader was his fearlessness, which made everyone else, including me, braver in turn. Given that the recent turn of events had scared the bejeebers out of me, this bravery thing was going to be in short supply on my watch.

"Isn't there anyone we can turn to?" Mary Donohue asked. A long-time Savoy worker, she was of the North Bronx Irish, having come over in the '60s with that decade's wave of Irish immigrants. Her husband was a cop, and they were sending their son to Fordham on a cop's and waitress's pay, with her working a lot of double shifts and banquets over the years. As I said, she worried over all of us, especially Barney, and was more determined than any of us to set things right. "What about going to Pete Kelly?" She returned our stares of incredulity without batting an eye.

Pete Kelly was president of the hotel union council that included our trusty Local 909. He was ultimately responsible for the pricks we were plagued by. Whatever Kelly thought of Eliot and his indiscretions, we were a bigger menace. Kelly believed Barney and I, and the rest of the rank-and-file movement, were trying to steal his union from him. That he thought the union belonged to him and therefore could be stolen from him went a long way toward explaining why there was a rank-and-file movement. I didn't need to explain this to Mary Donohue. She had his number. As Pete approached where we were standing during the St. Patrick's Day parade last year, carrying his GIVE IRELAND BACK TO THE IRISH banner, she'd hollered at him, "Give the union back to its members, you fat son of a bitch."

"Why would he help us?" Betsy asked. "He hates Barney and the rank-and-file folks. That's why he put Barney and Brian over here. I'm sure he wishes someone would get rid of all of us."

"But Pete Kelly isn't the kind to chop a man's fingers off," said Mary Donohue.

Given a run-in we'd had not so long ago, I wasn't sure this was true, but I didn't debate it. He wasn't much of a democrat, but he was a union guy in his own way. He put up with the crooked locals because they supported him when he needed them, and, I suspected, because he knew if he took them on he'd most likely end up in a vacant lot in Canarsie. This kind of crappy local couldn't be good for him, though, and he might help if we did the heavy lifting. Failing that, he might at least put a leash on the thugs running it.

"It might be worth a try," I said. "Who wants to go talk to him?"

One of the features of our little group I liked best was that we didn't have the problem of folks falling over one another to volunteer for something. I actually couldn't remember a time when one of us did volunteer for anything, with the possible exception of Barney. In our group, you did something when you were talked into it by the rest of the group.

"Ah, go on," Barney would say. "Is there a better man in the place than you for the job?" And so it went this time.

"How about you, Mary?" I suggested.

"Ah, go on, Brian. What would I say to the man? I'd be speechless in front of him. You're the man to go, Brian. You're accustomed to these kinds of talks. He already knows you."

"Knows him is right," said Francois. "He tried to have him killed once."

Everyone looked at me.

I shrugged my shoulders. "It's a long story. He sent a couple of goons to scare me out of running for office a year or two ago." That episode and some things that happened at the time brought back too many painful memories, so I brushed off the rest of the questions. "A friend of mine back then arranged to have him talked out of it."

chapter three

I agreed to talk to Kelly, but only if someone came with me, and that someone turned out to be Betsy. As usual, things didn't go as planned. When I called the next morning to make an appointment with Pete Kelly, a brisk and businesslike but not unfriendly secretary told me to take up my problem with my business agent.

"I need to see Mr. Kelly personally," I said. "If you would tell him this is Brian McNulty and I'm calling on behalf of Barney Saunders about a couple of hundred hotel workers who need help, maybe he'd have a few minutes to chat."

"Mr. Kelly doesn't take this kind of phone call, hon. I'll connect you with one of the organizers."

"Never mind," I said. "I'll get back to you." Over the years, I've learned you can't argue with someone who's been given instructions.

"I'm nervous," Betsy said the next day as we made our way across 67th Street from the subway stop on Broadway, past tinkling bells and muted Christmas carols drifting from the store we passed, to the Central Park Inn. Tall and statuesque to begin with, this afternoon she looked like a Greek goddess, her long black coat unbuttoned and flowing behind her, wearing high heels and a long black skirt with a slit up the side and a low-cut scoop neck that made her neck look really long—and accentuated her breasts so that they now seemed to be pushed up and leaning forward, about to tumble out of the dress through the scooped neck; her hair was up in a bun and back from her face, so her blue eyes sparkled and her skin seemed soft and fresh as a child's. I didn't expect her to look this good. She looked good enough in her worn and faded waitress uniform in the dim light of the Savoy bar. Here on 67th Street in the December chill, with a flush on her cheeks from the frosty air and the slight exertion of walking, wearing fresh vibrantly red, sparkly lipstick, she looked too good. I'd glance over at her every once in a while, and my eyes would lock there looking at her, so she'd smile, and that would make it worse.

"Why are you looking at me like that?" she asked with a giggle.

I snapped my eyes away and grumbled, something bartenders usually can get away with with waitresses because there's a bar between you and them and you can walk to the other end. This time there was no walking away, so she hooked her arm through mine and hugged herself toward me, her rambunctious right breast bumping against my arm as we walked.

"Are you sure this is a good idea?" she asked. "I'm scared and excited at the same time. What do you think he'll say?"

I wasn't sure it was a good idea, but it was the only one I had. The union grapevine placed Peter Kelly in the Central Park Inn, a union establishment, for lunch every Wednesday. He ate by himself, but the owner, the manager, and the chef would stop by to pay tribute, and undoubtedly comp the lunch, treating him as a labor statesman as payback for labor peace.

My idea was for us to be there when he arrived, finish our lunches—which would not be comped—before he finished his, and stop by his table as we were leaving, to pay our respects. Betsy's role was to watch my back and look gorgeous, which she handled with aplomb.

Sure enough, just after our lunch was served, Pete was ushered into the garden room, which was decked out in opulent Christmas finery; the glass and the crystal and the white tablecloths had been given a seasonal touch with poinsettias and vases of ornaments, and Christmas greens were draped among the chandeliers. Betsy ate salmon with a lemon butter sauce. I had a hamburger and a beer. We were seated at a deuce against a wall, not far from the entrance to the kitchen. Trying to act natural and keep a conversation going, I made the mistake of asking Betsy if she'd been to see Barney. She looked away guiltily, and when she turned back, her eyes had reddened, as if she would cry.

"I'm afraid to," she said.

"What are you afraid of?" I asked without thinking about what I was saying.

Now her lip trembled.

"Look," I said. "This is an expensive lunch. Don't start sniveling and getting tears and snot all over it."

It was a weak attempt at humor, and she produced a weak smile in response. "Oh, Brian, what am I going to do?"

"You're going to stop sniveling and go powder your pretty nose; then we're going to talk with Pete Kelly, and you're going to smile and nod a lot, and when the time comes you're going to look fiercely determined. From there, you can play it by ear."

She grimaced, curling her lip and lowering her eyebrows. "I meant about my life." She drilled the message into my eyeballs. Thankfully, the crisis had passed. Her eyes cleared up and she went back to taking dainty bites of her salmon. I decided not to risk any more questions, so we sat there oblivious to one another, like a married couple.

I couldn't see what Kelly was eating, but whatever it was it took up a lot of room on his table and required a number of trips by the waiter, busboy, and captain to deliver it. True to form, the restaurant owner, a society man-about-town, who owned more than one of these glitteringly appointed restaurants, also stopped in to the Central Park on Wednesdays and made it a point to stop by Peter's table. With handshakes, pats on the back, a bit of banter, and a few chuckles and guffaws, they shared their bonhomie, letting the world know they enjoyed the good life, living high on the hog off the backs of the workers, as Pop would say.

When the owner moved along to his own party, Betsy and I finished our lunch. While I paid the check, she went to the powder room, then walked resolutely over to Kelly's table, which he almost knocked over when he jumped up to suavely greet her. By the time I moseyed over, Betsy's laugh was tinkling and Kelly's eyes were bulging. He made no attempt to hide his irritation as I sidled up to Betsy and she took my hand in hers to introduce me.

"Brian's a member of your union, too," she said. "He's stuck in this awful local, just like I am."

Kelly eyed me shrewdly. He was short and stocky, with what used to be called a flattop haircut back in the '50s. He looked as tough as he was reputed to be. I noticed he was drinking Perrier with lime and eating a whole fish that had lemon slices on it. His voice was gruff, and while he might have been smitten by Betsy, he wasn't making a fool of himself.

"It's nice to meet you," he said, eyeing me in a way that suggested he was trying to place me. "But where you work now, that's Local 909's jurisdiction and nothin' I can do about it."

"What if we helped you take them on?"

Kelly looked surprised, both suspicious and curious. "Why would I do that?"

I took a deep breath. "You know what happened to Barney Saunders?"

His expression didn't change and his eyes stayed locked on mine. "I know you, don't I?"

"Brian McNulty. I was a steward at the Sheraton. I ran for executive board." There was a bit more to this that I didn't want to go into, having to do with a Labor Department charge some of us filed against Kelly.

He brought it up anyway. "You and Saunders think you should be runnin' the union, right? Except the workers keep electin' me." His expression hardened. "Why you comin' to me now? Take your girlfriend and get the fuck out of here, before I get up and throw you the fuck out."

He didn't make any menacing movements or gestures, but his voice was a low growl—the kind you hear from big, mean dogs—so I believed he would do what he said.

"Give me five minutes." I tried to sound calmer than I felt.

He took a drink of his Perrier, picked up his knife and fork, and bent to his fish, giving no indication he listened. Still, he wasn't chucking me out the door, so I went on.

"What this guy is doing is wrong, Pete. The pay's below scale; the benefits are lousy. The boss walks into the kitchen and fires workers on the spot. That's not the kind of union you run."

Kelly continued his meal, as if I weren't there. It's unnerving, being ignored in a public place. You get the sense that everyone knows it, too, that you've been hung out to dry.

"Let's get out of here," I said to Betsy, grabbing her arm. She resisted. I pulled on her arm a bit harder, so she resisted harder. A fine kettle of fish. Pompous asshole, king of the domain, wiping his puss with a linen napkin, and now the beautiful princess, ignoring me tugging her arm, while the Christmas lights shone, the chandeliers twinkled, the crystal glittered, the silverware sparkled, and the upscale diners watched me, saying to themselves, *What's with this asshole causing a scene, spoiling everyone's lunch, making a spectacle of himself?*

We Irish embarrass easily. Most of us don't like to call attention to ourselves—at least not when we're sober. A thousand times when I was growing up, I heard from my mother, "What will the neighbors think?" For my mother, that was the worst part of the Red baiting, what the neighbors thought. I pretend to myself I don't care what people think, but the truth is it's hard to get out from under your upbringing. Now here I was the center of attention in one of New York's spiffiest restaurants. I didn't know what to do. For openers, I wanted to backhand Betsy, but that wouldn't do, so I stood there about to internally combust, until Betsy said, in her gentle, lilting voice, "Wait, Brian." Her pretty blue eyes smiled, holding in them comfort and steadfastness and encouragement. Having calmed me, she turned to Kelly. "Mr. Kelly," she said in a tone that would lull lions to sleep, "we came here because we believe in you."

Kelly could hear the sincerity in her voice and, unless his heart had rotted away completely, couldn't help but recognize goodness when it stared him in the face, flowing from an angelic, blue-eyed blonde with skin as soft as eiderdown.

"If you think we're trying to trick you, you're wrong. We came because we believe you're a person who helps people."

Kelly considered this for a moment. Betsy was smart enough to clam up and let him. Her earnestness got me. Seemingly, too, it found the two or three percent of Kelly's heart that hadn't yet calcified. He gestured with his eyebrows toward the empty chairs at his table. We sat.

"I don't know what you guys want with this dissident union crap," he said. "My local's got the best pay and the best benefits of any hotel and restaurant workers in the country, and you guys bitch about it. You think I need bosses tellin' me 'how do we know you can really deliver the union' when they're hearin' this dissident crap?"

"We're not against you here, Pete. We want to get rid of this guy, Tom Eliot."

"Yeh. Well, this guy has the local. You being a pain in his ass, what's he gonna do? You done the same to me."

"It's not the same thing."

Kelly considered this. After some deliberation, he pushed the remains of his lunch away and sat back in his chair. "First off, what you do is your business. I don't want to know nothin' about it. Number two, what the local does is their business. I don't like what happened to Saunders. I ain't sayin' I know who did anything, but I don't like it. I don't want none of my members gettin' whacked, even it's you."

The waiter took Kelly's plate away and brought him a small pot of coffee. He didn't ask if we wanted any. "You got yourself elected to the executive board, right? You must know somethin'. But you bring the feds into this one we're all gonna get fucked, not just the guys you're after."

Somehow, probably because I'd been deciphering the garbled life stories of incoherent drunks most of my adult life, I understood that Kelly was making an offer here. "We're doing this ourselves," I told him with some misgivings.

Gazing into the sparkling and twinkling center of the garden room, Kelly shrugged one shoulder in a gesture signifying something known only to him, following this with a sip of coffee, then a vacant glance at me and then toward the door. I stood up. This time, Betsy stood with me. Kelly made no effort to shake hands or bid us farewell. Instead, he stared through the windows at the barren trees in the park.

"Thank you, Mr. Kelly," Betsy said politely.

He glanced at her appraisingly for a second, though his expression was hard, then began to push the table away, as the waiter and the captain rushed over to help him. When he stood, I realized that although he was stocky, he hadn't gone to fat. His body was as hard as a boxer's. For one second, our eyes met again. In that second, I came to believe the rumors I'd heard that Pete Kelly had at some time in the past killed men who got in his way. I'm sure that in that same second he saw in my eyes that I did not kill people who got in my way. So we knew then who we were—and, much as I hated to admit it, knew, too, who had the upper hand.

Without really deciding or either of us mentioning it, Betsy and I began to walk downtown along Central Park West instead of getting on the subway. We didn't talk until after we'd left the park behind, crossed through Columbus Circle, and headed down Seventh Avenue with the herds of pedestrians. I wondered if Betsy had clocked the miniature standoff between Kelly and me, if she knew about the things that went on between men about who had the killer instinct. Then I remembered her husband and realized she did know about men who let you know up front they were capable of killing.

Somewhere around 56th Street, she broke into my thoughts. "You're going to have to explain to me what went on back there."

As we waited to cross a street, I noticed a tall brownstone apartment building, made of some substance only New York City buildings were made out of some time before I was born and never since. I liked the solidity of the building and the designs constructed into the stone and wished they still made buildings like that.

"This is what I think," I told Betsy. "Kelly isn't a gangster. He knows the gangsters. Like our guy Eliot, they probably control a couple of locals in the hotel council. He leaves them alone because they deliver him votes when he needs them, and he can count on help from their thugs when he needs to teach someone a lesson, like he tried to muscle me one time. What they do, Pop says, is work out deals with the bosses. The workers get weak contracts that save the boss bundles, so the boss kicks back some of the money to the business agent. The boss saves money, the thugs make money, and the workers get screwed.

"Why Kelly lets them do this is more complicated. The gangsters divvy things up and try to keep their unique version of order. As I understand it, from my years of reading the *Daily News,* there are different crime families. I don't remember their names, but they have Italian last names like the kids from Bensonhurst I played baseball with. So say Pete Kelly's got some loose connection to the Banana family, and they've helped him when he's needed help. And say Eliot's hooked up with the Bonono family. Somewhere in the past the Bonono family boss and the Banana family boss sat down—that's what gangsters do, they have sit-downs—and they agreed that they'd help Kelly with this and that but he'd have to let this jerk Eliot have the Savoy Hotel. They don't say, 'Hey, Kelly. Stay away from the Savoy or we'll kill you.' They talk in euphemisms and make oblique references. Kelly comes to understand he's been asked to do a favor for a guy who has a good friend whose cousin needs to have Local 909 and the Savoy so he can skim enough money to put his kid through reform school or something."

Betsy stopped stock-still in the middle of the sidewalk, disrupting the throng of hustling New Yorkers headed downtown. For some reason, when it gets close to Christmas, traffic in Manhattan—in the streets and on the sidewalks—increases in volume and intensifies in determination. Since she stopped, I had to also, getting myself bumped and shoved by the hurrying herd.

"That's the dumbest explanation of anything I've ever heard, Brian. What the hell are you talking about?"

"Well, to put it another way," I said, grabbing her elbow to get her moving again before we were trampled. "Kelly will check to see how important Local 909's hold on the Savoy is to his associates. If it's relatively unimportant to the Banana family and not a life-or-death thing to the Bonono family, Kelly will let us duke it out with Eliot. If we win, we get the local and he gets loyalty from us now, since he's kept us alive to enjoy our victory. If we lose, he'll live with that, too, and no one can say it was him who tried to grab the local. If, on the other hand, his principals tell him the local is important to them, Pete will let them know we are relatively unimportant to him. He'll then get word to us that it will be dangerous to continue our efforts. But that's all he'll do."

Betsy thought this over as we walked. "So what do we need him for if that's all he's going to do?"

"These crime families are said to hold crime to a higher standard than the run-of-the-mill criminal. That's why everyone likes them so much."

"So Kelly will tell the gangsters not to kill us?"

"The way I understand it, the thugs are supposed to get permission from the higher-ups before they kill someone."

"Do they really do that?"

"I wouldn't bet on it. They didn't get to where they are today because they played by the rules."

"That's encouraging," said Betsy.

chapter four

That evening when I went to visit Barney at the hospital, he wasn't as doped up as he had been.

"The whoores," he said, waving around his bandaged hand. "I would've beaten the pair of them bloody in a fair fight."

What had happened, Barney told me, was that he was jumped on his way to work; two guys dragged him into an alley, worked him over, then taped his right hand to a loading dock and lopped off the tops of four fingers on his right hand with a cleaver.

"I got the best of them, though," Barney said, holding up his good left hand. "*Ciotóg.* They cut the wrong one. I'm left-handed." He sounded triumphant, as if there had been a victory there.

"I was careless," Barney said. "There was an envelope for Eliot at the front desk. I made up a story about being on the way to see Eliot and wouldn't I take the envelope along to him. The desk clerk got suspicious and wouldn't give it to me. And so didn't the eejit tell MacAlister the very same day that I wanted the envelope?"

Barney grew tired quickly from the effort at talking. His usually ruddy face was ashen and a cloudy film dulled what were usually sparkling blue eyes. I hesitated to ask about the reattached fingers.

Barney called things as he saw them, though. He held the bandaged hand in front of him, pointed toward me. "I've got black and blue sticks at the end of me hand that may never be good for anything again."

"They're still there, though, eh?" I said tentatively.

"What good are they to me?" The pain in his voice went to my heart. "You don't know the fierce rage I feel, Brian." Those sincere blue eyes burned through the fog into mine. "The fookers have stolen the heart right out of me."

"The fingers are still there, Barney. There's hope."

"Ah, hope," said Barney. "I don't know how we don't lose hope altogether with all the cruelty in the world."

Barney's despair tore at me. Mine was never far below the surface. I tried to sound encouraging, though I wasn't much good at stiff-upper-lip pep talks. Why shouldn't poor Barney dwell on his misery? I should give him a hand whining about the injustice of it. I had to be nuts complaining about the guy feeling a bit down when someone chopped off his fingers. Instead, I'm there looking for help with my problem because I'm not sure what to do next. So I brush off Barney's troubles and bend his ear with mine. Hey pal, sorry about your fingers there. I hope they don't rot off. But I have a situation here we need to take care of.

I told Barney about our meeting at the hotel a couple of nights before and my talk with Kelly—and Barney being Barney is like Ruffian, a heart so gallant she runs the last half of the race on a broken leg because she knows her job is to beat the horse running beside her. Doped up, the pain causing his eyes to cross, his future with a maimed and crippled hand staring him in the face, Barney sat up, as if the strains of the "Internationale" called to him across his dreams.

"So God bless them," says Barney. "I knew the fookers wouldn't scare the workers off. And Betsy . . . with so much to bear already. She went with you?"

This reference to Betsy gave me a start because I didn't want to let on I knew about her triangle of troubles, nor about Barney's role in this triangle that could easily bring disaster on both of them.

"She came with me to see Kelly. We're ready to go. But I'm not sure if it might not be better to let things cool down first."

Barney regarded me as if I were an errant child. "Ah, what good would it do to wait, Brian? What's going to change for the better?

Much as we'd like to go our own way and let the world become a better place for us, what's ever happened to the benefit of the working man he hasn't made happen himself?"

He warmed to his plan. "For the time being, we need to keep things to ourselves. You'll be doing the work now, Brian, until I'm back on me feet. You'll need to expand the committee one person at a time, not letting on to anyone what we're about until you're sure they can be trusted. You'll meet in secret and talk only to those you trust." Beyond the clouds that veiled his eyes, I'd swear I saw a twinkle. "Just like in the old country, Brian McNulty. Your grandfather would have known well the approach we're taking."

Maybe I looked uncertain. I certainly felt that way, unnerved, too, by the hoses in Barney's arm, the blinking and beeping of monitors, and the man in the next bed with tubes in both his nostrils who hadn't moved or opened his eyes since I'd gotten there, only snorted now and again, making a desperate sound that each time I heard I thought was his final breath.

Barney ignored the accoutrements of misery that surrounded him. He waved his bandaged paw at me again. "If they don't know who we are or what we're about, they can't get us." He began to lose his concentration then. The nurse had adjusted his IV and whatever painkiller was dripping into his system, so his eyes lost their focus, his face lost even more of its color, and he began to drift away.

"Okay, old pal," I said as I got up to leave. "Mum's the word."

It was a New York City winter, deep-freeze night, the kind that comes rarely, but often enough to notice, when the temperature dips near zero as night deepens and the frozen wind blows in from New Jersey across the Hudson and howls along the crosstown streets toward the East River. This night, it came straight at me as I walked west across 23rd Street toward the subway. It wasn't that long a walk, but before I'd gone a block I felt like Dr. Zhivago crossing the tundra. You can't get a cab in New York when it's cold like this, and the bus limps along like an old lady with a shopping cart—actually, getting close to Christmas, it's filled with old ladies with shopping carts.

Head down, bundled into my pea coat, hands shoved deep into my pockets, body bent, I trudged into the wind. At the corner of Third Avenue, I stopped for traffic before crossing. The sidewalks were deserted. The cars jostled one another through the intersection. Waiting to cross, I stomped my feet and hugged my arms against my body. Then I heard something.

Next to me was what might have once been a food store, a Gristede's or Sloan's. It had burned out or been gutted for some other reason and was in the early stages of being rebuilt. The sound came from behind a chain-link fence. It took a moment to recognize that it was mewing that I heard. A cat. The light changed. I started to cross the street. A cat in the freezing cold, on probably the only night of the year the temperature in New York City might dip below zero. I remembered something Nelson Algren had written about the Chicago winter, an image that stuck in my memory of "a night so cold that cats froze to death on fire escapes."

The image rose up in front of me again like a billboard. I couldn't cross the street. I went back to the chain-link fence and after a few moments saw the kitten. I bent down and touched its nose through the fence; then, mewing all the while, it followed me along the fence until we came to a gate with a large enough gap for me to reach through. I picked the cat up and stuck it into the pocket of my pea coat, telling myself I would take the cat home, keep it until the temperature warmed up enough for cats to stop freezing to death on fire escapes, and let it go again.

The trip uptown was uneventful, except the cat wouldn't shut up. On the subway, the kindhearted Christmas shoppers with their shopping bags loaded with brightly colored packages looked at me and smiled, while the distrusting and suspicious grinches looked like they suspected a catnapping. I picked up some cat food and litter at the West Side Market and threw the cat and his paraphernalia into my apartment, telling him to make himself at home until the weather got warmer.

I found Ntango, a cabdriver friend of mine, at La Rosita at 106th and hitched a ride down to the Savoy. Because of the damn cat, I was late for work, too late once more to eat dinner before my shift, going behind the bar as soon as I got there, a disruption of my evening work ritual that soured my mood. Ntango came in for a drink since he saw a parking space in the same block as the hotel, too good an opportunity to pass up. He drank a Beck's while I checked the fruit, juices, and beer stock. The day bartender, Sam Jones, had covered for me. A journeyman bartender, he took things in stride, so everything was usually in order, even when I didn't deserve it. We worked without a barback at the Savoy, so it was easy to forget some of the pain-in-the-ass stuff like refilling the beer cooler or cutting extra fruit, but Sam remembered.

He put on his civilian clothes and came back to sit down at the bar to have a beer with Ntango. They were talking about Patrick Ewing and the Knicks when a guy in a black overcoat that even I recognized as cashmere came in and parked himself at the middle of the bar, a few stools away from them. He took off his fedora and overcoat, folding the coat carefully and placing it on the stool next to him with the hat on top of it. He had slicked-back gray hair and a broad face that was almost square.

When I placed the bar napkin in front of him and waited for his order, he looked at me with a slight smile and what I'm sure he thought was a kindly and avuncular expression, but looked to me like the unctuous smile of a door-to-door Bible salesman.

Turned out the man was none other than Tom Eliot, business manager of Local 909. My heart went cold when he introduced himself and held out a flabby hand for me to shake. Since this was the guy I suspected had ordered his thugs to cut off four of Barney's fingers, I looked at his hand, then at the razor-sharp paring knife on the fruit-cutting board. Sam, who'd been exiled to the Savoy years before either Barney or me, clocked this exchange and followed my eyes with his when they went to the knife on the cutting board. He stood up, a wiry, muscular, black man, as energetic as Barney, if not as cheerful, his tightly curled black hair graying at the temples.

"Mr. Eliot," he said in a booming voice as he stood, moving in the same motion to cover the distance between them and taking Eliot's hand in his own catcher's-mitt-sized paw. "Sam Jones." He pumped the startled man's hand a couple of times. "Good to see you here at the old hotel. I thought you union guys had forgot all about us. You don't hardly ever make your way this far west no more. There's no union election coming up, is there?" Sam laughed heartily, and Eliot joined in with an anemic chuckle.

"Well, Sam, it's good to see you. I didn't recognize you when I came in, it being so dark in here and—" Realizing he'd put his foot in his mouth, he stopped and moved on to something else. "You know me, Sam. I like to stop by and see how my members are doing. Wish I could do it more often."

"One of them isn't doing so well," I said. Knowing Sam had stepped in to keep me from doing something foolish with Eliot, I tried to keep myself under control. I was shaking.

Eliot feigned surprise. "Oh? What's the matter?"

"Barney Saunders."

"The Irish fellow? He met with an accident, didn't he?"

I wanted to strangle the smarmy bastard till his smiling eyes popped out of his fat face. "There was no fucking accident. Someone cut off his fingers."

Eliot registered this information with a melodramatic expression of shock and sadness. "That's too bad, too bad. I'm very sorry," he said. "I hear the Irishman made a lot of enemies. The hotel wants to let him go, but you and Sam are the barmen, so I told MacAlister it wasn't that easy because I'd have to ask you. If you want me to put in a word with the manager to hold open a job for him until he gets back on his feet, I'll see what I can do."

"That would be good," said Sam quickly. "We'd appreciate your putting a word in for him, Mr. Eliot. We certainly would."

Eliot watched for my reaction. I glared at him. "What you need to know is that you don't scare us."

Eliot stopped smiling. "You're McNulty, right?" He didn't wait for an answer. "Don't make no insinuations about me. You got something to say, say it. I ain't scared of you neither. I could have you bounced out of here on your ass in nothin' flat, so don't give me any shit." His voice rose as he spoke; his face reddened; his chest puffed out like a rooster getting ready for a fight. "Come out here from behind the bar and talk that shit," he shouted.

I started to come out. The thought flashed through my brain that getting into a fight with the gangster-connected union business manager in my own bar might not be the best course of action. I was coming out from behind the bar anyway. At least I was, until I ran into Ntango as I entered the first turn. At the other end, Sam got an arm around Eliot's throat, and since Sam had arms like bridge cables, Eliot wasn't going anywhere, either. I didn't struggle against Ntango, who simply put his hand on my chest. It didn't make any difference whether Eliot struggled or not; he wasn't going to get out of Sam's grip.

"Now, Mr. Eliot," Sam said, turning his baritone up a notch. "That's enough of this foolishness. Time for you to take a walk. Tempers get too hot, and there's a nice December breeze out there to cool them down."

Eliot's color was returning to its normal pallor and his breathing was slowing down. "I don't need this shit," he said. "Let go of me."

"I certainly will, Mr. Eliot. Certainly will." Sam half-led, half-pushed him to the door, keeping up his chatter, handing him his hat and coat. "Let me just walk you to the door here. And don't you worry, Mr. Eliot. I been in the union a long time. I'll talk to Brian here for you and set him straight. Don't you worry; I'll set McNulty here straight. You won't have nothin' to worry about from us, Mr. Eliot."

"You better set that son of a bitch straight," said Eliot as Sam closed the door behind him.

When he was gone, Sam came back to the bar. I went back behind it, and Ntango sat down with Sam. I poured both of them and myself shots of Powers and refilled their beer glasses.

"Sorry," I said, when I'd downed the shot.

Neither man said anything for a couple of minutes. Then Sam said, "Think you could have taken him, McNulty?"

He and Ntango sized me up over the rims of their schooners and began chuckling. Then they looked at each other, put their glasses down on the bar, and began laughing out loud. After a few seconds, the laughter so contagious and good-natured, and filled with meaning, I couldn't help but join in.

Before he left with Ntango, Sam called me over. In the meanwhile, a few regulars had wandered in, as well as a couple of hotel guests, and business picked up in the dining room, so the waitresses were sliding up to the bar. It wasn't enough activity to have me hopping but enough for me to keep my eyes open. Talking to Sam wasn't a problem, because if I happened to be facing him, he'd be clocking the bar behind me and raise an eyebrow if something needed my attention.

"This MacAlister," he said. "He says he do the inventory this month. The bar cost been too high."

"I heard. Barney told me."

Sam looked at me significantly, nodding his head, before he spoke again. "Somethin' about him . . . Know what I'm sayin'?"

Sam was the head bartender and usually did the inventory. This meant he could do a juggling act to make the numbers come out and cover a variety of indiscretions for all the bartenders. I didn't know what it meant that MacAlister wanted to do the inventory, but I said I'd keep my eyes open. Sam seemed satisfied with that.

chapter five

Later that night, when the bar traffic slowed after the supper rush, the devil himself, as my mother used to say, showed up at the bar. James MacAlister wanted to go over the drink dupes the waitresses had turned in to get their drinks.

"Mr. McNulty, do you check these dupes before giving the waitresses drinks?" Pissing off Barney wasn't enough for this guy; now he was starting on me. I didn't like bosses to begin with, and I especially didn't like bosses that hovered over me, but I was still in my probationary period, so I needed to be careful.

"I check them."

"Some of them are unreadable. How do you know they're accurate?"

"I ask."

MacAlister was worried that a waitress might have slipped a drink containing forty cents' worth of liquor to a good tipper at one of her tables. If she did, I'd know about it. Smart waitresses didn't try to get over on their bartenders.

"Mr. McNulty, the barman is responsible for the liquor that goes out over the bar. If you're not vigilant, you'll be taken advantage of."

It always amazed me that when someone becomes a boss, he begins to think he's smarter than everyone else, as if infused knowledge came with the job. MacAlister was the know-it-all type. He was bigger than me, with broad shoulders and a deep chest. His movements were quick, his eyes alert. His air of self-confidence bordered on recklessness. Some bosses are respectful in dealing with their workers; they understand we're all part of the same species. Others think they're better than those who work for them. MacAlister was one of those. I'm the boss, says he, so I must be the best man in the room—and he let that attitude hang in his words and in his expression, as if he hoped someone would challenge him. He'd already summarily fired a couple of the kitchen workers, and Francois was ready to kill him.

For the moment, though, I was using the "discretion is the better part of valor" approach. "With all due respect, Mr. MacAlister," I said politely, "I've been a bartender for twenty years—"

"Perhaps, Mr. McNulty. But when you work for me, you do things my way. This means reading each dupe the waitress puts on the bar."

As fate would have it, a waitress appeared at the service bar as he spoke. To make my point, I examined the dupe she handed me. It had *S/W* written on it. I pulled the well scotch with my right hand and lifted it toward the glass as if I'd free-pour, but at the last second snapped up a shot glass with my left hand and held it over the iced glass the waitress placed on the bar. I poured into the shot glass and dumped the scotch into the highball glass in the same motion. MacAlister kept his eyes glued on my hands. I could pour the same amount with or without the shot glass. If he was any sort of manager, he'd know that. I could also pour long or short with or without the shot glass.

"I'm glad to see you using the shot glass, Mr. McNulty. Prevents waste."

This was bullshit. Probably he knew that. There were managers who trusted their bartenders and those who didn't. He was one who didn't. If he didn't trust me, I didn't trust him.

When he left me, he began prowling around the service area of the bar, making the waitresses jittery—the way the fox in the children's books prowling in the hill beyond the barns makes the chickens nervous. The waitress he zeroed in on was Mary Donohue, a nervous wreck anyway because she was such a conscientious waitress. You got used to her antsiness and fidgeting pretty quickly because you saw she was high-strung and that was how she got her job done. The important thing was she was fast, didn't make mistakes, and was watching out for her customers because she really believed she should do a good job for them. What she didn't need was someone hovering over her when she was fluttering around the bar, mumbling to herself, setting up her drinks, and getting her checks in order.

MacAlister, for reasons he alone knew, picked her. At the moment it was happening, I thought back to what Barney had said about him lording it over the Irish. I was pouring a drink at the service bar and watched over the shoulder of the waitress at the bar as MacAlister went up to Mary in the small waitress-station area next to the service bar where she was icing glasses and arranging them on her tray. He said something to her, but she was concentrating on what she was doing and waved him away. This was a characteristic of Mary's that anyone might find dismissive and irritating, especially a boss. But when you got to know her, you realized she was as kind as a saint and only did this because she was afraid of losing her concentration and having everything she was juggling collapse into chaos. MacAlister either didn't know this about her or, if he knew, didn't care. He was on his high horse, looking for an act of insubordination he could crush. That this was an Irish woman probably made it all the better.

He spoke. Mary waved him away. He came back at her, saying something else. Good old Mary, refusing to give up her concentration, waved him away again. This time, when he came back at her, I did hear him. "You'll bloody well listen—" said he, reaching for Mary's tray. He was trying to pick up her checks, I guess, but so shocked and unnerved her that she jumped and in doing so almost dropped the tray, tipping it sideways. What happened next depended on who you talked to. What I saw was MacAlister lunge for a glass falling from the tray, and in doing so catch Mary Donohue's not insubstantial breast with his right hand. If they were playing football and it was a face mask instead of a boob, it would have been only a five-yard penalty because he let go right away—but not quickly enough for Mary, who, still holding the tray after the glasses fell, wheeled and smacked him with it—hard—right alongside his left ear.

MacAlister's face exploded into shock and rage. I've seen lots of angry people, and I've even shocked a few people in my time, but this was a sight to behold. I wouldn't have been surprised to see his head erupt and spew out molten anger. I got over the bar and to him before he could get to Mary, if he was going to, and both busboys were there to back me up. He took a couple of deep breaths and stomped away toward the kitchen. Everyone who saw what happened, mostly we of the hired help, stood in shocked silence, until Mary unfroze and burst into tears. A couple of waitresses comforted her; the busboys cleaned up the mess; the rest of the crew went back about their business. By the time I got back behind the bar and made Mary's drinks, she'd pulled herself back together and was ready to haul them off into the dining room.

We didn't have much time to speculate on what would happen next before MacAlister was back in the service area, this time with the dining room hostess and the night front desk manager. Everyone knew what was coming. Well, not quite. Everyone knew the first thing that was coming: He fired Mary for insubordination. She who'd been an exemplary employee for more than a decade, fired in the blink of an eye by an arrogant bully.

Since I'd taken over for Barney on the rank-and-file committee and since Mary was one of our folks, I thought it my duty to intervene. Diplomacy not being my strong suit, and doubting MacAlister would be having any of it anyway, I gave it a try nonetheless. I told him there was a union contract and Mary was entitled to a just-cause hearing and couldn't be fired on the spot. This is by and large true in a union house, except when the employer has the union in his pocket, as in our case. Already Eliot had let MacAlister get away with firing the kitchen workers. Now he had the bit between his teeth.

"Take it to your union, Mr. McNulty. Have the business manager speak to me. I doubt he cares any more about what you think of the situation than I do."

I didn't have a reputation throughout the city's hotel industry as a hotheaded malcontent for nothing. But I wasn't about to let myself be baited into one of my famous throw-the-baby-out-with-the-bath-water responses. Instead, I spoke calmly, first about unfortunate situations and tempers needing to cool, then about loyal workers and company morale.

"Come, Mr. McNulty. The woman struck her superior—"

"Supervisor," I corrected him.

He caught my drift. Raising his eyebrows and lowering his head, he actually looked down his nose at me. "The woman is terminated, McNulty. I'm her superior enough to do that. If you'd like to join her, I'll provide you your termination papers also."

We glared at each other, as I choked back the bile rising in my throat. One of the reasons I could never quite get myself quit of Pop's workers-of-the-world philosophy was the overabundance of assholes like MacAlister, who saw the squashing of the human spirit as part of their bossly rights. I swallowed my anger because I needed the job. There were larger issues: my child support payments for my son Kevin, for one; what happened to Mary Donohue, for another.

I gathered myself together. "Look, Mr. MacAlister. The night's pretty much over. Why not put the discussion off until tomorrow morning? We'll get Eliot in and resolve this. Maybe you'll fire her. Maybe you're right and I'm wrong. But maybe, just maybe, it'll turn out that I'm right. You don't want to be in a position of having fired her and then having to take her back."

MacAlister looked me over with pity born of contempt. "She's fired, and I'm not taking her back." He waited with a smirk for my reaction.

The waitresses and the busboys were listening. They didn't gather around, but the busboys slowed on their way to a table or took longer filling the water pitcher; the waitresses took longer adding up a check or paused pulling a glass from the shelf or the ice bin at the service bar. It was unusual for the entire waitstaff to be within earshot of the bar at the same time, but they all were for this. This wasn't a case of throwing my apron on the bar and taking a hike, as I'd done many times. What I did here would affect all of these folks and many others. There was responsibility to be taken, and I hated responsibility. I wanted someone else to take charge. I knew what to do, but I was afraid to do it. Afraid to do it and afraid not to. Frozen with indecision. Damned if I did and damned if I didn't.

Fortunately, Francois burst out of the kitchen at that moment to put an end to my Hamlet impersonation. He went straight for MacAlister—and he did throw his apron onto the bar. "*Dictateur!* Who the hell do you think you are? Fire everyone, numbskull!! You cook the dinners!"

Francois returned to the kitchen and hollered something in French and then in Spanish. A few minutes later, he came back through the bar, the entire kitchen crew marching in formation behind him. I called the waitresses and busboys together at the bar while Betsy went for the banquet crew. MacAlister blustered about for a while, threatening to fire everyone if we didn't get back to work, but he was too late. Our defiance had already taken on a life of its own.

Pretty soon, MacAlister had his hands full with a rowdy banquet in the function room and a dining room half full of patrons who wanted their dinners or their drinks or their checks. He came back to the bar once, flushed and harried, and bellowed a few more threats, but we were in heated discussion about what to do next, so no one paid any attention. In the end, he went back into the dining room to try to put his finger back in the dike. By then most of the diners had caught on to what was happening and screwed, so he made a short speech to the stragglers finishing up dinner about difficulties in the kitchen and circumstances beyond his control. The patrons who hadn't been served got up and left. Those who had dinners sitting in front of them finished up and beat it themselves in front of the trouble they saw brewing. The banquet was a different matter. The cacophony of shouts and boos and catcalls was something to behold. It turned out to be an operating engineers' Christmas dinner, and MacAlister made the mistake of telling them the problem was a work stoppage. I expected to see him come out of the banquet hall tarred and feathered riding on a rail.

By then, we actually were on strike, so when MacAlister tried to give us one minute to get back on the job, his threats fell on deaf ears.

One of the waitresses grabbed the waiter/waitress phone number list from the hostess stand and the two busboys did an "I'll distract the guard and you grab the list" act on the front desk clerk and got the phone numbers for maintenance, engineering, and housekeeping. We divided up the lists and the jobs, and walked out as the squad cars were pulling up in front of the hotel.

chapter six

Oh, Jesus," said Barney, pronouncing the *e* in "Jesus" as "ay" in "hay" so it sounded like "Jaysus," the Irish pronunciation he favored when a calamity presented itself. I'd snuck into the hospital, using an approach I'd learned long ago from Pop: quick and decisive movement, head up, no eye contact, following a few steps behind someone who looked like he belonged there. Security guards don't bother people they think might be more powerful than they are, according to Pop. Like most people in authority, they prefer to step on someone who's already had a fall rather than take on the hale and hearty.

Whisking by the security desk, I was lucky enough to grab an uptown elevator as the doors were closing and in another stroke of fortune happened to remember Barney's room number. I woke him up, and that's where the "Jaysus!" came in—actually a couple of them, followed by a long probing look into my eyes.

"Bejaysus, McNulty, you're a terrible whoore." He said this gleefully, so I took it as a term of endearment. "Bejaysus, we'll have to take the bastards on now. It's time I got meself out of here."

Barney began squirming around on his bed, so I thought he would jump right up and go running down the hospital hallway, his tubes and wires flailing out behind him. I lunged at him to keep him from getting up just as the nurse arrived. She let out a scream. Not only was I an intruder in the hospital in the middle of the night, it looked like

I was trying to strangle Barney. Fortunately, this being New York, no one paid any attention to the scream, and Barney and I were able to calm the nurse. Barney, who wasn't really planning on jumping up out of bed anyway, settled back in. I assured the nurse I would leave quietly that minute, and Barney said he would ask his doctor in the morning when he could leave the hospital.

The picket line was a bit scraggly when I arrived shortly after six the next morning. The first objective of a strike, I learned at Pop's knee, was to make sure no one went into work. This wasn't as easy as it might seem, so I figured I should get there early. The longtime union members would be okay, but others were new to the hotel, to the union, to the country. They were scared. However badly the Savoy might treat its employees, for most of them it was a better place to be than the one they left behind. Many of them were illegals. They certainly didn't trust the company to have their best interest at heart, but they didn't trust the union, either. They'd got to where they'd gotten by relying on their own wits and weren't going to change now.

Francois, the French chef who'd gotten us into this mess in the first place, had the good manners to show up at six also and, as he spoke Spanish, kept the kitchen crew solid. Some of the kitchen crew knew some of the housekeepers and brought most of them along. The main problem areas were a contingent of Russians who worked in the housekeeping and engineering departments, the front desk clerks, who all hoped to become hotel managers, and the lunch dining room waitstaff, a collection of ballet dancers, concert musicians, and budding actors and actresses keeping a roof over their heads until stardom. When the first of the actors arrived, a gay guy who was a dead ringer for Adonis, I showed him my Equity card and told him I'd have Equity pull his card if he scabbed on a strike. He passed the threat on to the rest of the crew as they arrived, so they stayed out, too, milling around 48th Street as if they'd arrived early for a casting call. The Russians gathered around the employee entrance, waiting to see how things played out before they decided which side they were on.

MacAlister and the other managers came to the windows every few minutes to watch worriedly what was happening outside. We didn't care about the folks checking out, and check-in wouldn't be until the middle of the afternoon. The managers had their hands full just checking people out, moving baggage, and hailing cabs. As long as we kept the workers out, we were okay.

We spent the morning getting ourselves organized, picking out leaders, and shoring up those who doubted the wisdom of the strike. Around eleven, as we were herding the last of the lunch crew into line, Eliot and one of his henchmen, the weasel who'd been in the bar the night Barney was attacked, arrived on the scene, climbing out of a Lincoln Town Car. True to form, Eliot looked disdainfully at the picket line, then went inside to talk to the bosses.

Before long, I was sure, Eliot and MacAlister would get their act together and come out and address the workers with the unimpeachable sincerity of a couple of Louisiana snake oil salesmen. When that happened we'd have to convince our fellow workers—using hand signals with most of them, as far as I could tell—that a couple of waitresses, a bartender, and a chef could take on and win against the corporation that ran the hotel and the gangsters who ran the union. What would we say? Why should anyone listen to us? We didn't know half the people working in the hotel. We didn't know what the hell we were doing.

Then, at the moment of my deepest gloom, our rescuer arrived— not on a white horse and wearing a white hat, but riding a Yellow Cab and wearing a scally cap. Out of the cab climbed Barney Saunders, holding his damaged paw like a blunderbuss in front of him. Everything stopped. The picket line collapsed around him.

"Y'er a heluva crew," said Barney. "I'm proud to be one of ye." He spoke softly, yet his voice carried, as everyone leaned closer to listen. His little speech cheered everyone, making us all feel stronger and braver than we thought we were. We had to stay strong, Barney told everyone. If we stayed strong, we'd win. That was all there was to it.

It was good to have Barney back and good to hear him. We all knew there were a couple of holes in this theory of solidarity winning the day—as there might soon be holes in some of its proponents—but with a little luck we'd beat back the first assault by Eliot and MacAlister when it came.

And it did. Around twelve thirty, MacAlister came out and set up the portable banquet-room sound system under the canopy in front of the hotel. Eliot spoke first. His attempt to sound like a tough labor leader who had pushed through a deal fell flat. When he began talking about how the union couldn't "countenance insubordination"—two words, some of us figured, that had entered his vocabulary that very morning—a few of the assembled started to boo. By the time he got to the strike being illegal, he was drowned out, sound system and all, by boos, catcalls, and Bronx cheers. I stood off to the side, not much of a catcaller myself, but he found me anyway and glared in my direction.

MacAlister took the microphone then, but before he could say anything, Barney, who stood next to me, hollered, "You're a beaten man, MacAlister. Your days are numbered."

MacAlister froze. He heard what I heard in Barney's voice. It sounded like more of a threat than I thought Barney meant it to be, yet when I took in the hotel manager's stunned expression and Barney's steely-eyed glare, I wasn't so sure. MacAlister looked stricken, as if Barney had threatened his life, and Barney's expression did nothing to dispel this notion.

Eliot looked around uncomfortably, with that "Who are these people and what do they want?" expression, as he turned away toward the hotel entrance. His departure elicited a good-natured cheer from the workers, causing him to pick up his pace as he headed back inside.

Around three, when the guests began arriving to check in, the next shift of cops showed up, too, and began setting up blue sawhorse crowd-control barriers in front of the hotel. We'd been doing a pretty good job of stopping the would-be guests before they got out of their cabs and sending them on their way. Some of the desk-clerk crew had made a list of other reasonably priced hotels, and the cabdrivers, some who supported the strike and others who didn't want their windshields smashed, were taking off before their startled fares had much of a chance to think our proposition over.

The sergeant in charge was a no-nonsense, stocky black guy, with a habit of jerking himself around and grabbing the handle of his baton every few seconds, as if he were tired of talking and ready to sap someone. Luckily, it turned out he knew Sam, so they had a quiet conversation, and his attitude improved. When Betsy and Mary Donohue, both cops' wives, showed up, we put them in charge of the evening picket line, and, good-natured and chatty as they were, they had the uniformed cops eating out of the palms of their hands in no time.

I figured for once Betsy's husband would be an advantage for our side. This bit of optimism lasted about an hour until I saw one of the cops watching Barney and Betsy cuddling together at the corner of the building. Whatever else you can say about cops, and from my perspective the less said the better, they've got an unerring instinct for things that are not as they should be. On top of this, they don't trust anyone who isn't a cop, and they especially don't trust other cops' wives. So this cop, clocking the scene between Barney and Betsy, has his ears perked since she's introduced herself to him as a cop's wife. What was going on between Barney and Betsy was the tenderness and solicitousness of as-yet-unacknowledged puppy love. If I could see it, this cop could see it. Whether he'd pass this information on to Betsy's husband was anyone's guess, but if hubby showed up on the picket line, fur would fly. So Barney the Innocent had a lot more trouble than he thought he had just for letting sweet Betsy caress his damaged paw as he talked to her and brushing a few wisps of her golden hair back from her eyes when she spoke to him. The cop was gawking like he'd caught them in the sack.

Later, uptown, when Barney and I stopped at Frank's Bar for a ten-dollar steak and a couple of beers, I bit the bullet and broached the topic of his indiscreet behavior. I hated to bring it up. For one thing, it was none of my business, and Barney hadn't asked my advice. For another, Barney blushed like a schoolboy at the very mention of relations with the fairer sex. On the rare occasion when I spent an evening making a fool of myself over a pretty lost soul scoffing up rum and Cokes at the bar, Barney acted like he and I were strangers. On the even rarer occasion when I'd wander off into the night with one of these pretty waifs, he'd cast his eyes down, so as not to notice we were leaving together, and never ask where I'd gone or what had happened. So barging into his love life was something I did with great reluctance.

After hemming and hawing through the steak and a couple of beers, I managed to say. "Look, Barney, it's none of my business. Betsy's a sweet kid, but she's trouble. She doesn't mean to be. It's just the help she needs brings with it big problems. That guy she's married to is a wacko."

Sure enough, Barney's face turned bright red; his eyes sought out the ceiling and then the ground. He seemed to be gasping for air as he tried to speak. When no words came, he stared at the table, then looked at me in disbelief. He was so mortified I couldn't face him any longer and dropped my gaze to my beer glass.

We sat there in silence. I started to say, "I mean—" Of course, he knew goddamn well what I meant. And he might have begun some kind of denial. But we both knew that wouldn't wash. So there we were. Frank's was a brightly lit joint and not especially noisy, so there was no place to hide. We were sitting at a booth, also, so we were right across from one another. When you sit at a bar to talk to a guy, you can turn to look at him if you want. If you don't want, you can stare straight ahead at the mirror or the bottles, or the tropical fish, or the lady bartender's ass if you're in that sort of joint. Here, there was only down at the table, up at the ceiling, or across at poor Barney suffering acute mortification on top of his throbbing-with-pain reattached fingers.

Finally, I said, "Look, like I said, it's none of my business. You just should know I'm not the only one noticing." Then I changed the subject back to the strike, and after I'd speculated on this and that possible development, Barney caught up with himself and found his tongue.

"It's that whoore MacAlister that needs something done about him."

I raised an eyebrow. "Done about him?"

No embarrassment now. "He won't see reason, Brian. He'll have his own way. Eliot's not man enough to stand up to him, and MacAlister's not the man to give in."

Neither was Barney, I saw now. Remembering the troubles in the north of Ireland that Barney grew up into, I realized that as much as we had in common, he'd fought his battles under different rules than the ones I was used to.

"Other bosses have given in," I said. "If we keep the strike together, we've got a shot."

Barney shook his head. "Ah, Brian, you're as good a man as they come. I wish we had a hundred like you. We'll stay on the picket line then as long as you like." His expression grew serious, his blue eyes intense. "Two men stand in the way of the good we might do—Eliot and MacAlister. We can't take our eyes off either of them. And, Brian, me good-hearted friend, some one of us will need be as ruthless as they are."

chapter seven

When I got back to my apartment, I noticed the cat-food bowl was empty and the litter box had been used. I still hadn't seen the cat, though; he'd been hiding under the couch since he got there. I threw myself on the bed thinking I was exhausted and would just conk out, but I didn't. My mind started whirring. I was scared. What the hell was I doing? Barney already had his fingers chopped off. Did I think these guys were going to say, "Well, gosh darn it, McNulty, it looks like you got us beat. Come up tomorrow, we'll turn the union over to you"? Since I was a kid on Pop's picket lines, I'd known that strikes were often life-and-death struggles. People got killed, and people killed. And I didn't want any part of being killed or killing—in that order. Eliot was a stone-cold gangster. Now here was Barney, reliving his IRA days. What the hell was I going to do when bodies started dropping around me?

My body was rigid with the tension I'd talked myself into, so when the phone rang, I sprang out of bed like I'd been catapulted.

It was my ex-wife.

"Kevin's been arrested," she said breathlessly.

"Jesus Christ!" My heart fell at my feet. "What? What happened?"

"Your son was caught smoking pot in the playground across from your father's apartment building."

This is my ex-wife true to form. When Kevin does something

good, she says "my son Kevin" or, if she's feeling generous, "our son Kevin." He gets picked up by the cops, and it's "your son Kevin."

"Is he okay? Is he out of jail?"

"That's right!" she screeched. "That's just like you! Kevin's ruining his life, and you sound like a goddamn hoodlum lawyer." There was a pause until she screamed, "Your son has been arrested. He's a goddamn criminal. What are you going to about it!?" Her voice was like an air raid siren in my ear. Karen doesn't handle crises well. She's like Chicken Little crying, "The sky is falling." She's borderline hysterical because she's worried about Kevin. I understand that. She still drives me nuts.

Truth be told, I was at least as hysterical as she was, if not more. I'd been in jail, and I'd tear my heart out of my chest with my own hands to keep Kevin out of there. "Listen to me, Karen!" My volume was now close to matching hers. "Where's Kevin? Is he locked up?"

"A lot you care. Where were you when you could have stopped this from happening? What good is it doing anything now?"

"Karen," I bellowed, "where's Kevin? If he's in jail, we need to get him out right now. Now!!"

"Maybe it would be good for him to stay in jail. Maybe the stupid kid will learn something if they keep him there and scare the pants off him."

I tried to keep my voice calm. "Karen, no kid should be in a New York City jail. Things happen in those cells that kids never recover from. Kids like Kevin are tossed in with every kind of deranged misfit." My voice started rising again in spite of myself, not because of anything Karen was doing but because I was picturing Kevin in a cell and it was driving me crazy. "Please tell me where he is," I pleaded.

"What do you think you can do to help now?"

I told myself to be calm, to not get mad. When I thought I was ready, I tried again. "Karen, please tell me where my son is."

A pause and then, "He's here." Relief flooded through my body. I could have cried.

"Can I talk to him, please?"

She hesitated, but seemed to be losing her enthusiasm for the fight, because the next thing I heard was Kevin's bored, angry, insolent voice. "Yeh, what?"

"Kevin," I said, hoping to communicate by the sound of my voice the anguish in my heart.

"Oh, c'mon, Dad. It's only a ticket. It's no big deal."

"No big deal!!?" I screamed. "Are you crazy? Have you lost your mind? You can't get arrested. You can't smoke pot. Are you nuts?"

"Right," said Kevin, the kid with the chain around my soul. "You never smoked pot. You never got arrested."

Ah, the sins of the father. I must have known this would happen, that all I wished for for Kevin would crumble to dust because of his no-good father. A child of divorced parents, with a father who couldn't find a place in the respectable workaday world, who spent his life in bars and dreamed he was an actor one audition away from the part that would make him a star, what did I expect? What the hell kind of role model was I? What happens to a poor kid with a bum for a father? I didn't need Karen to browbeat me. I could do it fine without her.

After hanging up, I lay back down on top of my bed, remorseful and despairing. Kevin, my heart and my soul, was headed for more trouble than he could imagine. I'd been in jams in my life; I'd been scared for myself, plenty scared, but never like this. This time it was my kid. I pictured the cops coming for him—the boy I'd always been able to comfort ripped out of my hands, the steel door slammed shut between us. Tears gathered in my eyes. I didn't have the right to ruin a kid's life.

When I got to the picket line early the next morning, Sam Jones, the day bartender, saw me and walked over. As usual, he was energetic and cheerful, pumping my hand and clapping me on the back. "Awright, Brian! I never seen you up and around at this hour before, 'cept maybe you on your way home from the night before." He laughed heartily. "Better watch out for this daylight. You don't look natural." He clapped me on the back again, then spoke softly. "Eliot call me last night, sayin' he want to meet me. I told him I didn't know about what was coming down here. He need to talk to you."

"What about Barney?"

Sam squinted, scrunching up his face as if he were in deep thought. I didn't think he really was. He'd already made up his mind, I suspected. This pause for deep thinking was for my benefit. He had this habit of making believe he treated things said by white folks with great seriousness.

"Barney's okay," he said, "but this one's for you and me." He nodded as he said this, compressing his lips and looking me in the eye—a quick hard look. Sam was like that. His confidence left me feeling it wouldn't do much good to argue. For myself, I would have discussed this with Barney and a half-dozen other people before making a decision. So it struck me, as it often does, that I tend to be buffeted about in life by folks who are more confident about what they choose to do than I am about what I've chosen to do.

We met Eliot at his office on the second floor of a loft building in the garment district. It was still early enough in the morning to have to dodge the dress trolleys as we walked from where the cab dropped us on Seventh Avenue. The garment district was one of the places in Manhattan I really liked because folks actually worked for a living there—making things, moving stuff around. Over the years I'd known it, the area had both changed and not changed. Young Latin guys still pushed or pulled the racks of dresses or coats or jackets through the streets, and there were probably still hundreds of small textile wholesalers in the staunchly working-class, broad-fronted loft buildings. But some of the buildings and streets had the ominous look of conversion about them—Latin guys in hard hats instead of Latin guys pushing hand trucks. You could see that in a few years another piece of the real New York would be turned into outlandishly priced condominiums and trendy restaurants overseen by chefs who put their names on the menu. Still, the changing face of New York, however much it saddened me, was not my concern this morning.

The office we entered had a door with a frosted glass window that looked like the one with SPADE AND ARCHER printed on it. The office had the same large wooden desk and metal file cabinet you might expect behind such a door and the same dusty wood floor. There was an inner office also. But that door was closed. Eliot sat at the desk in the outer office, looking out of place and uncomfortable. I suspected this was because the office served as a larger than normal post office box and not much else. In addition to trying on the desk for size, Eliot seemed to be trying on the aspect of a reasonable man as well. He didn't look any more comfortable in that role than he did behind the desk.

"You guys are making a mistake," he said, then waited for this to sink in. "I don't gotta do this. I don't gotta put up with your shit. But I'm a good guy." He snuck a look at each of us, I assumed because he expected an argument about his good-guy assertion. Sam and I waited to see what would come next.

What came next was an envelope from Eliot's inside suit jacket pocket. When he reached for it, I panicked, thinking he went for a gun, but the hand went in and the envelope came out so fast, I hadn't time to react anyway.

"What's in there's for you. I'm putting youse on the payroll with the union to get the strike over." He brushed his lapels with his hand to flatten the front of the suit jacket. It was brown, and he wore a blue shirt and a darker blue tie. Everything looked crisply ironed, and his silver hair was slicked back. "Settle it any way you want." It seemed like he was hiding behind his thick eyebrows as he spoke. "Only thing is, you gotta settle it quick, and the broad don't go back."

This was cool, I said to myself. I'd never been offered a bribe before; probably I'd never done anything worth bribing me to do or not do. I was curious as to how much was in the envelope, but it wasn't likely I'd find out.

I stood up. Sam stayed sitting, so this gave me pause, but I went ahead anyway. "Nice of you to offer, Mr. Eliot. But no thanks."

Sam didn't say anything. I looked at him. He looked at me. I gestured with my eyes toward the envelope. He didn't take his eyes from mine. His expression was frank, not evasive, nothing to hide.

Eliot seemed troubled by my answer. The idea of someone refusing a bribe must have been outside his frame of reference. He mumbled a sort of gangsterland pep talk, a soliloquy that contained a lot of youse guys on the one side and dem assholes on the udder side, ending up something like wese guys had heart and knew how things were and would do the right thing, while dem guys—the assholes—would be persuaded by the force of our argument, the emphasis being on force.

I was about to tell Eliot he could stick his envelope up his ass, when Sam said, "Excuse me, Mr. Eliot, what Brian's sayin' here is we don't want to take your money until we show you we got the goods. You understand what I'm sayin'? You keep that envelope, Mr. Eliot. But keep it where you can get your hands on it, because when me and McNulty finish up, you'll be needin' that envelope again."

Eliot nodded. "Youse guys know how it is."

One of us guys for sure didn't know how it was. I didn't know what the hell Sam was doing, but he didn't seem to care. I wouldn't say he was whistling as we walked along Seventh Avenue to the subway, but it sure seemed like he was. The only thing he did say, just as we entered the subway, was that we probably didn't need to mention the meeting to anyone.

I didn't want the money. I wanted the strike. This was a fine kettle of fish. Sam was no better than Eliot, selling out the workers for a few bucks, even for a few thousand bucks. This was what happened when you had secret meetings. I sat on the subway getting more and more pissed off, until we got off at 50th Street.

"What's the matter with you?" Sam said as we walked toward the hotel. "You wanna go duke it out with Eliot again? When you gonna learn, man? You stand up there all noble and tell Eliot you too good for his money. See where you wind up." I was staring at him, probably with my mouth open. "What we got now is some time if you can keep your mouth shut." He looked me over and his expression clouded up. "What you gawkin' at, McNulty? You never seen me before?"

This was a New York thing. I knew too many people like Sam. You're supposed to know. If you don't know, too bad for you. You're going to have to guess because no one explains anything to you. It would seem simple enough to ask Sam whether he was willing to take Eliot's money, but he figured I should already know. I didn't though. First I thought he was. Now it sounded like he wasn't.

"I don't understand," I said.

Sam eyed me suspiciously. "You ever think about movin' to the country, McNulty? A small town somewhere maybe? You ain't cut out for city life. Things move fast here, man. You gotta be quick on your feet."

He waited a few seconds for me to put together a response. It was in vain. I couldn't think of one. Maybe he was right. A small town, a slower pace . . .

We found Barney in the Greek diner across from the hotel. The shop was union, and the Greek guys were friends with Barney and a lot of the hotel workers, so they'd set up an office of sorts for us in a small function room at the back of the restaurant. It gave us a base—a place to go inside and warm up, and even more important, a bathroom. The owners of the diner were tough guys, too, who themselves worked six or four days and had a weak spot for the toiling masses, who were by and large their customers.

I didn't feel right not telling Barney about the meeting with Eliot, but on instinct, I chose to throw my lot in with Sam for the time being. I hoped I wouldn't regret it.

Barney told us what had been going on at the picket line. A couple of housekeepers had gone back in, but the Russians were holding on. The day dining room crew was restless and planning a meeting with Equity to see if they really had to stay on strike. Everyone else was strong. The picketers had turned the provisions and laundry trucks and, most important, the trash haulers, around. Most of the cabdrivers were avoiding the hotel, too. I didn't know how long any of this would last once word got out that the union wasn't going to sanction the strike. We needed something to happen pretty quick.

That evening, Betsy, Mary Donohue, and the night crew again had things under control on the picket line, so I went uptown for some rest and peace and quiet. Barney lived even farther uptown, in an Irish neighborhood in the North Bronx. I'd gone up there a few times with him to the Irish bars in days gone by, and he invited me up this evening, but it's a long trek on the train and an even longer trek back home when you're tired and half drunk, with the alternative, sleeping on a lumpy couch and taking the subway back in the morning grubby and hungover, even less appealing, so with that to consider, on top of my having to keep secret my talk with Eliot, I said no and went home.

When you live alone, sometimes the walls start closing in. The excitement of the day crashes around your feet and you're left with a lot of emptiness. Sometimes, you don't notice. You've come from somewhere and you're thinking about that, or you'll be going somewhere later and your mind is on that. Other times, like this night, you're too aware of the nothingness around you. Other people have lives they go home to—kids and wives, fathers and mothers, friends and lovers— but this night I was having a hard time with the end of the day. I should go and see Pop; I hadn't been out to Brooklyn for a while, but I didn't feel like making the trip to Flatbush either.

Thinking of Pop, I thought of Kevin. I had to deal with him. I would see him this weekend for his regular visit. He'd been skipping the visits once in a while lately, so I should have figured he was up to no good. I got careless and let my guard down. Kevin's a great kid, but the teen years are tough. Like most kids his age, he needs a leash, and I hadn't been doing that. I don't like saying no to him. I don't like throwing my weight around. But this weekend would be a showdown.

As soon as I started thinking about Kevin, my mood changed. The empty places began to fill up. I remembered I was a guy with something important to do in life. I had a kid to take care of. When I got into my apartment, I caught a whiff from the used litter box and remembered I had a cat to keep up with, too. I hadn't seen him, but knew he must still be there. The food bowl was empty again, and he certainly found his way to the litter box. It was amazing how much shit one little cat could produce. I didn't much care that he hid. My job was to keep him until the weather warmed up, and it was already warm enough for him to find an alley to set up digs. I'd left the kitchen window open, so he could slip through the bars and out into the alley if he decided to leave early, but he hadn't taken the hint.

After rummaging through the refrigerator and finding a TV dinner in the freezer, I considered heading out to one of the neighborhood bars for a couple of pops, but decided against it. Too often, a couple of pops led to another couple, and the later it got, the more interesting things got, or so I might have thought. I seldom drank at home alone, either, and I didn't have any pot. So I found myself in a dreadful state of normalcy for the evening.

I read for a while and fell asleep earlier than I usually do. Somewhere in the night, I felt something moving on the bed, then a soft pressure against my thigh. I didn't wake fully, just reached out and felt something furry. This startled me awake enough to realize it was the cat. I thought about giving him the boot but realized he'd come up for warmth after the boilers shut down in the wee hours of the morning, so I left him alone.

Since I'd gone to sleep so early, I got to the picket line early the next morning again, leaving the cat in the kitchen, giving him some food in his bowl, and showing him the open window. The line looked more professional that morning, with printed picket signs someone had arranged for, and the blue police barricades. Pop was there when I arrived. This didn't surprise me. Strike support was one of the Communist corporal works of mercy. He was walking beside Barney preaching class solidarity when I caught up with them. Barney was beating his drum again, too, telling Pop about the whoore MacAlister and how something must be done about him.

"It's him holding up the works," said Barney. "He's a hard man and he won't give in."

"You can't let this get personal," said Pop. "The workers want their money. They don't care about grudges."

Barney nodded. We were all three of us thinking about this as we walked slowly in a circle.

"You'll need to get this settled before Christmas," said Pop. "You won't hold them once they see the holidays. You can't explain a strike to kids waiting for presents."

Barney and I nodded about this also. We had less than two weeks. If MacAlister didn't throw in the towel by then, most of the workers would start drifting back into work, if not stampeding. It was cold, even though we were walking, so after another half hour, I sent Pop home, asking him to round up Kevin and hold on to him until I called him. I was reluctant to tell Pop about Kevin's latest escapade, more for my own sake than Kevin's. I still couldn't handle Pop's disapproval.

After he left, Barney and I picketed for a few more minutes in silence. When I said I was going to the Greeks' for a cup of coffee, Barney cleared his throat a couple of times, scuffling around, looking at his feet.

"There's a bit of a problem came up last night." His tone suggested it was more than a bit of a problem.

"Oh?"

"It's Betsy. Her husband came by the picket line and told her to go into work." Barney faced me squarely. His blue eyes weren't twinkling. "She said he'll be stopping by today to have a word with me."

chapter eight

We stayed on the picket line all day into the evening, dealing with small problems that came up: a couple of tense moments with a belligerent guest and the hotel security guards. Then a wiseguy Russian cabdriver, who most likely saw the strike as the return of the Bolsheviks, harangued us for a good few minutes, but his accent was so thick no one understood what he saying. We also had some work to do with our own members: some housekeepers with cold feet and a desk clerk we figured out was a stooge for MacAlister. The real problem was yet to come, in the form of Betsy's husband.

Late in the afternoon, the buildings around us swallowed up the little bit of warmth the sun provided, so a deeper chill descended with the darkness. The street was mostly deserted by then, except when the light changed at Ninth Avenue and a scraggly herd of taxis, cars, and trucks galloped through to the east and the next traffic light at Eighth Avenue. We stomped our feet and burrowed into our coats, waiting for the looming confrontation.

One of the bad habits bartenders develop is thinking we have to be the peacemaker if we see a fight brewing. We see it as part of our job to head off this sort of trouble, mostly to keep the combatants from breaking up the joint. With me it's worse, another legacy of Pop's "no man is an island" brainwashing. So I was already thinking that if Betsy's husband showed up, it was going to be up to me to turn him around.

This waiting for a battle I hoped wouldn't come reminded me of myself as a kid in Brooklyn, waiting one night on the corner, a gang of us—five or six, maybe seven or eight—waiting for the Puerto Rican kids from Sunset Park, who said they'd be coming for us, after our baseball game that afternoon broke up in a fight at home plate between Pat O'Hagan and the other team's catcher. I didn't know what the other kids felt that night—like I didn't know what Barney felt this night, though he seemed calm enough. Maybe some of them looked forward to the fight, but I dreaded it, hoped and prayed they wouldn't come. That night, the Puerto Ricans didn't come. Probably a grown-up, one of their dads maybe, clocked what was going on and headed them off. This night, though, Barney and I were the grown-ups, and there wouldn't be anyone to head it off.

The night crew was sparser than it had been earlier in the week. There were a couple of waitresses, a handful of kitchen workers, and one of the night desk clerks, who pestered me with questions as to whether the strike was legal, and would the hotel hire strikebreakers and replace us all, and when did I think the strike would be over.

Like most people, I don't like trouble. Unfortunately, there are people who look for it—far too many for my money—and one of them was heading our way tonight. I didn't even remember the jerk's name. So I'm going to say, *Look, Betsy's husband, you seem like a reasonable guy*—a lie to begin with—and then *you don't want any trouble here*—another lie because to create trouble is precisely why he was coming here.

Half a block away I saw him, walking with the unmistakable gait of a drunk holding himself stiffly in line, pretending he isn't staggering. He was well built and muscular, and his leather bomber's jacket didn't hide that his body was hard. As cold as it was, he didn't wear a hat, and his hair was longer than you'd expect for a cop. He walked right up to us, his eyes lively with drink, something between a smile and a sneer on his lips.

"You the guy telling my wife not to go to work?" he asked, his face inches from Barney's.

"Good evening," said Barney, his eyes just as lively and his stance as challenging.

I was standing there with squirrels running around my insides and these guys looked like they were having the time of their lives. "Watch his hand," I said to Betsy's husband. "It's hurt."

He saw Barney's bandages and seemed confused for a moment, as if dimly remembering a prohibition of some sort about slugging a cripple, but this didn't hold him back for long. He tapped Barney in the chest with his forefinger. "Maybe someone didn't tell you Betsy's married." His words rang with menace. "Maybe you don't know she's married with a baby at home. Maybe you think you got some business taking advantage of a girl that don't know much and ain't been around. You the big union guy so fucking tough. I'll show you how fucking tough you are. Your hand wasn't bandaged I'd smack you down right now—"

I stepped in then. He was working his way up to a rage, and he might just smack Barney anyway. I didn't want that to happen and Barney try to smack back and leave a couple of his fingers in the gutter. Usually, if you get a guy's eyes off the person he's going after and onto yours, you can short-circuit the frenzy long enough to get a few words in. This didn't happen. That I'd stepped up didn't register on the guy.

Adrenaline or instinct—the call of the wild, perhaps—took over. I thumped him in the chest with the heel of my hand to get him off Barney and onto me. Not surprisingly, this worked. In the blink of an eye, he'd grabbed me by the collar of my coat with both hands, thumbs at my throat, and had lifted me onto my toes. I saw what was coming, so before he could fling me backward, I grabbed for something of his and came up with a handful of hair. When he shoved, I brought him with me to the sidewalk. His resistance to coming along broke my fall, even though I yanked out a good chunk of the hair I grabbed, but he landed on top of me, and the collision smacked my head into the sidewalk. He managed to get off a punch, too, a good one that smashed into my left cheek and hurt all the more because my head was already pressed against the sidewalk and had nowhere to go to absorb the punch.

He didn't get off a second shot because amidst a chorus of shrieks and screams, two shadowy bodies attached themselves to him, one to either arm, and in the melee, he was dragged off of me, while soft-yet-firm Betsy tumbled across him to take his place on top of me. My ears were ringing from the punch to my cheek but not so much that I didn't take pleasant note of Betsy's arrival and her squirming around on my midsection to get herself righted again. When she did, she lit into her husband. "Dennis, you asshole. Are you crazy?" She screamed this into his face, all of us watching. The other shadowy shape, I realized, was Mary Donohue, who just then, unfortunately, let go of Dennis's right arm.

Dennis looked at Betsy stupidly. "Don't—" he said. I noticed him become conscious of everyone watching. As soon as he did, he grabbed Betsy's arm and yanked her toward him.

"Let go, you son of a bitch," she said, and tried to yank her arm back. She twisted to get away, and he held her arm until she was bent forward. When he loosened his grip to let her unbend, she swung with her opposite hand and grazed his chin. He let go then and backhanded her across the face, a glancing blow because she saw it coming and rolled with it, but he'd swung hard.

This was enough for the boys in blue to intervene. Two of them grabbed Dennis and walked him away down to the corner. He was agitated and talking a mile a minute to them, but I was pretty sure he was done with us, for the evening anyway. They wouldn't arrest him, most likely, but they'd get him out of there, probably to a cops' bar in Brooklyn, where he'd spend the rest of the night telling his fellow workers about what a bitch his wife was.

The picket line was a somber place after the commotion. Barney and a bevy of waitresses led by Mary Donohue fluttered around Betsy. Me, who'd had his bell rung pretty loudly, no one paid much attention to, although the kitchen crew eyed me with some interest. This thing with Betsy's husband, bad enough on its own terms, was the kind of problem Pop always said could scuttle a strike. So when I took a break and went to the Greeks' for a cup of coffee, I called him.

"Not good," he said right off the bat. "Something like this lets people start crying the strike is falling apart and gives them an excuse to give up."

"I know it's not good. Tell me something I don't know."

"You might have to get rid of Barney."

I didn't like to hear this talk about getting rid of Barney. First off, he was my friend. He was also our leader, and I wasn't sure that anyone could take over for him.

"And that young woman. Is she going back into work?"

"I don't know, but I doubt it." Pop was irritating me, bringing up these realities I didn't want to deal with, so I told him I had to go and hung up.

Back on the picket line, I fell in behind my fellow workers, all of us walking a kind of desultory march in front of the hotel. After a few moments, Betsy sidled up beside me, hooking her arm into mine.

"Thanks for what you did, Brian."

"Think nothing of it. It was a moment of temporary insanity. Besides, if I remember correctly, you rescued me."

"Think nothing of it," said Betsy with her coy smile. "A moment of temporary insanity. You're still my hero."

We circled the far signpost and entered the backstretch. The street was quiet, darkness in full swing. I noticed for the first time colored Christmas lights blinking from a few windows in the apartments on the far side of the street.

"What am I going to do, Brian?" She tightened her grip on my arm.

The kid was in a tough spot. Some things you get yourself into, you don't get out of again. I didn't want to tell her this. She probably knew what to expect from her husband better than I did.

"Poor Betsy," I said in spite of myself.

She loosened her grip on my arm, so I put the arm around her shoulder, and she leaned in against me. "Not poor Betsy. If it wasn't for Kate, I'd kill the son of a bitch."

"Nice talk. This is New York. We don't allow killing here."

She looked at me quizzically.

"Seriously. It's against the law."

"You'd never know it. Anyway, I'm going to pick up Kate from the babysitter and stay at Mary's tonight." She said this last thing like a question, as if she weren't quite sure of it.

For good reason. "Isn't that where Barney's been staying since Mary figured out he wasn't able to feed himself with his bum mitt?"

"He's not staying there now. He moved to a monastery or something."

"A what?"

"It's a place the priests have up in the Bronx where men can stay for a short time—a retreat house."

"Even so. Mary's is where your husband would expect you to go if he thinks Barney is there." I could see that I'd embarrassed her, but I envisioned a middle-of-the-night confrontation with women screaming, children crying, and Mary's husband Pat going for his service revolver when Daddy Dennis broke down the door coming to get his wife and kid. A lot was at risk here, so a bit of embarrassment for causing all this difficulty might not be such a bad thing for Betsy. She had a lot of things to work out, with the kid and all, and Barney shouldn't have a role to play yet.

She walked silently for a while, her head down. After a few minutes, she said so softly I barely heard her, "I don't have anywhere else to go."

After an even longer time, I said, "You can stay with me until we figure something out." Stray cat. Lady with a baby. What the hell?

Some hours later, Betsy rang my bell, accompanied by a harried cabdriver carrying a half ton of baby equipment. When the cabdriver left, Betsy looked at me, then looked around nervously.

Kevin had arrived in the meantime, so I told her this, assuming it created a higher level of propriety.

It seemed to work. Her face lost its strain, and she worked her way though the foyer. "Oh, Brian," she said as soon as she entered the living room. "You have a kitten." The baby noticed this, too, and screeched. The cat, having grown less timid, was now sleeping on the couch instead of under it. He still hadn't shown any signs of moving on.

"What's his name?" Betsy asked, heading over to pet the creature.

"Otto."

"That's a strange name for a cat."

"It's a strange cat," I said, as the animal hissed and dove out from under her hand.

Betsy seemed quite efficiently motherly as she tended to the tyke, who took in the surroundings without much comment. Betsy seemed different with the kid, sure of herself, almost showing off, but in an endearing way. She wore black jeans and a black sweater. Her blond hair was tied back, and her lips glistened. Despite her troubles, her blue eyes sparkled with life. There was no awkwardness between us. The tyke went to sleep pretty quickly, and Betsy's eyes began to droop as soon as the baby's closed.

They slept in my bed. Kevin and I slept on the fold-out couch. Early in the morning, the blaring phone woke me up.

chapter nine

W e got trouble!" It was Sam. Before I could ask him what it was this time, he told me. "Someone offed MacAlister."

I knew the term, though I hadn't heard it for a while. I knew what Sam was telling me. Maybe this idea of offing coming at me from out of the past threw me. I knew what he said. I just didn't want to believe it.

"What?" I asked. "What do you mean?"

"You heard me, man. You know goddamn well what I mean."

"How do you know?"

Sam hesitated. "I heard it from the cops as soon as I got here this morning. They had the hotel entrance taped off."

"MacAlister was killed in the hotel?"

"I guess. You better get your ass down here. Barney says he ain't comin'."

"Who did it? Why won't Barney come down?"

"Did what?"

"Killed MacAlister."

Sam hesitated. "You tell me."

"I don't know. How would I know?"

"You better know somethin', man, and we all best be able to account for ourselves pretty quick."

"Why?"

Sam let out a deep breath. "McNulty, you know who got killed? You know what we been doin' lately? Who they gonna think killed him? Where were you last night?"

"Home. I was here with—" I stopped and looked at my bedroom door. This was great. I'm going to tell Betsy's crazy husband she spent last night at my apartment?

"Well."

"I was home."

"You gotta do better than that, McNulty. Better say you were with me. Better if we're all together last night. The cops won't believe it. But there's nothin' they can do if we keep our story straight. You, me, and Barney playin' cards all night. Relaxin', chillin', gettin' away from the strike, playin' cards on 129th Street—Moxie's—the cops know it. It's been busted a dozen times. I know everyone there last night. Our story'll be as solid as a brick shithouse. You and me—you and me and Barney—playing cards all night at Moxie's. You got it, man? Let the motherfuckers try to break that story—"

"Hold on, Sam—" I tried, but he'd hung up. Great! I hate phony stories. I'm a lousy liar. I should have told him I was with Betsy, but I wasn't sure Betsy's crazed husband would buy into the platonic nature of her overnight visit. I also didn't know why Sam jumped to the conclusion I needed someone to cover for me. Then, maybe it wasn't me.

Betsy, her face wrinkled with sleep and concern, came bounding out of the bedroom as I was hanging up the phone. She was wearing one of my white dress shirts that I guess she'd borrowed for a nightgown. It reached about to her midthigh, but she hadn't buttoned it all the way down, so when she moved a certain way, it gaped open and her lacy black panties peeped out, the vision of her lace-shrouded crotch taking my breath away for the moment, despite the crisis. When she realized I was transfixed, she looked worried for a second but caught my drift pretty quickly and blushed. She turned and trotted back to the bedroom, the tails of my shirt swishing against her own cute little tail as she left.

When she returned, fully attired, I regained my composure and told her what happened. She was shocked, and the awfulness of what happened began to sink in for me, too, as I told her about the murder. I didn't like MacAlister. He was arrogant and used his power as a boss to humiliate workers, the kind of boss workers do rise up against when humiliation becomes too much to bear. Still I didn't wish him dead, but I guessed Sam was right. When the boss is killed in the middle of a strike, you've got yourself a whole picket line full of suspects.

I hoped that as soon as the cops figured out MacAlister's connection to Eliot and the gangsters, the emphasis would shift. But I wasn't going to bet on it. What MacAlister's murder meant to the strike was an unanswered question, and why Barney didn't go to the picket line where he was sorely needed was an even bigger one. He didn't, though, so I figured I'd better get down there if for no other reason than to put the ix-nay on Sam's cock-and-bull story about the three male strike leaders playing cards all night at an after-hours poker palace in Harlem.

I asked Betsy to stay put in the apartment, taking care of her baby, the cat, and Kevin, who was buried under pillows and blankets on the couch. "Tell Kevin to take the cat for a walk when he gets up," I told her. "Show him some of the neighborhood alleys. Maybe he'll see something he likes." She looked at me strangely, but I left before she could say anything.

As soon as I went through the outside door and saw the police cruiser, I sensed trouble, but I was wrong about what kind. I looked left and saw a flash of blue. At about the same moment, something pushed me hard in the chest, and right behind that something whacked me in the stomach. I went backwards, pushing the door to my building open with my back and shoulders, into the vestibule. I recognized Dennis's grim expression a foot or so in front of my face just before the lights went out.

When I woke up, I remembered being jostled, and I remembered Dennis's face and the thumps in the front and the back. Pretty soon, I recognized my own apartment and that Kevin was holding an ice pack on my head—one of the ice packs I'd picked up when I coached his rec league basketball team a couple of years before. Sitting across from me, in my easy chair, was Betsy, holding another of my ice packs to her cheek and sobbing.

"He took Kate," she belched out between sobs, as soon as she saw I was awake. "He took Katie," she wailed again. I rolled my head to the side to try to see her better and a pain shot up from the base of my neck through my head to the tip of my nose. I started to say something, but I had no idea what, and it came out as a moan anyway.

Kevin was staring into my eyes. "Can you see me?" he asked. His expression was serious and, strangely to me, confident. There was a kind of reassurance in his calmness. I started to nod my head and got the shooting pain again. This time, I was able to get out a word, which was "Yes." He held up two fingers in front of my eyes. "How many fingers?" he asked.

"Eleven," I said.

"Don't joke around, Dad. Lie still. How many fingers?"

This time there were three.

The door buzzer rang. Whatever Kevin saw in my eyes caused him to put his hand gently on my forehead. "Relax. I called EMS. It's the ambulance."

Sure enough, it was. They checked me out, shining a flashlight in my eyes, taking my pulse, blood pressure, and temperature. Temperature? They wanted to take me to the hospital, but I wouldn't go. I had a concussion and it was possible my brain was bleeding, they told me. Even though my head hurt too much for me to move it, I didn't buy this brain-bleeding idea. I'd watched too many cowboy movies when I was a kid, where the guy in the white hat gets clunked on the head but a few minutes later picks himself up from the ground, finds Stewball waiting patiently at the hitching post, and rides off into the hills after the desperadoes. I wasn't so hurt that I didn't remember the strike and know I needed to be there—Pop would never forgive me, throbbing head or not. If I could get rid of these EMS folks and get to my stash of codeine pills, I figured I could hang in. When they finally did leave, I asked Kevin if he would track down Ntango through the car-service dispatcher and get me my codeine pills from the medicine cabinet.

Betsy had only a busted lip to worry about, that and her hijacked daughter. She'd calmed herself by the time the EMS folks packed up, assuring me—and herself—that Dennis wouldn't hurt Kate. He was just getting back at her. She didn't want to call the cops, something I understood, even though I suggested it. Domestic cases aren't the NYPD's strong suit, especially so, I'd bet, when it was one of their own who slugged his wife and grabbed his kid because she shacked up for the night with a ne'er-do-well bartender.

"I'll find him," said Betsy. "I'm sure he went home. He thinks he can do whatever he wants."

At the moment, it did seem like hubby Dennis held all the good cards. If she was right that he went home, he had the house, and now he had the baby. Betsy was out in the cold. If she went to the cops, even if they believed her, she didn't have a place to live and at the moment, because of the strike, wasn't even fully employed. The only thing she had going for her was that he smacked her. But it wasn't like he'd held a gun to her head or beat her within an inch of her life—and who cared if he beat up the bartender she was with?

"You need a lawyer," I told her. "Right away. You're gonna have a custody fight, you gotta do everything right from the beginning." I knew from bitter experience.

Betsy shook her head, her expression one of hopeless understanding that you see in the eyes of a welfare woman sometimes after a session with her caseworker. "Not a custody fight. He wants me back. That's all. He wants me back on my knees." Her eyes reddened; her voice, though it was barely above a whisper, filled with anguish and rage. "Did anyone ever own you?"

I didn't answer, but she didn't want one anyway. You want your baby, get down on your knees. Roll over when I tell you. No. No one had ever done that to me, but there was a time I thought I might not see Kevin again. "You gotta go to someone for help," I said.

"Who, Brian? Who do I go to for help? Hire one of Eliot's goons to kill him?"

"For now, get a lawyer."

She shook her head. "For now, Brian, I've got to go to him to be with Katie."

Kevin came in from the kitchen to tell me Ntango would pick me up in half an hour. I didn't know what to say to him. You'd think finding your father lying on the marble vestibule floor of his apartment building would freak a kid out. Instead, he gets me into my apartment where he'd just witnessed a kidnapping and there's a woman there—closer in age to him than to me—bleeding from the lip and hysterical because someone snatched her baby. He takes all this in stride, tends to the wounded, calls the ambulance—but not the cops without asking first—and doesn't ask questions until things are under control.

Now, I'm the father here, providing wisdom, sage advice. I'm prepared to read him the riot act because he's been caught smoking pot—I want to read him the riot act. I don't want him smoking pot or drinking or doing any of the crazy things kids do. I'm scared for him. But this doesn't seem like the right time to lecture him. He's calm. He's mature. He's taking care of me. I'm confident in him. I'm proud of him.

So I told him that.

"Is this connected to the strike?" Kevin asked while we waited for Ntango. "And who's she anyway?" He nodded toward the bedroom, where Betsy was getting herself ready.

The codeine had kicked in, so the pain had dulled and seemed to be coming from far away. I was beginning to feel at peace. "Betsy's one of the strikers, and she's having trouble with her husband. That's who came to pick up the kid."

"Why did he smack you down?"

"I guess I was in his way." I asked Kevin to keep Betsy company until she was ready to return to her better half and then come down to the picket line. He said he was supposed to play basketball with some of his friends in Brooklyn around noon and could he meet me at Pop's later. I hesitated.

In mock exasperation, he rolled his eyes. "Jocks and nerds, Dad. They're straight."

"Maybe you'd want to consider becoming a nerd."

"Yeh, Dad. Right." said Kevin.

———

When I got to the picket line, I found yellow police tape cordoning off the hotel entrance and the picketers fenced in with wooden police barricades on the opposite side of the street. Since they were in front of a Greek coffee shop and not the hotel, they'd given up picketing in favor of gawking at the police activity. Mary Donohue arrived just before I did. She and Francois were trying to buck up the troops, but she was out of sorts and jittery herself, so she was having the opposite effect, undoing whatever enthusiasm Francois conjured up, raising the tension level of the group so high I expected everyone to turn and run.

As I gawked at the hotel from in front of the Greeks' like everyone else, I noticed that the holiday season had arrived during the night. Decorating had probably been delayed by the strike, but the old Savoy was decked out in its Christmas finery this morning—wreaths and candy canes, ornaments on the potted yew trees in front of the doors, a tasteful string of white lights around the lobby windows. They must have done the decorating after we closed the picket line down for the night. I wondered if MacAlister had been there supervising the operation, thinking he'd gotten over on the union one more time. I suppose if you get to do one last thing in your life, putting up Christmas decorations isn't such a bad choice.

Having reflected enough for one morning on life's ironies, I went over to the front of the hotel to see if I could find out any more about what was going on and got a cop's baton in the chest for my trouble.

"What's happening, officer?" I asked politely, nonetheless.

"Police business."

"No shit. What police business?"

"Move along, wiseguy. You can read about it in the newspaper."

"You've been a big help," I said, "but you guys are denying us our legal right to picket. I think you need to get your sergeant."

"I told you to fuck off. This is police business. We got our rights to conduct police business."

The cop wasn't a kid. A bit bulky, with gray hair showing under the edges of his cap and a belly bulging over his belt, probably fifteen or twenty years in, still standing on his flat feet keeping the crowd back, this wasn't a guy who'd do any strategic thinking about the situation. So I went back behind the wooden barricades to conspire with Francois and Mary Donohue. They rounded up our fellow workers. This time when I went back, I did so after kicking down the barricades and with thirty workers, led by Mary and Francois, marching menacingly behind me. This time we got the sergeant.

As Sergeant O'Day and I walked down the block together in quiet conversation, while the workers and the uniforms faced off, he, a narrowback mick like myself, said there'd been a murder in the hotel. He couldn't tell me any details, he said, because they were investigating. But if I'd keep the picketers calm for a couple of hours, he'd make sure no one registered in the hotel during that time. "Better than a picket line, if you ask me," he said.

"I don't suppose you could give me any information . . . off the record, maybe?"

He shook his head. "They don't tell me anything either. The detectives think their shit don't stink." He appraised me, his blue eyes intense. Sympathy in his expression, I would have said if I didn't know better.

"Well, I mean," I tried apologetically, "we're not suspects or anything, are we?"

He shrugged a shoulder and raised an eyebrow. "You'll lay off for a couple of hours, right?"

Back again behind the wooden barricades, I told the crew we were shutting down the day shift. They were gone before the last word left my mouth.

Sam showed up as everyone was leaving, so we went into the Greeks' for coffee. I wanted Mary to come, too, but she'd left with the rest of the crowd.

"Where were you?" I asked him.

"I had some things to take care of. What's it to you? No one else wants to be around here when there's any trouble. Did you find the Irishman?"

When I told him I didn't, he made clear by his expression that he held me responsible for Barney's no-show.

Things didn't improve much from there. I tried to talk him out of using the card-game story he'd come up with, but he didn't bite.

"Your story's no good," Sam said. "If you had a better story, I could see it."

"But it's the truth. I was home."

"Alone?"

I clammed up.

"Don't fuck me on this, McNulty. Keep the story. If something better turns up when we find Barney, we'll change it."

Sam said he was going home but would come back and cover the night shift until Mary or Betsy got there, if I'd try to track down Barney. When he left, I had another cup of coffee and thought things over. Mostly, I thought about what I should have done instead of what I had done. For one thing, I could see the whole strike escapade going ass backwards down the dumbwaiter shaft: everyone freaked out by MacAlister's murder; the wicked witch dead; Barney on the lam; Betsy duking it out with her husband; everybody with too many troubles of their own to be trying to run a strike . . . and comin' on Christmas. I wished I had a river . . .

One recurring thought had to do with a parlay between Barney's fingers being chopped off and MacAlister dead. Tit for tat? An eye for an eye? Maybe Barney was better left to his own devices, strike or no strike. This left me, Sam, and Mary Donohue to carry on the class war, everyone else too busy with their private wars.

Enough thinking. We'd posted a list of the strikers' phone numbers on the wall next to the pay phone in the Greeks', so I tried to phone Mary and got no answer. I stared at Betsy's phone number for a solid minute, then decided not to call her. I did call Kevin and told him I'd meet him later at his grandfather's house for dinner.

"I think the cat's gone," he said.

chapter ten

Before heading back uptown, I checked out the hotel to make sure Sergeant O'Day was a man of his word. He was, so I began my trek toward the subway on Seventh Avenue. I'd gotten about half a block when I noticed a black Lincoln Town Car keeping pace with me along the curb. At the very moment panic gripped my heart, the Town Car's window rolled down and a hoarse whisper said, "Brian, over here. 'Tis me, Barney."

I took a quick look around, then climbed in the car.

"Jaysus," said Barney. "It's a lovely bollocks we've made of things."

"Where've you been, for Christ's sake?"

"My friend and neighbor, Jim Ryan," said Barney, introducing me to the driver, a pleasant enough chap with a workingman's thick paw to shake hands with and a brogue as thick as the fingers.

"Barney," he said, "I'll need to drop you off. I'm to pick up a bride in Bay Ridge at five. By rights, I should be already on my way."

"Jaysus," said Barney, squirming in his seat to look out the back window, as if the posse were closing in.

The logical thing was to ask Barney if he'd killed MacAlister, but when I looked at his hand, I realized he probably couldn't have. Then I thought of Jim Ryan's hands and decided to mind my own business.

"The strike almost went down the drain this morning," I said with a clear note of rebuke in my voice. "If it wasn't for Francois and Mary, the street would have been deserted by noon."

Barney shook his head, pursed his lips, and turned to me with enough sadness pouring from his blue eyes to almost bring tears to my own. "I couldn't take the chance, Brian. Begod, it tore the heart out of me leaving ye on yer own, but bejaysus, I couldn't take the chance."

"If it's any consolation, Sam made up a cock-and-bull story to cover all three of us for last night."

Barney's expression was wistful. "It's not a story for last night I don't have. It's a story from the past that I do have." He clapped me on my shoulder. "Ah, the things that were done in the days we were young." The anguish rose again in those sincere and sad blue eyes.

No one was after anyone, as far as I knew, I told Barney. The cops would be questioning us soon, though, and unless I came up with an alternative pretty quickly, I'd have to use Sam's stupid story, if only because he would, so I'd have to cover for him.

One of these days, I promised myself, I'd find a group of normal friends who didn't need alibis and hideouts. We'd go bowling, watch football games. I'd hang out with guys who thought cops were the good guys, the mayor an honest civil servant, and the president the leader of the free world. What the hell was I doing involved with another murder? There's something wrong with your life if every time you turn around someone you know is either getting murdered or being accused of murder. I should sign on for a self-help class. I needed a new line of work. I should have stayed in college and become a pharmacist. Instead, I thought I was an actor. That's what got me into this crazy nightlife world in the first place. If I'd gotten one good part, I wouldn't be worrying about who murdered whom. I wouldn't be covering for my friends or hiding them out when the law was looking for them. Why wasn't I respectable?

When I returned from my reverie, I realized Barney was watching me intently. He didn't say anything, just nodded as if I'd been speaking to him. The Irish understand dreamers.

Since Jim Ryan was headed out to Brooklyn, I told Barney we could go to Pop's apartment and talk things over. He wouldn't mind an extra guest for supper and, having been "on the run" himself during the

McCarthy era, might have some compassion for Barney's troubles, whatever they were.

True to form, Pop greeted us cordially. He'd cooked lamb stew, so there'd be enough for everyone, and he liked company—and adventure. Kevin was there, watching rap music videos on TV, and mumbled something incomprehensible when I asked if there was anything on the news about MacAlister's killing.

Barney told us the bare-bones version of why he had stayed away from the picket line: He needed to avoid contact with the police since everything wasn't quite on the up-and-up with his immigration papers.

After dinner, Pop got around to the reason he'd wanted me to come out that night in the first place. After assigning a grumbling Kevin to clearing the table and getting the dishes into the dishwasher, he went to his desk and brought back some papers he'd found in MacAlister's rubbish. He told Barney he'd had some experience breaking up deals between bosses and crooked business agents in one of the garment unions, so he could smell a crooked deal from a block away.

"The payoffs are usually in cash," he told Barney. "But the cash has to come from somewhere, and that's where you can pick up the trail. Maybe not enough proof for court, but enough for you to know. I'll show you what I mean in a minute.

"The hotel collects the dues and a health and welfare fund contribution and is supposed to send the money on to the union. The hotel deducts dues from your check, say ten bucks a paycheck—two hundred workers, that's two thousand bucks. Just for instance, say MacAlister sends the union a thousand bucks and a list of a hundred workers. So far so good for him, except the dues don't come in cash. The money's in the hotel's account. How's he get it out? He writes a check. To Eliot? That wouldn't work. To himself? Nope. How about to Acme Produce? Who's that? It's MacAlister. In this case, it's MacDonald Produce." Here, Pop laid out canceled checks on the table, showing the signatures on the front of the check, MacAlister, and on the back of the check, MacDonald, looking quite similar.

"Now, I've looked high and low for MacDonald Produce, and there is no such place. But there is a street address." This time, Pop laid out two envelopes, one addressed to MacDonald and one to MacAlister. The address on both: 153 W. 38th Street. "Wanna guess?" asked Pop.

"Eliot's office," said Barney.

"Right you are," said Pop. "So there's that. But the real money is in the health and welfare contributions. That could be fifty bucks a week per worker. What happens is you have immigrant workers, many of them illegal. A maid's kid gets sick and needs an operation. She goes to the union welfare office and is told she's not a union member and doesn't have any health benefits. What's she going to do? She screams. She cries. She pulls her hair out. Who's she going to complain to? So she sends the kid to Kings County or one of the other city hospitals and hopes for the best."

Pop's investigative work—its origins in the hotel's wastepaper bins—came too late, I was afraid. It would have been great to use the dirt he came up with against MacAlister were he still alive, but I didn't know how it would help us now. Maybe Kelly would care, but I doubted it. That Eliot was corrupt wasn't news to me and wouldn't be to him, either.

"It wouldn't surprise me," said Pop, "that MacAlister got in over his head with that crooked business agent and whoever he's tied to and paid the price for getting greedy."

This information tucked away for the time being, we worked out a plan for the present. Pop agreed Barney should lay low until New York's Finest got their act together and solved the case of the murdered innkeeper, or they would violate him on the immigration problem. Meanwhile, we'd try to keep the strike going without Barney, despite the distraction of a murder.

Barney said he had a place to stay up in the Bronx and could lose himself among the other illegal Irish, veterans of the Troubles, working on fake papers, living half a dozen to an apartment, fighting again the wars of home in the Irish bars along Bainbridge Avenue.

I called my cabdriver pal Ntango, himself a political exile, to ask if he'd take Barney up to the North Bronx. It was a long haul, the kind of ride another cabbie might remember if pressed by detectives investigating a murder. I was probably overly cautious, but this would protect Barney. Having Ntango drive him meant I could get a ride home myself and not have to take the subway from deep in the heart of Brooklyn, where subways had a tendency to go astray and not show up at their appointed place at the appointed time late at night.

Kevin wanted to spend the night with Pop. He had sets of clothes at all three of our apartments, so it shouldn't be a problem. I told him he could stay if his mother said it was okay, but he couldn't go out that night after I left. I expected an argument. Instead, he said quietly, almost politely, he wanted to talk with me, indicating the conversation should be private. We went outside and leaned against the low brick wall in front of Pop's apartment building. It was quiet and dark, chilly but not cold, no traffic on the street, the parked cars settled in for the night against the curb, the ancient streetlights struggling halfheartedly against the dark, the flickering Christmas lights in the windows of the four-family houses down the block.

With all that was going on, I'd half-forgotten about Christmas. It was still a big deal for Kevin, even though he pretended it wasn't. Christmas had always meant something to me, too, because it had been important to my mother. She collected Christmas ornaments and decorated the apartment from top to bottom each year with nativity scenes and Santas, shiny bulbs and blinking lights, while Pop stomped around snorting like Scrooge. I tried to keep something of the peace on earth, goodwill to men stuff alive for Kevin, in memory of my mother, I guess, but I wasn't having much luck with the jolly season this time around.

"I'm having a lot of trouble with Mom," Kevin began. "All she does is criticize me."

I nodded but didn't respond. This was touchy ground. Divorced parents aren't supposed to criticize one another. We were told to stand shoulder to shoulder, not to let the kid divide us on issues of discipline and not to join in his criticism of the other parent.

"She criticizes you all the time, too."

I tried to smile.

"Whenever I get in trouble she says it's your fault because you're a bad influence."

"Maybe she's right."

"She probably is," Kevin agreed. "What I want is to come live with you for a while."

"You what!!??" This came out of nowhere. For fifteen years, he'd been happily growing up in Brooklyn, visiting his dad on weekends and school vacations; his dad always available, visiting the kid whenever he wanted him to, his mom taking all the responsibility. What was wrong with that? "Whoa, Kevin. Let's take it easy here. Your life's all wrapped up in Bay Ridge."

Kevin didn't raise his voice, but it resounded with determination. He'd thought this through, I realized. One of his characteristics since he could talk was that when he wanted something badly, he planned his attack. He didn't lose his cool like he might when I asked him to take out the garbage or clean up his room. Nope. When he really wanted something, there was no weeping and gnashing of teeth. He chomped down and held on like a bulldog.

"She's driving me crazy, Dad." He made sure to look me meaningfully in the eye. "I'm afraid something might happen. She makes me so mad, I'm afraid I might punch her if I don't get out of there."

I knew that feeling, too. But Christ, what kind of change would this be? There were too many things rushing at me for me to think straight. I didn't have an answer. "You gotta give me some time to think about this," I said, stalling for time. "Besides, it's getting near Christmas. You'd want to be with your mom for Christmas. And you can't punch her."

He was too quick for me. "Decide whatever you want. I'm not going to stay there anyway."

"Now, wait just a minute—" I said as authoritatively as I could. He turned his back and went inside the building.

"Kevin, look—" I said, chasing him through the lobby.

"Leave me alone—" he screamed, and I heard the tears in his voice, so I let him go.

By the time I caught up with him in Pop's apartment, they were on their way out to the Jamaican ice cream store down the block. Neither asked if I wanted to come or if I wanted any ice cream—another slight, on top of the other barbs and arrows fate had thrown at me lately. The last codeine pill I'd taken had worn off. My head ached; every time I moved my eyes, pain streaked across my forehead. I was sick and tired. I wanted to go to sleep and not wake up again unless I'd been transported to Oz or maybe Shangri-la. Everyone should go away and come back another day; I was tired of them all.

Why I decided just then to call my service is anybody's guess. Out of habit, maybe, or boredom. Or perhaps I thought that with all the crap happening around me, justice would provide that I'd get some good news for a change—like the lead in a Broadway play my agent forgot to tell me about.

The message, however, was to call Betsy; it was urgent. I should call her at her mother's, and she'd left the number. When I called, an older woman answered. She didn't seem especially glad I'd called, so I stammered that I was looking for Betsy at this number and started to repeat it. The woman cut me off and told me to wait. As I did, I could see Barney on high alert. He watched me the way the candy store proprietor used to when I was a kid.

Betsy's tone was even more hysterical than it had been that morning. "Oh, Brian! You've got to help me. You've got to help me. My God! My God, Brian! Katie is missing. She's gone, Brian. She's really gone now—"

"But . . . but—" I stammered.

"No! No!" she screamed, cutting me off. "Dennis is dead!! Someone killed him. He's dead. The fucking asshole is dead . . . and Katie is gone—" A torrent of wails and sobs overcame her voice.

chapter eleven

Her mother got back on the line, having subdued Betsy for the moment, and explained more coherently that someone shot and killed Betsy's husband and the baby was missing. The police were on the case—and they'd tear the city apart to find the child and capture the animal who did this.

"My husband was a police officer," Mrs. McIntyre told me proudly. "When it's one of their own that's killed, they don't rest until they get the murderer. We've known Dennis's family for years. The police families here stick together. The police will find whoever did this, and they'll find Katie before—" Reality must have caught up with her then, because the rest of what she was going to say caught in her throat.

I told Betsy's mother I was sorry for what happened and asked if I should come out there to Gerritsen Beach, if Betsy needed company or if there was something she wanted me to do. She told me no before I'd finished asking, as if she were afraid if she didn't get it out fast enough, I'd show up on her doorstep. She said that Betsy was better off with her family and that the police were doing all that could be done, so all we could do was wait and pray.

I didn't like her tone when she said this, the implication that, whoever I was, I represented the part of the world that had brought this trouble that wouldn't have come Betsy's way if she'd stayed in Gerritsen Beach. I could see why Betsy might have married young—to get away from her mother—and a cop because he was the only game in town. I might have married a cop myself to get away from Betsy's mother.

When I hung up the phone, I thought Barney would try to shake the story out of me. Then, as I told him about the murder and the missing baby, his spirit seemed to leave him. "God has forsaken us," he said when I finished, blessing himself.

I could buy that God had forsaken us, all right. I didn't understand, if that was the case, why Barney blessed himself. Nor did I understand Betsy's mother praying for Katie's return. What good would it do praying to a God who allowed this to happen in the first place? Betsy's loss was unimaginable to me. I wouldn't know how to comfort her, because nothing or no one could comfort me if my child were lost.

"What the hell is going on, Barney? What are we going to do?"

Barney shook his head woefully. "My heart goes out to poor Betsy. Her husband dead and the baby gone, it's more than a heart can bear. Please God, they'll find the infant soon. Sure, no one would hurt the child." He looked to me for affirmation.

I stared at him blankly. MacAlister dead, now Tierney, I couldn't believe there wasn't a connection. But what? And why would someone take Betsy's baby?

"I can't understand what's happening," I said. "Why would MacAlister and Tierney be killed one after the other?"

Barney shook his head. "I can only think there were things going on around us we didn't know about." His expression was thoughtful, as if he were thinking out loud. "We're carrying on our strike, thinking it's what's most important in everyone's life, and with no one the wiser, these men were entangled in something far more sinister that led to their murders."

"We don't even know that they knew one another, Barney. It could be what you say, but there could be a dozen other reasons. The two murders might have nothing to do with one another." Or they could have to do with the strike, I could have said but didn't.

Barney made the connection for me. "Bejaysus, Brian, looking at the murders and who'd be the man most likely to have committed them, you could say it was meself." His expression was that of a wronged man searching for understanding. I was hard-pressed to offer any.

MacAlister the one man holding out against the strike according to Barney; Dennis Tierney standing between him and Betsy—the possibility made too much sense. What was worse, Barney and Betsy could have engineered the murders together. Where had Barney been since the tussle with Betsy's husband on the picket line? Where did Betsy go when she left my apartment after my second run-in with Dennis? My head was spinning. I imagined Barney's open and honest face turning suddenly evil, him pulling out a gun, and telling me I was next because now I knew too much.

Kevin did stay at Pop's that night, and I said I'd talk to his mother. A real treat that was going to be. By the time I got home, I felt like something the cat dragged in, which, of course, reminded me of the cat; gone now, I remembered as I looked around. Good riddance. At least I wouldn't have to shovel cat shit anymore. Still, I did look outside the window and make a couple of halfhearted attempts to call him. This was New York, though. You had to be careful hollering "Otto!" out the window. There was no telling who the hell might show up.

My mind was clogged with many things, including the effects of the joint I'd shared with Ntango on the trip over from Brooklyn. Betsy's baby missing, the baby's father dead. What did it mean, the kid gone? Nothing good came to mind. I couldn't get rid of the idea that for Barney, even though he had to hide out for a while, two major obstacles to his future happiness were gone. Yet, I couldn't see the baby as an obstacle to anything, and no way, even if in a weak moment I might think Barney put MacAlister and Betsy's husband out of their misery, could I think of him doing anything to harm the baby. Maybe he would, though, it occurred to me, not hurt the tyke but sell her. Start a new family with Betsy, without someone else's kid. Even have a few extra bucks from the sale of the kid to set up housekeeping.

This is what happens inside the mind of someone who smokes a joint after sucking on codeine pills all afternoon. I was crashing now.

Death all around me, depressed about everything I could think of, I threw myself on top of my bed, still in my clothes, barely getting my shoes off, not bothering to turn off the light.

After what must have been only a few minutes, my doorbell rang. It's shrill and obnoxiously loud to begin with, but coming at this moment with my head splitting from the pain, it pierced my brain. I tried to ignore it. Someone ringing my bell this late only meant trouble. Then I realized it might be Kevin, so I dragged myself over to the intercom and asked who was there. No one. Just another long push on the bell. I live on the first floor, a few steps across the lobby from the front door. Most of the time, I skip the intercom and buzz people in, waiting on the little stoop in front of my apartment to see who it is. This is what I did next, but no one came through the big front door of the building. Just another long pull on the buzzer. Remembering myself lying in the foyer not many hours before, I propped my apartment door open and went for a look.

When I opened the door, my heart stopped—I was sure for good. My mind reeled. When my heart started up again, it sent a rocket-launch shot of adrenaline through my body. Parked in the foyer, underneath the row of mailboxes, was a baby stroller—and in the contraption was a blue-eyed baby staring up at me with something resembling a cute little smile on its face. Worse than the initial shock, on second look, I realized the kid looked like Betsy's baby—Katie—but with only her eyes and red nose showing beneath her wool cap and the rest of her wrapped in blankets, I couldn't tell for sure. Bound up like a mummy, she was gurgling, kicking, and smiling, as cheerful as the Christmas pup.

I looked around outside the building. No one there. I called Betsy's name out the door. Of course, no one answered. I looked around the lobby, but I already knew it was empty. So I picked up young Katie, stroller and all, and carried her into my apartment, my heart thumping, my head pounding, my brain shooting out distress calls. I was as panicked as if I'd kidnapped the tyke.

Then, at the height of my panic, I heard a sound from the kitchen. At the same instant, the baby's eyes widened. Fear crawled up the back of my neck and stood my hair on end. I let out a yelp and turned just in time to see the cat scramble off the windowsill and scurry across the kitchen floor.

"You fucker!" I yelled, grabbing a book from the shelf to throw at it. This scared the baby. I saw the accusing look in her eyes, the bottom lip begin to curl. Oh Jesus, I knew what was coming. Sure enough, she began blatting. This was just great. Once she began crying, she must have realized all the problems she had. Number one, where's her mother? Number two, who's this guy with the big loud, scary voice? And where is she and where has she been? I want to go home. I WANT MY MOMMY!! She cried and she hiccupped and cried some more. I had visions of everyone in the apartment building calling the police. Strangers on the street calling the police. Not only did he snatch the kid, they'd say. He brutalized her.

I cooed to the baby, made clucking sounds, and tried for funny faces, but my heart wasn't in it. Not surprisingly, this made things worse. I shook the kid's rattle that I found in the stroller. There were lots of things in the stroller, a couple of changes of clothes, a sweater and a little jacket, diapers, a couple of toys, and a bottle. A bottle! Of course. I grabbed the bottle and ran to the refrigerator. Great! What was I going to do, fill it with beer? The West Side Market. I could get milk at the store. I made a beeline for the door. Wait! I couldn't go out and leave the kid in the apartment alone, and I'd be damned if I was going to wheel a screaming baby down Broadway.

All of a sudden, the baby's eyes grew wide again; she hiccupped and stopped crying. She gurgled a couple of times, waving her hands, kicking her feet, and craning her neck. The cat! The kitten had come out from under the couch and was crossing the living room heading toward its food bowl, stopping every couple of steps to check that the coast was clear, and garnering the rapt attention of the little one. During this lull in the action, I came to my senses, called my service, and got Betsy's mother's phone number.

Betsy answered the phone on the second ring. Her screech when I told her I thought I might have Katie with me must have roused her mother and half the neighborhood, if not half the dead of Brooklyn.

She first had me make sure the kid had a tiny earring, then a small mole on her neck. After this, questions and giggles and terms of endearment tumbled from her as I tried to calm her enough to figure out what to do when Katie started crying again.

"Are you sure she's all right, Brian? She's not hurt? Is she dirty? Is she hungry? Did you check her diaper?"

"She looks fine to me. I'm afraid I'll scare her half to death if I touch her."

"She won't cry, Brian, or not for long. She knows you love her."

"How does she know that?"

"Don't be silly," Betsy gushed. "You're so wonderful, Brian. Everybody loves you. I'm so happy!!"

"Easy, kid. I didn't do anything. She showed up on my doorstep."

Betsy was breathless. "How could that be? Who brought her there? Did someone find her? You're sure she's all right?"

"She looks all right to me. You want me to take her to the hospital?"

"No! No! I'll be there in no time."

"I could get Ntango and bring her out there."

"No! No! Brian. I want to come there. I'm so happy. I can't believe it. Thank God! Thank God!"

I started to suggest that for the sake of propriety she be a little bit less happy since her husband's dead body had barely gone cold, but thought better of it.

"The car service is on standby, Brian. I'll be there in less than an hour. There won't be traffic this time of night."

"Says you. What do I do when she starts screaming again?"

Betsy became the efficient mom again. "She'll be hungry. She must be. And she'll want to nurse. But she only nurses for comfort. She can eat baby food and drink from a bottle."

When I told Betsy about not wanting to leave the baby to go to the store, she said, "Don't be silly," again.

I didn't think silliness had anything to do with it.

"Katie loves to go in the stroller. Take her for a walk."

"It's two o'clock in the morning."

"Take her to the store, Brian. People understand that babies sometimes can't sleep. No one will think it's weird. Buy some milk and some baby food. Then feed her a little—maybe just fruit for now, apples and apricots. Feed her some of that. Then take her out of the stroller and give her a bottle . . . and don't forget to check her diaper . . . I'm just so happy!" Betsy said again, and began sobbing.

The cat was finishing up dinner when I got off the phone, so I grabbed him before he could jump out the window again. I figured I might need an ace in the hole. Katie let me work her back into one of the sweaters and put a blanket over her, cooperating because I more or less dangled Otto in her lap. The kid loaded up, I put on my pea coat and stuffed the kitten, who'd grown some and now barely fit, into the side pocket. I thought he might squirm and try to jump out; instead, he settled in and I think went to sleep.

By the time Betsy arrived, the tyke was asleep. We'd gone to the market. I'd fed her the baby food, hoisted her out of the stroller to take off her sweater—bit the bullet and laid her on the floor to change her diaper. There was a package of Pampers and a packet of wipes in the stroller. The job went more smoothly than I dared hope. I carried her around the apartment for twenty minutes or so showing her assorted things, then put her on my bed with her bottle and the cat. She whimpered for a while between slugs from the bottle but finally conked out, as did Otto. What a helluva day she must have had. I wondered if she was there when her father was killed, if she'd remember, if it would haunt her life.

After watching her sleep for a few minutes, deciding I'd had quite a day myself, I went and poured a healthy shot of Jameson from the private stock I kept on hand for such days. I put on a John Coltrane record, sat down in my stuffed chair, and marveled at all that had happened since Sam phoned that morning to tell me MacAlister was dead. How strange it was Betsy and Katie spent last night in my apartment and would again tonight—at least what was left of it. In the interim Betsy became a widow.

When the doorbell rang this time, I buzzed without asking, and as soon as I got the door open Betsy flew into my arms and knocked me back into the apartment. She squashed me into her arms, loosened her grip, then squashed me again, burying her face in my chest. The bedroom door was open, so she saw Katie on the bed. Letting out a yelp, she ran to the baby, holding on to my arm and dragging me along. For a moment, she just looked. Tears came, then she scooped Katie into her arms and squashed her. At this point, I managed to sneak away back to my Jameson.

After cooing and crying and kissing and hugging, Betsy seemed to be coming back to earth. Her smile was beautiful, and her eyes, even though glassy and streaked with red, sparkled with happiness. She was a tall girl, Betsy, as tall as me, with a thick mane of blond hair that made her look robust, but she was actually slim and fit easily in my arms when we hugged. I watched her with the baby, thinking there might be something to this madonna thing that artists get off on.

She sat down on the couch, still with that beatific smile, and opened her blouse, unclipping her bra in the middle, pulling it apart and exposing her breast. I thought I should politely avert my eyes, but I didn't want to, and since Betsy was smiling, her pretty eyes meeting mine, with no sign of shyness, I didn't and watched her hook the baby onto her breast.

Soon after, the baby fell asleep, and Betsy took her into the bedroom and laid her on the bed. When she came back, she sat on the couch and said, "I feel so content, so at peace." She talked softly about how worried she'd been, how relieved she was, what a miracle it was that Katie showed up on my doorstep. She pondered how Katie got there and why Dennis was murdered.

I soaked in her presence next to me. I was worn out, barely awake; my mind wandered. She was so pretty. The softness of her body, the clearness of her skin, the silkiness of her hair, the slight puffiness of her lips, it wasn't fair for her to be so desirable and so close—and I was sure, so oblivious to her effect on me. When she turned to face me, my eyes met hers, and I wasn't sure what I found there—sympathy, tenderness. There was an echoing silence around us, and she looked into my eyes for a long time. I don't know what she found there either, but I was sure they were pretty much glazed over by that time.

When I awoke for the second morning in a row on my own couch, the strike, the picket line, murdered bosses and murdered husbands, kittens in windows and babies on doorsteps, my son, my ex-wife, all of it came rushing back at me. I rolled off the couch and went to the shower.

Later, when I got back with coffee and bagels from the corner, Betsy had changed, fed, nursed, and given Katie a bath in my kitchen sink. The baby was now dressed and sitting in the stroller.

"Brian, something terrible happened!" Betsy said, as soon as I came through the door. "The kitten jumped out the window. He was out and gone before I could stop him. I'm so sorry. Katie and I were just going to look for him."

"Don't bother. You wouldn't find him. You can take the cat out of the alley," I told her, "but you can't take the alley out of the cat. He'll be back."

Over bagels and coffee, while the tyke gnawed on a bagel half and smeared cream cheese across her face, Betsy told me again about finding her dead husband and not finding Katie. "I didn't feel. I just acted. Called the police. Called my mother. Called Dennis's mother. Looked in every room. Ran next door. Ran down the street, ringing doorbells and knocking on doors. All I thought about was Katie. Before long, the entire neighborhood was out on the street. I had started in to do everything all over again, was heading down the street, when my mother found me. She gave me two Valium. I went into a trance and stayed in the trance until you called. I didn't think about Dennis being dead at all. I thought about Katie being gone. It was like a gigantic hole opened up where I once had a heart." Betsy finished her bagel and we drank coffee, both tied up in our own thoughts.

"You must think I'm awful not to be sad that Dennis was killed," Betsy said, "but I'm not. I'm sorry for him that he's dead, but I'm not for me. Whoever killed him gave me back my life. I was trapped. Dennis told me he'd kill me before he'd let me go, and I believed him. I think I always believed he'd either kill someone or be killed anyway. He had this reckless streak. When we were kids, he was never afraid of anyone or anything. That wildness and craziness attracted me then. After we were married, I knew I'd been wrong. He was cruel. Not just mean, he was sick. At a bar once, when I was waiting for him, a guy bought me a drink and was kind of coming on to me. Nothing serious. Polite. Kind of charming. When he got there, Dennis shooed him away, but the guy wouldn't take the shooing. Dennis embarrassed him, so he had to save face. You know how that thing is with Brooklyn guys." Betsy paused. She hadn't been looking at me as she told me this but did now. "Dennis beat him bloody. Way beyond the fights you see sometimes in a bar. And he liked that it made me sick and repulsed because he knew that meant I was really afraid of him."

"Do you know who wanted to kill him?"

"Besides me? Probably a lot of people. People he arrested. Street hustlers he harassed. Dennis liked throwing his weight around. That's why he liked being a cop. He was already investigated by internal affairs for hurting people he'd arrested, and he'd only been in the department not even two years. People tried to warn him. Mary Donohue's husband Pat did—he's been in twenty years and never hurt anyone. We had dinner with them a couple of times, then never again. Mary made excuses, but I knew it was because her husband didn't like being around Dennis."

We talked for a while longer trying to figure out how Katie ended up in my doorway but couldn't come up with anything. Betsy wondered if it might have been Katie's guardian angel. For all I could figure out, it might have been.

Even though I was shaken by the murders and bewildered by the return of the missing baby, the strike continued to weigh heavily on my mind. Sam and Francois and Mary Donohue were holding things together, but I needed to be more help, especially since Barney was likely to be out of the picture for the foreseeable future. I was preparing to make my way down to the picket line when a new problem arrived. Betsy called her mother and found out her front yard was crawling with reporters and photographers and that the police investigating Dennis's murder wanted to know where Betsy was. Fortunately, Betsy's mother didn't know where I lived, or for sure she'd have blown the whistle, but she did tell them I was one of the bartenders on strike at the Savoy.

When she hung up, Betsy said she wasn't going back there, but I could see the handwriting on the wall. "It seems to me you better get back to Gerritsen Beach and play the role of the grieving cop's widow, like it or not," I said.

Betsy's face crumbled; her lip quivered. Chalk another one up for Diplomat McNulty. "What I mean is, all hell's going to break loose until the cops find whoever killed your husband. Won't matter if he was the worst prick who ever walked, or if every cop in New York hated him. He's a dead cop now."

There were tears in Betsy's eyes. "Now you think I'm awful—"

"No. I don't. That's not what I mean—"

"Yes, it is what you mean." Betsy's voice rose menacingly.

"No, it isn't. Calm down, God damn it. You wanna be on the front page of the *Daily News* tomorrow, 'Murdered Cop's Widow in Love Tryst'?"

Betsy hung her head. "No," she said quietly. She looked at me beseechingly, and I felt heartless, as if I were sending a mutt to the dog pound.

Okay McNulty, I told myself. Time to step up. Take some responsibility here. Be a man. You don't have to push Betsy out the door to take her lumps. You could go with her. Stand up for her. In truth, there was something appealing about the little scene of domesticity I found myself in after so many years, something appealing about Betsy—and the tyke, too. Why couldn't I be a family man? Me and Betsy and little Katie . . . and Kevin . . . and the cat . . . What the hell was I getting myself into?

"Are you all right?" Betsy had leaned closer to try to get a better look at me, her brow wrinkled with concern. "Your face just went all pale."

chapter twelve

When I left for the picket line, Betsy headed to Gerritsen Beach to face the music—a symphony played by her
mother and her dead husband's relatives gathered at her mother's
house, plus a dozen or so cops' wives from the neighborhood, along
with a handful of off-duty cops, some of whom were already probably mean-drunk and ugly. She didn't ask me to go with her, but I suspected she wanted me to. Maybe a better man than I might have gone.
But even if I was inclined, I didn't see how showing up with the bartender she spent the night with would help anything.

The picket line at noon, when it should have been bustling with a
dozen Sunday brunch waiters and waitresses in addition to the kitchen
staff and the housekeepers, looked like one of those small Mexican
towns you see in western movies when the hero comes riding in at
siesta time. Sam and Francois pulled themselves away from the rem-
nants of the crew staking out the front of the hotel and came toward
me with disgusted looks on their faces.

"The polices!!" bellowed Francois. "They scare the shit out of
everyone." He waved his arms excitedly. "Off in all directions, like
chickens!"

Sam was scowling. "I didn't know you'd put in for vacation time,
McNulty. You and Barney. Did you find him?" His stance was challenging, as if to say the next move was mine; he'd handle what I came
up with.

What I came up with was an abject apology. I knew how slowly the hours passed on the picket line. I told them about Barney's immigration difficulty and him making himself scarce until things blew over and about Betsy's murdered husband. The story was in the paper, and the cops had already been there, so they knew about the murder, but not about the lost kid being found.

"A babee on your doorstep, Brian? Magnificent!" Francois said, and kissed me on both cheeks—just like in the movies. "Your heart is pure!" Sam and I both must have looked surprised by this because Francois took umbrage. "*C'est vrai!* It's true! Such things happen only to the pure of heart." He jutted out his jaw and waited for an argument.

"What I want to know is who put the kid there?"

"Angels, maybe," said Sam, glancing at Francois.

I looked at Sam to make sure he was joking. I wondered if he'd talked to Betsy.

"Who the fuck you think put the kid there, McNulty?" asked Sam, presumably not buying the pure-of-heart explanation—or the angels.

Was I supposed to know? Had I missed something? Perplexed, I turned to Sam.

He shook his head.

Over coffee at the Greeks', we decided whatever was going to happen with the strike, stay and fight or throw in the towel, we should all do it together. I said that was fine but before we did anything we needed to talk to Mary Donohue, since she was the issue in the strike. When I said this, Francois hemmed and hawed. Even Sam did a little dance with his eyes to keep from looking at me.

Finally, Sam said, "Mary Donohue may have made her own peace." Then he glanced at Francois.

Distress clouded Francois's expressive dark eyes. He hemmed and hawed again, then, his eyes filled with sympathy and his tone consoling, said, "Jeanne, the French girl who is the night front desk manager? You know her?"

I nodded.

"She saw Mary put in a secret visit to MacAlister."

My eyes sprang open. "When?"

Francois shook his head. "Thursday. Perhaps Friday, when Jeanne told me. A day or two before the unfortunate event of MacAlister's death. In the excitement, I didn't get a chance to tell you. Today, I wonder where Mary Donohue has been, and Sam announce Mary Donohue said to him she had enough. She would get a different job. No longer persevere. And I say, 'Oh my God, of course,' and I tell him what Jeanne has said to me."

Even though Francois spoke apologetically, I still got mad. "Are you sure, Francois? That doesn't sound like Mary. How do you know MacAlister hadn't put Jeanne up to telling you this? She's management."

Francois puffed out his chest, raised his eyebrows, and looked down his nose at me—the de Gaulle influence, no doubt. "A French woman," he said, his accent more exaggerated than normal, "she would not lie to me!"

I hoped she had, because if Mary called it quits, we would have two hundred workers on the street holding the bag. Half of us would go back to work, our tails between our legs; the rest of us would be fired. I couldn't believe she'd do it. "Mary was here on the picket line yesterday at lunch. She organized the demonstration when we went at the cops."

Sam harrumphed a couple of times. "He told you what she said, McNulty. You got too much faith in human nature, man. Been listening too long to that solidarity-forever bullshit."

I winced. Betrayal came in many forms and from all directions, I knew from experience. Before the cock could crow three times, just about anyone might flip on you. Even so, you couldn't believe rumors you heard on a picket line. Pop warned me about splits when the workers hit the bricks—day shift against night shift, dining room against housekeeping, other Slavs against Poles. African American and French against the Irish? Who knows? I had to admit the Irish weren't holding up their end of the fight, what with Barney hiding out in the hills of the Bronx, Betsy taking on the *Daily News* photographers in Brooklyn, me deserting my post last night, and Mary seeming to have thrown in the towel. I wanted to hear it from Mary herself before I'd believe it, though.

We set the meeting for Wednesday night at the Lord Byron Hotel on 27th Street, something of a sister ship to our own lovely Savoy. This gave us a little time to get our ducks lined up. Francois went to activate the phone tree, Sam went home to sleep, and I joined what there was of a picket line. The half-dozen Guatemalan and Salvadoran dishwashers and kitchen slaves smiled wearily, giving the impression they were glad to see me, when I knew in their hearts they hated my guts, since I was one of the gringos that got them into this mess. It was chilly—not freezing as it had been early in the strike, but cold enough, and colder still when the sun dipped behind the buildings. I shivered into my pea coat and the kitchen guys shivered into their windbreakers, none of us outdoor guys to begin with, and them especially sensitive to the cold, coming from warm-weather countries and spending sixty hours a week in overheated kitchens. We walked for a while, me by myself, them in groups of two or three, talking quietly in Spanish— probably about getting me alone in an alley. I suggested we take breaks in groups of two or three to go to the Greeks' for coffee and to warm up. When my turn came, no one came with me, except that one of the two uniformed cops watching the picket line peeled himself away from the other one and stopped me at the door of the restaurant.

"You McNulty?" he asked.

My heart stopped. Here it comes, I thought. "Let's say for the sake of argument I am."

He stiffened, the expression in his eyes hardening. He looked like he wanted to kick my ass but instead reached inside his jacket and came up with a business card that he handed to me. "One of the detectives wanted me to give this to you."

On the card was written SERGEANT PATRICK SHEEHAN NEW YORK POLICE DEPARTMENT DETECTIVE BUREAU.

"What did he say?" I asked the cop, I'm sure with a quaking voice.

"He said you were an asshole," the cop said, walking away.

———————

Cops are never much help to workers on strike. It's not all their fault—the laws are stacked against the strikers—but too often the cops make it personal: A challenge to the law is a challenge to them, *mano a mano*. If that's not bad enough, everything gets worse when a cop is killed. On that point, Betsy's mother was on the money. The cops figure every outlaw is fair game until they get the cop killer. Every bad guy should know this—and if they don't, they learn it once the manhunt begins. The experienced bad guys lie low. In some cases, they turn the cop killer over to the police. In other cases, they take care of the killer themselves. The cops get a million tips. Every punk who gets collared has a tip on the cop killer. He's made everyone's life miserable, so no one gets the mark of the squealer for dropping a dime on this one.

Now that Betsy's mother had connected her son-in-law's murder to the strike, the cops might very well drop a net over the entire picket line and haul us all in to try to pressure someone into talking—and somehow Sheehan, the only homicide detective I've ever met, gets involved. He must have a computer that tells him if my name comes up in an investigation, so he can come out and lean on me. There'd probably been a thousand murders in New York since the last time our paths crossed. This wouldn't stop him from marveling over the coincidence that he's found me with another body at my feet, so to speak—and this one a cop.

I grabbed a cup of joe and called my service from the Greeks' pay phone to get even worse news. Another emergency message from Betsy. Call her at her mother's.

"They think I killed Dennis," Betsy announced breathlessly. "What should I do? They asked where I was and didn't Dennis and I have a fight and who were the guys on the picket line who assaulted Dennis." She was practically panting when she finished.

I went dizzy and had to grab the pay phone to hold myself up—that old getting hit on the back of the head with a two-by-four feeling I know so well. "Oh my fucking word!" I wailed, loud enough to halt the buzz of conversation at the counter behind me. "Everything can't be this screwed up."

"They act like I'm a criminal," Betsy said self-righteously. "You'd think they'd be sympathetic. What about the blue wall and all that?"

"It doesn't extend to wives. Cops don't like other cops' wives. A lot of them don't even like their own wives."

Betsy was silent for a few seconds; then she went on. "What should I do, Brian? They wanted to know where I was last night and the night before—" She paused for a deep breath. "And what's worse . . . this I can't believe. I can't believe anyone could say this . . . the pricks—"

"What, Betsy?"

"The fat blubbery bastard—his breath stinks, on top of everything else—he said Katie being lost was a hoax. He said maybe I forgot to tell him something. Maybe Katie was with one of my friends and I kept it secret because I didn't want anyone to know where I was the last two nights. He asked my mother who my friends were . . . anyone I might leave the baby with. What should I do, Brian? I'm scared . . . I can't believe this is happening."

I was ready to bang my head against the wall. Why hadn't I seen this coming? Mexico, I thought—or Ireland, if they don't have an extradition treaty. This was ridiculous. Betsy didn't kill her husband and hide the baby and have someone leave her on my doorstep . . . Did she? Where was Barney when all this was happening? Betsy and Barney? Bonnie and Clyde? I had to calm down.

"Okay, let's take this one step at a time. You could tell them you were with me, but that's not going to help much. It's you and me saying that's where you were. They might decide we're both lying. What you should do—"

"Brian—"

"What you should do is get a—"

"Brian!!" Betsy shouted. "I already told them. . . ." Her voice went soft. ". . . I thought it would be enough . . . In the beginning, I thought they were trying to help . . . Is that really bad?"

It took a few seconds to absorb this—like trying to keep down the first couple of bites of breakfast after a bad night. The good thing was, she really was with me. The truth is easier to keep straight than a lie. The bad thing was, contemporary mores would frown on hearing—via the *Daily News*—about the slain police officer's widow and the bartender. We might have gotten away with one night chastely spent—but a second night, and the hapless bartender finding the missing kid? I didn't believe the goddamn story, and it happened to me.

"It's not so bad," I said.

"I don't believe you."

"It's just a lousy set of circumstances. I'm not sure you saying you were with me, even if the cops believe you, helps. Dennis was at my apartment turning out my lights at what time? Then what time did you find his body? Where were you in between?"

"I don't know. I don't know." She began crying.

Remembering Peter Finch's advice in similar circumstances, I told Betsy not to answer any more questions. "I'll have a lawyer call you. He's a friend of mine. His name is Peter Finch."

"I can't afford a lawyer."

"We'll work it out. The poor bastard's used to not getting paid."

I hung up and headed for the picket line with way too much on my mind. The door to the Greeks' had barely closed behind me and the chilly late afternoon air had scarcely worked its way through my pea coat when a muscle-bound blue and white police cruiser pulled to the curb in front of me. Detective Sergeant Sheehan climbed out of the passenger side.

chapter thirteen

Since I'd mentally prepared myself for Sheehan, this wasn't a great shock. Nor was it the high point of my day.

"Let's go back inside and talk," said a grim-faced Sheehan. No "hello." No "long time no see," or "how are you?" Sheehan never was much on small talk, but this was rude, even for him. Public servant, my ass.

"I don't have time. I need to be on the picket line," I said, trying to match his gruffness. Since he was wearing only his sport coat, let him freeze if he wanted to question me.

"Whatever you say." He grimaced as he followed me across the street. The kitchen crew watched this new development warily. Sheehan ignored them. "Let's go through this once, McNulty. A cop was killed and you know something about it. This time, I'm not buying any of your hoity-toity 'citizen protecting the rights of the bad guy' bullshit."

"It's not always clear who the bad guy is, Sergeant."

Sheehan stopped dead still. "There you go. That's the crap I mean. You try that shit with someone besides me, you're gonna get slapped, McNulty."

"I've already been slapped—twice—by the deceased. The guy should have been on a leash."

Sheehan began walking again and caught up with me. "I'm not interested in your psychoanalyzing, McNulty." He moved closer, bellying up to me when I stopped. "Just tell me what you know. Like his wife. Were you fucking her?"

Sheehan was no fool. He said this the way he did on purpose, to piss me off and provoke me into saying something I didn't mean to. The problem was that knowing this didn't help. He did piss me off. Thickheaded people do that. Everything's simple to them. This fucker Dennis Tierney abused and terrorized his wife. The simpleminded cops didn't care about that. They wanted to prove there's a slut behind every man's problem. Glaring at Sheehan, I kept my mouth shut until I'd swallowed back most of the bile. "It wasn't God who made honky-tonk women," I told him.

"Be an asshole if you want, McNulty. You're gonna be sorry. I happened to hear your name, so I said I'd take a crack at you. You wanna wait, I'll let the guys from Sheepshead Bay—Tierney's buddies—loose on you."

This presented a dilemma. Sheehan wasn't going to do me any favors. Our cynicisms were of a different order, his to see the worst in those society left behind, mine to see the worst in those society enabled to live high on the hog. Then again, neither was he out to get me, so I considered taking a chance. If I told Sheehan what happened, even if he didn't entirely believe me, he'd have to think something might have happened that was different than what the cops now thought happened, which was that Betsy, possibly in cahoots with an illicit lover, killed her husband. Well, here goes, said I, who should have known better.

"Tell you what, Sergeant. I'll make you a deal."

Sheehan raised his gaze to the heavens and took a deep breath. "You're a real piece of work, McNulty." His eyes met mine, the expression in them as unyielding as ever. "Shoot. It better be good."

"I'll tell you everything I know. You'll tell me you'll look through Tierney's records—arrests, shakedowns, personal feuds, internal affairs records—and check out everyone you come across who might have had it in for him."

Sheehan's eyes went wide with disbelief. "That's great, McNulty.

Such a grasp of the finer points of police work. If I didn't have an eye for the job myself, I'd put you up for chief of the homicide division." I tried to get a word in edgewise here, but he was having none of it, just thundered right over me. "Who the fuck are you to tell us how to conduct a murder investigation? You've been breathing too many liquor fumes."

I told Sheehan to stop with the wounded-pride crap and agree to investigate some other possibilities, no matter what the precinct detectives thought happened. He finally said okay, so I told him pretty much what had happened, as it happened, including the attack on Barney and Barney's suspicions about MacAlister and the crooked business agent being borne out by Pop's investigation. I told him pretty much straight up about Betsy being afraid of her husband and my letting her stay at my apartment, her husband arriving the next morning, later finding the baby on my doorstep, and Betsy coming back, emphasizing the purity of her overnight stays.

Sheehan rolled his eyes. "That's a lot to swallow, McNulty. So this Tierney babe stayed at your apartment the night the hotel manager was murdered? And the next night you found her baby on your doorstep, just sitting there none the worse for wear, and so the Tierney woman comes back and spends the night again. But nothing's going on between you, right?"

"Right. It wasn't that kind of thing. Her husband was just killed, for Christ's sake."

He took out his notebook. "The night the hotel manager was killed, she was at your apartment, right?"

"Right. She told the cops that."

"Funny, McNulty. I've always known you to be a truthful guy—" Here he guffawed loudly for the benefit of an invisible audience. "Why do I have written here that you spent the night in question playing cards at a poker club in Harlem with a Sam Jones and Barney Saunders? In front of a half-dozen or more witnesses, no less?"

Involuntarily, I let out a groan and smacked myself on the forehead with the heel of my hand. Sam's goddamn alibi story! I glanced out of the corner of my eye at Sheehan's triumphantly beaming face and wanted to smack him. There was no way out. No matter which story I chose, he wouldn't believe it.

Sheehan put his pad back in his chest pocket. "Your girlfriend's in trouble, McNulty. I'll tell you that. We'll look at other possibilities. We would've done it without your advice. If I were you, though, I wouldn't go too far out on a limb for her."

I was going to tell Sheehan that the card game story was a fake, but I thought better of it. I knew Betsy was with me that night, so the cops weren't going to prove she was somewhere else. Sam and Barney were a different story. Maybe one of them—or both of them, for that matter—did need an alibi.

Sheehan didn't seem surprised by my decision. "Remind me not to look you up if I need an alibi. You're the worst liar I've ever come across."

"For what it's worth, Sergeant, when everything comes out in the wash, you'll find that Betsy didn't kill her husband."

Sheehan waved his hand dismissively. "Thanks for the tip."

I got exasperated. I knew what the goddamn truth was. Betsy didn't kill her husband. Where was this fantasy coming from? "C'mon, Sergeant. Did you ever talk to her? She's the last of the innocents. Like Snow White and the fucking dwarfs. Ask anyone at the hotel. Her husband was the jerk, not her."

Sheehan shook his head. "I've known sweet little fifteen-year-olds pulled in on murder charges and later admit to cutting the dicks off of grown men."

This gave me pause. I tried to bounce back. "Do you think Betsy went on a killing spree and knocked off MacAlister also?"

Sheehan looked suspiciously around him, as if someone might overhear, then spoke in a conspiratorial whisper. "I don't know why I'm telling you this—especially after you just tried to get over on me. Anybody can get turned around by a piece of tail, so I got some sympathy for you. I understand she's a bombshell."

My dander was rising again until I noticed Sheehan's expression, which, strange on him, suggested sympathy.

"You may not be so far off on this Tierney guy. One possibility is he found out the hotel manager was banging his wife, so he took him out. Later, this came up between them, so your sweetie grabbed one of his prized collection and blew him away. We don't have the gun, but the bullets in both cases were from a .38."

Sheehan looked the picket line over as he made ready to leave. "This doesn't mean you and your labor warriors are off the hook. You think your lady friend should walk, you might tell us more about the card game in Harlem, about this guy Barney, who no one seems to be able to find, and this black guy who thinks he's a Philadelphia lawyer."

Reading between the lines, I realized Sheehan wasn't as confident about his suspicions as he sounded. "So what you're saying is that you don't really have any evidence connecting Betsy to the murders."

Sheehan deliberated before he spoke. "Yes and no. I'm not going to tell you about evidence. I will tell you we don't go thinking something for no reason."

"Why do you want to know about the other guys, then?"

"We're told she was screwing one of the bartenders. She might have had help."

This one got me. "Jesus Christ, Sheehan. Stop talking like Betsy's fucked every guy in the hotel. The fact is she didn't. As far as I could see, she was faithful to her asshole husband. Partly because she thought that's what she's supposed to do—partly because she was scared of him, which as far as I could tell she had every reason to be."

Sheehan assumed a thoughtful pose, which in his case meant pursing his lips and fiddling with his ear, checking me out, as if he wanted to believe me but wasn't going to. "This is what contradicts you, McNulty," he said after an appropriate lull. "Why did Tierney come down to the picket line to pick a fight with a couple of bartenders the other day—if I'm not mistaken, one of them being you? Second, why did he go to see the hotel manager a day or two before the murder, which we're told he may have done?"

Sheehan opened his eyes wider in mock surprise to let me know he clocked my own surprise and confusion. "You think you know everything's goin' on, McNulty. But someone was talking to Tierney about his wife—and someone's talking to us, too." He gave me one of those cop-to-pathetic-criminal looks they like to use. "Let's put it this way, McNulty. You're all on the list. Someone killed a cop—and that doesn't go down easy with us. So we'll get whoever it is. You want to protect the wife, fine. Being with you, if she was, don't say much for her. You lying about it makes it worse. I know from the past you ain't too swift about knowin' what's goin' on with your friends. And you don't like cops. You think you know better who's good and bad. One of these days you're gonna make one wrong choice too many and get your ass blown off."

When Sheehan left, I went back into the Greeks'. Barney had come up again. Now that the cops were looking for him for sure, he'd have to stay in hiding. We'd arranged that I could leave a message with Mary Donohue if I needed to get in touch with him. At the moment, it was just as well that I didn't know where he was. He and Betsy both had explaining to do that I couldn't help them with. I called my lawyer pal Peter Finch, a red-diaper baby like myself and, more important in situations such as this, a criminal lawyer. He also did labor and civil rights law and was helping out—pro bono—with our rank-and-file caucus and now the strike.

"Hey, Peter," said I cheerfully, a tone of voice coming from me that was bound to put him on alert. "I've got another bono to throw you."

"Ha. Ha," said Peter. He was a humorless bastard anyway, doing this for-the good-of-the-people work only to salve his conscience—given how much he bilked his clients for his criminal cases—and to keep his father, an old Commie crony of Pop's, off his back.

I told him quickly about the murders and Betsy, leaving Barney out of the equation, at least for the time being.

"You're talking about a criminal case here, McNulty. I charge for those. That's how I make my living. It's bad enough I don't get paid for the other work I do for you guys."

"Your reward will come," I told him solemnly, "when the international working class has become the human race."

"Fuck you, McNulty."

"I'll tell Pop, and he'll tell your old man you've turned your back on the working class." I paused but went on before he could complain. "Look, she's on strike at the hotel—one of the leaders, a rock. The murders might have something to do with the strike . . . I don't know how, but it's possible."

"All right. All right. Jesus, Brian. I'll call her, but this isn't just sending a letter or quoting the law to someone. If they charge her, and if it goes to trial, we're talking about a lot of money. Not just my time but out of my pocket." He paused. "You've got time on your hands. If there's any legwork to do, I'll be calling on you to do it, old buddy. You can consider it your own pro bono work."

"Bartenders don't do pro bono. Cash on the barrelhead, preferably under the table."

"We'll see."

What a fucking day, I said to myself, as I left the Greeks' once more. Brooding on my own troubles, I didn't pay much attention to a Cadillac limousine parked in front of the hotel. The joint still functioned, the strike and the murder notwithstanding, even if it was running on three cylinders. Some picketers had left; others from the night shift had arrived. I didn't expect Betsy, Barney, or Mary but was heartened to see Mary did show up,

She spent the first ten minutes gushing over Betsy's baby being found, thanking God and talking about miracles. I didn't have any better explanation for Katie's good fortune, so I let her go on. After that, as we picketed and talked, Mary seemed to grow more dispirited, no longer the tower of strength I'd pegged her for. I didn't know if the general malaise that had settled over everyone on strike after the murders had gotten to her, or if she really did feel the whole mess was her fault.

Even though I was uncomfortable doing it, I told her what Francois said about her visit to MacAlister. When I saw her reaction, I wished I hadn't. Visibly embarrassed, flustered, she stammered and stumbled.

"I imagine what you must think of me," she said, "sneaking into the hotel in the dead of night to meet with the devil himself." She didn't look at me when she paused, so I didn't know if she was waiting for me to say something. Anyway, I didn't, so she went on. "I thought I might put things to rights, Brian. I went to apologize, to crawl on my knees and ask forgiveness, and if that wasn't enough, to say I'd leave and let the rest of you get back to work. I knew if I talked to you first, you'd tell me not to go, that it was everyone's fight, not just mine . . . but I'd made up my mind, and you know we Irish are a stubborn lot."

"Why would you think he'd listen?"

"I'm a foolish woman, Brian. I thought he'd be satisfied with the opportunity to humiliate me."

"Did the police ask you about being in his office?"

"Why would they?" She stopped walking and faced me. "Sure, why would they care?" Her eyes widened. "My God, Brian. What are you saying?"

"They might want to know if you saw anything that would help with the investigation."

"But that was days before the man was killed. What would I see or know?"

I shrugged my shoulders. "Was anything different? What did he seem like?"

"The same as he always was, no better and no worse. He didn't have the time of day for me."

We talked for a while longer, and I had just finished telling her about the cops questioning Betsy and Sheehan wanting to know where Barney was, when I noticed a coterie of broad shoulders in suits coming out the front door of the hotel. Recognizing my fearless leader Pete Kelly, with Slick Willie Eliot trotting behind, froze me where I stood.

Seeing me had the same effect on Kelly. He stopped in his tracks, stared for a moment, then sent one of his hangers-on over to get me. This offensive-lineman-sized oaf was not to be trifled with, so I went willingly. One of the thugs—the group comprised Kelly, Eliot, and two of Kelly's associates, whom I refer to as thugs, perhaps unfairly because I'd never seen them do anything thuglike, though I'd never seen them do anything else, either, only follow Kelly around looking like thugs—one of the thugs, then, opened the back door of the Caddy, letting me know, by a slight movement of his eyebrow, that I should get in, which I did, despite a thousand misgivings and a quick inventory of my life to that point. Kelly got in beside me. The gracious thug got behind the wheel and we drove off, leaving Eliot and Thug Number Two standing on the sidewalk next to the pint-sized Christmas trees with blue lights.

"You made a fucking mess," Kelly said, not to put too fine a point on it.

Scrunched into the seat, I rolled my eyes in his direction because I didn't want to face him directly.

He didn't notice because he was looking straight ahead, too, not at me. "I put in a word for you and what do you do to me?"

Believing the question to be rhetorical, I didn't answer.

"You think whacking the guy is going to settle the strike? You're nuts."

Under normal circumstances, I might have interjected here that I didn't "whack" MacAlister, but I knew Kelly was taking me for a ride in this limousine because he wanted to tell me something, not because he wanted me to tell him anything.

"You made angry some guys you shouldn't make angry. Bad enough the hotel guy gets whacked. You gotta be nuts someone kills the cop."

This time, I forced a word in, to the effect that he needn't worry; I didn't kill anyone.

"What you gotta worry about is you don't get whacked," said Kelly.

We drove around a couple of blocks and returned to the front of the hotel, whence we'd begun.

"What can I do?" I asked Kelly when the car stopped.

Kelly shrugged his shoulders and turned his right hand palm up. "I'm tellin' you how it is."

The visit with Kelly left me more than a bit rattled. I thought things were bad when the cops suspected Betsy was the killer. That paled by comparison to how things were now. The folks Kelly was talking about were the guys who sent Jimmy Hoffa through the cement mixer. Their idea of civic duty in this situation was to track down the cop killer and drop the miscreant's body on the precinct doorstep.

"Good heavens! What will you do, Brian?" Mary Donohue said when I got back to the picket line and told her of my predicament. Her brow was furrowed, her blue eyes probing mine. She had those Irish washerwoman traits I remembered from my mother: A gang of neighborhood bullies picking on my mother's son would be chased down the street by a middle-aged woman wielding a broom, FBI agents chased off the stoop with the same weapon, doors slammed on nosy newsmen and landlords who thought they had a grievance about overdue rent. Mary was like that, too—the ferocious-protector-of-your-own sort of woman who may not be exclusive to the Irish race but is certainly found there.

Now, there was fire in her eyes. "The blackguards. And wouldn't you think that Kelly or Eliot or the two together are the ones responsible—and them trying now to put the blame on you? And the police, the eejits, why aren't they out after them, instead of bothering with poor Barney, and Betsy, for the love of God?"

I didn't have answers to her questions. I thought Kelly might be being straight with me, trying to warn me. That snake Eliot was a different story. I'd bet even money it was Eliot who told Kelly and the gangsters Kelly dealt with that either Barney or I was involved in the murders. He was probably the source Sheehan meant when he said someone was talking to the cops about Betsy. As to how we would turn the cops around to get them off of us and pointed at Eliot, I had no idea.

When I told Mary this, she thought it over for a couple of laps around the picket line. "Brian," she said then, "this is the thing. Pat knows well how the detectives operate. Come up now for dinner and we'll have a talk with him. Maybe he can get us off on the right foot."

chapter fourteen

We rode the D train to the last stop on the line at 205th Street in the North Bronx and walked the few crowded blocks to her house under strings of colored Christmas lights that gave the street even more of a festive air. The term "hustle and bustle" was invented to describe the main commercial street in a New York City neighborhood at dusk in the winter when folks hurry home from work, some stopping at grocery stands, butcher shops, and delis, others for a quick pick-me-up in the local tavern, of which there were more than a few along Bainbridge Avenue. With everyone bundled up into coats and scarves, you couldn't tell off the bat it was an Irish neighborhood, not unless you listened in the doorway of one of the bars to the jukebox playing Irish music, or asked directions, or happened to strike up a conversation with the dark-haired, blue-eyed young man behind the counter in the corner grocery, where you could buy a six-pack of beer—or Guinness, if you so desired, as I did.

Mary lived in a two-family house on 203rd Street, a block off Bainbridge Avenue. She'd lived there in this little Ireland since the late 1960s, through two or three waves of Irish immigrants, the last one bringing a wave of refugees from the Troubles in the north, among them Barney Saunders, lately of the venerable Savoy Hotel—and presently, surprise to me, sitting on the couch in Mary Donohue's living room, sharing a couple of pints with Pat Donohue, Mary's husband, still wearing some portion of his NYPD blues.

With his dimples and impish smile, his easy laugh and dancing blue eyes, topped off with his contagious friendliness, Barney, as usual, was having a helluva time, finishing up a tale of his youth having to do with the neighbor's pig and him cutting through a peat bog, but none the worse for wear, as my mother might have said, for being on the run.

He, too, had already heard of the found lost baby, and spent the first few minutes shaking my hand and pounding me on the back as if I'd gone off into the jungle and wrestled the tyke away from a herd of lions.

"The kid just landed there on my doorstep," I told him. "I have no idea where she came from."

Everyone stood back and marveled over this again, and since I didn't want to get into another round of guardian angels, saints, and miracles, I tried to change the subject by reacquainting myself with Pat, whom Mary insisted I'd met years before, but which meeting neither Pat nor I remembered.

Pat Donohue, as gregarious as Barney, had an easy laugh and good nature riding on his sleeve, with none of the hard edge you expect to find in even the friendliest of city cops. Tall and thin, with a kind of graciousness and gentleness you'd associate with a priest or a minister, he was as generous and welcoming as a lord of old.

"Welcome, Brian McNulty," he said, shaking my hand and clapping me on the back again. "A good Irish name and a fine cut of a man. You'll have a drink," he said in something between a statement and a question. "A shot of Powers to get the chill out?"

I demurred, mumbling something between denial and acceptance, a stance I'd learned from Barney, who thought it impolite to come right out and accept something being offered to him. When I first met Barney and would offer now and again to buy him a drink, I'd say, "Can I buy you a drink, Barney?" and he'd say, apologetically, "I don't mind." A response only the Irish would understand.

So I mumbled and demurred, which was enough to send Pat off to the corner cabinet for the bottle of Powers and three shot glasses,

Mary not being included in the manly ritual, though Pat did ask if she'd like a highball, which she declined.

"*Sláinte!*" said Pat, and we tossed down the shots. By then Mary had come from the kitchen with a glass for me and bottles of Guinness for all of us. Pat took a swig of his and, looking at it, said, "It's not the same as what you'd get in Ireland, you know. Guinness was always said to travel poorly." I wondered if that was true of the Irish themselves, who seemed always to be in exile.

Mary and Pat's younger son, a student at Fordham, living at home for a semester, he said, joined us for dinner, ham and cabbage and boiled potatoes, that we ate while we continued to drink Guinness. The boy was quiet but cheerful and handsome, with Barney's black hair and blue eyes, looking enough like Barney, in fact, that I might have suspected some hanky-panky if Mary and Barney had been closer in age and Barney not a wild young man in Ireland until just a couple of years ago.

After dinner, the boy slipped away as quietly as he'd arrived, and Mary and Pat began cleaning up, leaving Barney and me alone for a few minutes. Taking the opportunity, I told him about the detectives questioning Betsy and later Sheehan asking me about him. It didn't seem to be much of a surprise.

"Ah, Brian, t'was only a matter of time till they came round to me." He tried to sound philosophical, but I could see the suffering in his eyes. "If it wasn't for my bloody immigration mess, I'd set the coppers right in no time. The bastards thinking Betsy could have anything to do with murdering her husband, they have to be eejits." The sadness was in full force now, where when I arrived he was his bubbly and cheerful self. It made me wonder if some profound hurt might not always be lurking beneath the cheerful surface.

Pat and Mary joined us in the living room, and we grown-ups got down to the grisly business of talking about murders and those who commit them. As we talked, it became clear that my dinner companions believed Eliot either killed MacAlister or had him killed. They didn't have any reason to know this to be true but had many reasons why he might have done it. After all, it was well known, said Pat, what happened after there was a falling-out between thieves.

That these arguments didn't take us anywhere Pat Donohue recognized himself when I suggested he make the case about Eliot to Sheehan and maybe succeed where I had not.

He shook his head. "Aragh, you're right, Brian. It'd do no good to tell the detectives anything, with us not having the evidence to back it up. What do they care about the thinking of the likes of us? No. By rights, we'd have to show them something to make them stop and think."

I'd regret this in the morning, I knew as soon as I began, but with a willing audience and a boost from the Guinness, I expounded on the principles of criminal investigation. That this was an area of my expertise should have come as a surprise to everyone, including myself, but Pat, an authentic NYPD cop with more than twenty years on the force, cheered me on. So Pat and I traded opinions, taking turns explaining, for the most part to one another, how the keen-eyed man of the world—someone like the cop on the beat, or a man who works behind the bar and has a knack for listening and watching what goes on about him—knows how things work and can find out things the run-of-the-mill detective doesn't find out.

The plan we worked out—before Pat staggered off to his bed, Barney hauled himself to the spare room, and I crumbled onto the couch—was that Pat would use his network of PD contacts to get a line on what the detectives had in the way of evidence and suspects, while I would pay visits to Eliot and Kelly to see if I could trip them up and find out some things they didn't want me to know. Barney would continue to lie low. Mary and Betsy, as much as she could, would help Sam out at the picket line. We hoped to have some better information by the time of the union meeting the following night.

I woke up the next morning with a throbbing head and digestive difficulties that would cause a nun to blaspheme. Pat had left for work, and I pitied the lawbreakers who ran afoul of him before his hangover wore off. Mary made breakfast while Barney and I sat across from one another holding our heads in our hands. Every minute or two, I'd remember something from the evening before that I wished I hadn't said. At the top of the list was this idea of going to see Kelly and Eliot. After breakfast, I felt a bit better. Barney wasn't so sure.

"I think I left me liver in the toilet," he said.

On the way downtown, I thought about Sam and the bribe from Eliot that I hadn't told anyone about and decided if I was going to talk to Eliot, Sam should come with me. Now that the night had met the morning sun, I'd regained my critical faculties, so I didn't figure it was a sure bet Sam would buy into the plan we'd come up with last night. I was no longer sure about it myself.

Sure enough, the first thing he said, wearing that irritated, skeptical expression he'd patented, was, "You're nuts, McNulty. You and that crazy Irishman are gonna get us all killed."

I'd caught up with him on the picket line, where he was attempting to keep things moving while trying to placate three kids, the oldest of whom might have been six or seven but carried himself like a thirty-something, the youngest was two or three but the squirming sort of kid who doesn't much go for being held. With his hands full, literally, Sam wasn't interested in small talk—or large talk, either.

I also broke down and told him about my faux pas of telling Sheehan I was with Betsy after he told the cops I was with him and Barney in Harlem. My being with Betsy caused Sam to raise an eyebrow and then to look me up and down a couple of times. A slight smile on his lips and in his eyes spoke volumes.

We went round and round until I convinced him we could see Eliot on the pretense that we were ready to end the strike and pick up our pay. He wouldn't fall for that from me, but he might from both of us because he wasn't sure what to make of Sam—as I wasn't quite sure what to make of Sam. For instance, I hadn't known about all the kids.

"My second wife," he said. When I looked at the baby, he caught my drift. "We tried a reconciliation. You know, man, one of those getting-back-together things."

"I thought you had teenage kids." A boy I thought was his son had played basketball against Kevin the year before.

"That's my first wife. We have two kids."

"Five kids?"

"Six," Sam said sheepishly, then, to the question marks in my eyes, "The woman I'm with now."

I guess I looked astonished.

"Why do I work three jobs?" he said gruffly. "And I can't afford to be on this goddamn strike much longer."

I thought about the bribe from Eliot and tried again to tell myself I understood why Sam would keep the money. He didn't owe the union or anyone else in the majority camp a hell of a lot of loyalty. I told myself these things, but it didn't change what I felt: that because I liked Sam and thought him a stand-up guy, he should live up to my expectations.

Finally, he said he'd go with me to see Eliot but not until the next day, when he wouldn't have his kids to look after. He took off with the kids, and I took over the picket line for an uneventful day. Late in the afternoon, Mary showed up, and a little behind her, Betsy. Mary had spent the afternoon on the phone shoring up our fellow workers, and most of them were hanging in, though the rumblings of discontent were getting louder. They'd wait for the meeting before they did anything. This might have been more reassuring if I had any idea what we would do at the meeting.

I left Mary and Betsy to man the picket line. Betsy's expression was sad and she was jittery, looking at me beseechingly, as if she had something important to say. She didn't say it; only our eyes met now and again with helpless expressions. Before I left I grabbed her hand and squeezed it. She seemed to understand, smiling and squeezing back.

"We'll talk," Betsy said, as I turned away.

Uptown, since it was cocktail hour—or a-couple-of-beers-after-work time, depending on the crowd you ran with—I stopped in at Oscar's, my neighborhood bar, where, having fallen on hard times, I'd once worked, and still did now and again when Oscar was short-handed and I was in short pants, which was pretty close to my current financial state. There was a guy I wanted to see—a man called "the Boss," our neighborhood numbers racketeer, who ran a half-dozen store-

fronts above 79th Street and below 125th Street that, with trinkets—
or, in the case of the 107th Street store, lingerie—in the display window, fronted for numbers parlors, for which he paid tribute to the
same powers-that-be that Pete Kelly had said were angry with me.
Talking to the Boss was not so easy because even though everyone in
the neighborhood knew what he did for a living, no one ever mentioned it to him—a sort of emperor-has-no-clothes kind of thing.
This meant conversations were usually founded on euphemisms.

He was sitting at the bar with another neighborhood fixture, Sam
the Hammer, who'd also spent most of his life on the outskirts of the
law. The Boss was drinking Johnny Walker Black. Sam, who only
drank alcohol when someone else was buying, drank coffee. Sam was
usually no more forthcoming about "how things were" than the Boss.
Despite my financial straits, I bought them both a drink, asking Joan,
the bartender, to put it on my tab. Joan was new enough on the job to
lack the confidence of a true neighborhood bartender, so she went to
ask Oscar, who was as usual perched at the end of the bar drinking
Budweiser. He whispered to her for quite a while, telling her God
knows what, but seemed to okay the transaction.

"Did Oscar tell you I was bad news and to stay away from me?" I
asked her.

She looked flustered as she tried to decide whether to tell me the
truth, ultimately deciding to ignore my question.

"I saw your kid," Sam said, gathering in his Miller Lite.

"What?" I snapped to attention. "When? Where?"

"At the Olympia, pretending he wasn't there."

Kevin was supposed to be at his mother's. I didn't want him hanging out on Broadway when I didn't know about it. My brain was
bursting to know more, but asking Sam questions was sure to get him
to clam up, so I waited a minute to see if he'd say anything else. When
he didn't, I went to the pay phone and called my ex-wife.

Her greeting was nasty and hysterical. "You fucking idiot. Don't
you ever go home? Don't you ever check your messages? Still a goddamn alley cat. When are you going to grow up?"

"Nice to talk to you, too. Where's Kevin?"

"What do you care? You're no kind of father." She paused, and I recognized for the hundredth time, though it did no good, that the nastiness came because she was scared for Kevin.

"He's gone," she said flatly. "He walked out last night, and as far as I'm concerned he can stay gone."

"Are you crazy? What are you talking about? He can't be gone."

"He is gone, and he'd be at your apartment if you were ever home. He's probably staying with one of his friends. Last night, I thought he was with you, so I wasn't worried. But since you weren't there, I don't know where he went."

Now it was my fault. Switch the blame to me—and it worked. I wasn't home. I was swilling down Guinness up in the Bronx when my kid needed me. First things first. I had to find Kevin. I wanted that even more desperately than I wanted to murder my ex-wife. "You have to call everyone he knows," I said.

"Why can't you call them?"

"I don't know who they are. I don't know their numbers. Please, will you call?"

She snorted. "Don't think you're so goddamn smart. It's not my fault he left. You're the one who gives him these ideas about being independent, who lets him hang out in bars and argue with his parents. You've never stood up to him. Now look what happened."

Although I was rapidly coming unhinged myself, I tried to understand that she felt as awful as I did, that she loved her son as desperately, worried just as much, felt as helpless as I did.

"Should I call the police?" she asked in a resigned and uncertain voice.

Probably I should have told her yes, but I couldn't bring myself to. For reasons I couldn't even explain to myself, I didn't want the cops looking for Kevin. I had a fear of being hunted, probably going back to Pop and the Red Scare of my own childhood, that I had a hard time shaking. Even though the police would be trying to help, I felt like I'd be turning Kevin over to them, instead of taking care of him, which was my job. I told her to wait an hour; I'd call back.

Since Kevin knew everyone I knew in the neighborhood, I figured

I'd ask around. The first person I thought of was my cabdriver friend Ntango, but Ntango would have called me. I checked my answering service; the only calls were from my ex-wife. I went in the couple or three bars on Broadway where I knew the bartenders, checked out the arcade near 113th Street, the pizza-by-the-slice and falafel joints near Columbia, and walked around the Columbia campus, even though it was too cold for anyone to be hanging out. I was on my way to check with the counter guys at the Olympia when I thought of Eric the Red. The on-again, off-again chef at Oscar's, Eric was yet another illegal, in his case from Yugoslavia, a devotee of the late Josip Broz Tito and the late Yugoslavia itself. We'd bonded over the years, drinking slivovitz and bemoaning the slow death of socialism in Eastern Europe. Eric was a loyal if disreputable friend, a joker, a smoker, a midnight toker, if there ever was one, fired from more jobs than me, at odds with society's mores and manners. Just the kind of guy a runaway kid might go to, with no fear of being turned over to any authority, including a parent.

I hiked up the five flights to Eric's top-floor apartment, which overlooked Strauss Park, at the intersection where West End Avenue blends into Broadway, following the blaring sound of the Grateful Dead, "Playing in the Band." Even in my frazzled state of mind and alarming physical condition, it was hard to keep from dancing up the stairs. Impossible, once Eric opened the door and I saw Kevin. My heart leapt, despite the fact he was sitting in Eric's ornate easy chair, next to a massive marijuana plant.

"Kevin!" I roared over the music, and he jumped a foot.

"Sorry, man," said Eric. "I wanted to tell you, but he wouldn't go for it."

"It's not up to him," I began in my stern-parent voice. "You're the grown-up." I took in the room, the pot plants, the black light, the psychedelic wall hangings and naked-women posters. "Never mind," I said.

"No. I told him, man. Running away's no good." Eric held his open palms up to me, and I saw in his stance and his expression that he really had agonized over this. "I didn't want him on the street, man."

Behind those slanted eyes that seldom saw daylight was the anxiety you saw in someone trying to do what was right. "I said okay. I don't call. I don't tell. But you stay in here." Eric held up his hands again. "That was what I could do. I'm glad you came, man."

"You didn't call him?" asked Kevin, who had sat glaring at us through the prior exchange.

"He didn't call," I said. "Sam the Hammer saw you in the Olympia. But Eric should have called. You can't run away. You'll end up in jail. You were a half hour from having the cops after you. And you had no right to put Eric on the spot like this." I was prepared to go on, but Kevin's expression warned me to stop. I didn't want him to bust out of there and be out on the street again. I let out a big, exasperated sigh, of the kind parents of teenagers know well. "You can go home to your mother, stay with me or your grandfather, or get locked up. Take your pick."

Kevin was astonished. His eyes widened, and he stuttered before he could speak. "You wouldn't call the cops on me." He said this with a mixture of disbelief and belief, the latter catching up with the former about halfway through the statement.

"You heard me." Through a massive effort of will, I kept my voice steady. If he knew how terrified I was that he'd call my bluff . . . but he didn't. Age and experience won the day, even as my knees began to give out.

I listened to Kevin's grievances about his mother—they were mostly of the defiance type—and told him he could stay with me until we worked things out, but there would be rules living with me also. He nodded his head gravely and agreed, but I could see the smile creeping in. I told Kevin to call his mother and left him with Eric while I went back to Oscar's to pick up where I'd left off with the Boss and Sam the Hammer.

They were pretty much as I'd left them, though Sam had finished his beer and gone back to coffee, and the early edition of the *Daily News* had arrived in the meanwhile, so he was reading that.

I sat next to the Boss and got right to the point. "You heard anything about me?"

"Should I?" answered the Boss. He always looked sleepy-eyed, but despite appearances was always alert, like one of those lizards that lies there with its eyes closed, then suddenly snaps at you and rips your gullet out, or whatever lizards rip out. I don't think you last very long in the Boss's business if you aren't alert. He didn't blab, either, only talked about things that were entirely irrelevant to his own life, like the Crown Heights riot and that Orthodox Jewish guy getting killed, which is what he was talking to the bartender about when I sat down.

Taking a deep breath, I got his attention when the bartender headed off for another customer and delicately described my situation. The Boss listened with no apparent interest, and if Sam the Hammer heard, he didn't let on. Having described my dilemma, I waited for comment.

"Not so good, McNulty," said the Boss.

"You got any advice?" I said with even more delicacy.

"You always been a gentleman. I know Peter Kelly. A gentleman."

"He's not who I'm worried about. Who are the guys he's talking about?"

"How would I know?" The Boss stiffened up. We weren't exactly friends—in fact, we'd had a run-in not long ago that proved embarrassing for the Boss and almost fatal for me—and the guy is nothing if not shrewd. If there was no percentage in his helping me, why would he bother?

Still I was pigheaded enough to keep at him. "Look. I need some help." The tone of my voice changed, so it sounded even to me like a demand.

The Boss made a movement, maybe adjusting himself on his bar stool or running his hand through his hair. The movement was slight but carried weight, like a barely perceptible wince you might see from a boxer who'd been hurt by a punch. Before the Boss could say anything, if he was going to, Sam stood up.

"Let's take a walk, McNulty. I got to see a guy at Murphy's."

I took the hint and followed Sam out the door into the chilly Broadway night. It was still early enough for stragglers to be hurrying along with shopping bags or briefcases. There were a lot more briefcases and dark wool overcoats in the neighborhood than when I'd first moved there years before, prosperity peeking over the horizon for a neighborhood that had been down on its luck for a decade or two. Folks like me were hanging in by the grace of rent stabilization.

Sam the Hammer had been in the neighborhood longer than I had, since the last time he'd gotten out of the slammer. A three-time loser, he was out of the rackets now for good, like the journeyman infielder who's lost more than just a step and finally hangs up his spikes. Sam never worked a day in his life at a straight job and still didn't. He kept body and soul together doing odd jobs and hustling barely legal stuff, so he held on to his phone-booth-sized studio apartment and had a few bucks for the two-dollar window at Yonkers a couple of times a week.

"The Boss told you what to do, McNulty. Kelly. Don't push him," Sam said as we walked along Broadway toward Murphy's.

"It's more complicated than that, Sam," I tried to explain. "I need to know how things work. Who's in charge. I need to get out from under this. I'm not asking—"

Walking with my head down, watching my feet, gathering my thoughts, I hadn't looked at Sam. When I did look up, he was gone. He'd peeled off from me and was under the colored lights, in amongst Christmas trees and wreaths and hearty winter flowers, chatting with the Korean proprietor of the 110th Street fruit stand, paying no attention to me.

chapter fifteen

The other Sam, Downtown Sam Jones, met me at the Greek coffee shop across from the hotel the next morning, still out of sorts about going to see Eliot.

"We got this meeting tonight. What you think about that?" said Sam, as he wolfed down his sausage and eggs. "You botherin' about this other guy when you should be botherin' about the meetin'."

"The meeting's not until tonight. Maybe we can invite Eliot."

Sam eyed me over a forkful of eggs. "That's dumber than your last idea."

"How's it going to hurt if we talk to him? Maybe we find out something. Maybe we don't. What do we got to lose?"

Sam eyed me again—the evil eye this time. "You think you can play it like that? You don't push. Nice an' natural, let it come to you? You go in for this, man, you gotta go all the way—whatever you got to do, you got to do it. You hear?"

His face went to granite, impenetrable. Why was everyone I ran across hard as nails? Whatever happened to those dear hearts and gentle people? Inside, that's what most of us were—even the hard ones. The city knocked it out of us. Pop would say it was greed. You had to like the Commies for that. No more dog-eat-dog once the capitalists were out of the way. No more "I'm gonna get what's mine, come what may." Nothing but dear hearts and gentle people, when the international working class becomes the human race. Even so, the heart grows hard on the way there. Poor Pop. Anyway, I needed to toughen up. I should go home and kick that cat, who'd come back through the window that morning.

While Sam finished eating, I wondered about him, where he'd come from, what he did before he began working the stick, where that toughness came from. In New York, you're always coming across someone running a corner grocery store at night or driving a cab and you find out he was a captain in the secret police in Iran or a surgeon in Libya before leaving hurriedly in front of the executioner, taking whatever work he could get when he arrived in the New World. Sam struck me that way, someone who left in a hurry, a guy with a story to tell, if he was of a mind to tell it.

He put in a call, and Eliot agreed to meet us in his little-used mail-drop in the garment district where we'd met the last time around. I didn't like going to the office. At least it was during the day when there was activity on the street, not late at night down near an abandoned pier where these kinds of meetings usually take place.

Eliot was sitting at the same desk in the outer office, with the door to the inner office again closed, still looking out of place, as we walked across the dusty wooden floor to sit in the two wooden office armchairs across from him.

"What's happenin', Mr. Eliot?" Sam asked cheerfully. "Sure has been a helluva week."

Eliot's expression was sorrowful and expectant. He spread his soft hands on the desk in front of him, as if he waited for whatever it was we brought him. Overdressed in a loud green wool sport coat and a shirt with green geometric patterns offset by a white tie, he looked like he'd been dressed by Damon Runyon.

"Youse guys were supposed to fix things. What the hell happened?"

"Well, Mr. Eliot, that's what we came here to ask you," said Sam. "I said to McNulty, we better check with Mr. Eliot because maybe all bets are off now. Maybe someone took care of things for us."

Eliot blinked a couple of times while he caught up with Sam. I was having a time keeping up myself.

"Youse guys know what happened, you better tell me. Whoever whacked those guys don't know the problems he got." He lowered his voice conspiratorially. "You know who whacked the hotel guy?"

"We were hoping you knew," I said.

He twisted his mouth into something resembling a snarl, then took a quick glance over his shoulder, causing me to wonder if someone might be in the inner office listening. "Whadda you talkin' about? You nuts? Whaddo I know about someone whackin' the guy?"

Sam's eyes were glued to Eliot's face, not missing a twitch or a grimace. I followed his gaze and saw the telltale tics and fluttering eyelids. Sam struck quickly. "MacAlister was screwing us, screwing you. So you took care of things. That's okay, man. Helps us out, too. We ain't askin' what went down. We just wanna make sure everything's the same with us."

Eliot looked over his shoulder, then back at Sam, his eyelids blinking rapidly. Sam is wiry and muscular, wound tight as a guitar string. Eliot is flabby, mushy, the consistency of marshmallow, and he was squirming. Because he was uncomfortable under Sam's scrutiny, he turned toward me when he spoke next and lowered his voice.

"Youse guys are on your own. I didn't have nothin' to do with either of the deceaseds, as you goddamn well know. Someone of youse knows somethin', and if you ain't gonna tell me, that'll be your hard luck. The fuckin' strike is outta my hands. This fuckin' guy MacAlister was skimmin', as you goddamn well know. So I got a problem and you got a problem, 'cause the corporation's comin' in to settle the thing with Kelly and nobody gives a shit what any of us thinks." His eyes did a quick flick behind him again. "I'm tellin' you how it is."

Not knowing how it was but knowing we wouldn't get anything else from Eliot, we saw no reason to prolong our stay.

"There was someone behind that door, wasn't there?" I said nervously, as soon as we'd left the office.

Sam rolled his eyes. "I can do a lot of things, McNulty, but seeing through wood and frosted glass ain't one of them."

" 'Right. But if I told you I just heard that door creaking open, I bet you'd run."

Sam's eyes went wide; he dropped into a crouch, snapped a snub-nosed pistol out of his belt, and spun to face to the door we'd just left. It was closed.

He didn't come out of his crouch laughing. By then, my eyes were wider than his, and I was frozen to the floor, the hair on my head, I'm sure, standing straight up. Sam put the gun away and kept walking down the hallway, down the stairs, and out of the building. I followed. He didn't say anything, so I didn't either, since he was rigid with rage, and probably trying to talk himself out of using his snub-nose on me.

We'd walked a lot of blocks at a fairly good clip before he calmed down. When his pace did slow, somewhere on Eighth Avenue in the Forties, he turned into a gin mill, a Blarney Stone look-alike. The bar was about three-quarters full, most of the daytime warriors nursing beers in the noonday gloom. Sam ordered a shot of Hennessy with a beer chaser. I had a draft.

Something went off in Sam's brain when he pulled the gun. I didn't think he was going to tell me what it was, but I wanted to stay with him anyway. I ordered a Virginia ham sandwich from the steam table guy and picked up one for Sam as well. The Hennessy would need more than a beer chaser to settle into. Sam took the sandwich without comment.

When he'd finished eating and was drinking a second beer—no nursing at our end of the bar—he appraised me for a long time in the mirror behind the back bar. It had been a while since I'd settled in for an afternoon of drinking—a good long while—but I felt one coming on. Sam was a hard-drinking man; he kept it under control, but they were there—those demons he couldn't drown. So we drank beer—after Sam's couple of shots of cognac—and talked, first about the Mets, then the Knicks, about when we worked where and who we worked with and whatever happened to them; that led to music clubs we worked in and who played there, like Howlin'

Wolf or Big Joe Turner, and of course that led to talking about the blues, so it was well into the afternoon, when Sam got to the personal stuff.

"You got some strange ways about you, McNulty," he said. "You're like a guy knows somethin' about the blues."

"What's that mean?"

"You had some hard times, man. You seen some things other folks ain't seen."

"To live without illusions."

"What's that?"

"Camus. Or, 'When life looks like Easy Street, there is danger at your door.' That's the Grateful Dead."

"That's the other thing about you, McNulty. You talk in circles."

"I'm passing along life's little jokes."

Sam was pensive, so I left him alone for a bit with his thoughts while I ordered another round; this one turned out to be on the house, a vanishing New York barroom custom. In days gone by, bar owners figured out a formula. A guy stops in for a drink after work. He's fine if he has one. Finishes it up and goes home. Same with a second. That's enough. Fine. He's done. It's the third one that gets him. Drink the third one, the beer starts to taste real good, the ball game comes on, he settles in. So the tavern owners figured out, slip the guy the third one on the house, and the sucker's in for another three or four pops before he realizes he fucked up. No one will admit this—they'll talk about having satisfied customers and giving something back—but take it from me; this is the deal.

I finally got around to asking Sam what I'd wanted to ask him. Probably without the couple of beers I wouldn't have. Probably without the pops he'd had he wouldn't have answered, but he did.

"I was a cop," Sam said, "in Charleston, South Carolina. You carry a gun; you get used to carrying. Not always. When I expect trouble."

His story rang true, even more so after he told me how he became a cop and why he wasn't one anymore. He'd fallen in with a Charleston woman when he was stationed at the naval base there. When he got out of the navy, he stayed on with her. It was the early '70s, when cities like Charleston were making an effort of sorts to diversify their departments.

"Pretty easy to get hired as a cop if you were military and black," Sam said. "I didn't think much about it. It was a job.

"We answered a call. A shooting. A wooden frame house with a wooden porch, not much more than a shack, a shantytown in the inner city. I went first and busted through the door. I busted through with my shoulder and half-rolled, half-dove into the room. I was on the floor, had my gun out, pointed at him. The guy had already shot his wife. She was slumped on the couch, holding her arm, bleeding from the shoulder. He stood in the middle of the room pointing a gun at me. I looked at him. He looked at me. I didn't shoot. Neither did he. I don't know why I didn't shoot. The guy dropped the gun. We arrested him. Then my partner told everyone what happened. You get what I'm sayin'? He told them, and all these guys—the cops—were really pissed I didn't shoot the guy. Word got around and that was it. I was an outcast, man. The cold shoulder from everyone, even the black cops."

"Why were they mad because you didn't shoot the guy?"

Sam took his time answering, though I suspected he'd known the answer for a long time. "It got so bad I left. I didn't want to be a cop no more. The reason? I know the reason. They told me right from Jump Street—no bones about it. That's not what a cop does. The motherfucker points a gun at you. You need to shoot that bad boy. You know what I'm sayin'? I made 'em look bad. Maybe they wouldn't be able to shoot the guy next time somethin' like that come up. You hear what I'm sayin'? I fucked things up for them, man. That's what."

We were done with drinking then and never did get back to who might have been behind the door at Eliot's office. I could guess: the thugs who took off Barney's fingers; whoever it was that Eliot reported to; maybe Kelly. The point was I didn't know, and it was fine with me that whoever it was, if it was anybody, stayed behind the door.

Drinking beer for lunch was never a good idea, because it beer-logged my brain and made me sleepy. Sam had things to take care of, so we agreed to meet at the Greeks' at six o'clock with the rest of our crew to plan the union meeting that night. I went to the picket line for an hour to walk off my beer haze. I knew what I had to do next, but I wasn't in any hurry.

chapter sixteen

For a couple of reasons, I needed to see Kelly. One, I wanted to know what Eliot meant about settling with the corporation. Second, I'd been dispatched by our brain trust in the Bronx to find out if Kelly knew anything about the killings he'd neglected to pass along to me. Finally, I needed to find out who it was who thought I'd killed someone. It was in my interest to get to the bottom of things—things other than the East River.

At least this time, I figured, he'd take my phone call, which he did, although it took some doing to convince the receptionist he would.

"I need to talk to you anyway," he said. "Be here in a half hour." That was it. As Snoopy said, "The anticipation far exceeded the actual event."

Kelly's office was in the same building as the banquet hiring hall, off Seventh Avenue in the Forties, about a ten-minute walk.

Though I'd been a member for years, I'd never set foot in the hallowed halls of the United Barmen and Hotel Workers of North America office before. The lobby looked like that of any other office building, with marble walls, a bank of elevators, and a security guard sitting at a desk that looked something like a judge's bench. Kelly's office was on the top floor. There were rugs on the hallway floor and big glass doors opening into the president's office, but the whole outfit didn't look any more posh than your run-of-the-mill doctor's office. Kelly sat behind a wooden desk. Behind him was a large window, and on either side of the window was a flag, the U.S. flag and the union flag, a symbol of bodiless hands shaking across a map of the United States on a blue background.

Kelly acknowledged me by a flick of his eyebrows.

"There's a problem," I began diplomatically.

This brought a wrinkle to his brow and a tightening around his eyes. "The problem you got to worry about is the strike. It's over. Tell me what you want. I'll get as much as I can. But when I walk out of those negotiations, you're done. Got it?"

"The strike isn't over until we go back to work."

He stared at me. I stared at him. Whatever else I thought about Kelly, I knew he was tough—a bartender in his time, who'd made his way up through the ranks and now controlled a union in a bare-knuckles industry in the highest-stakes city in the world. Who did I think I was talking to?

Kelly answered for me. "Don't bust my balls, McNulty. It's not about you and a business agent who thinks he's hot shit anymore. Other things have come into play."

"How about you get us the same contract the other hotels in the city have and give Mary her job back. We can start from there."

Kelly folded his hands and let his face muscles relax. No posturing. "That's a bigger problem than you know," he said quietly.

"Because Eliot and MacAlister were tapping the till?"

He took this without any sign of irritation, but he didn't respond.

"Did you consider that it might have been Eliot who killed MacAlister?"

This time his expression hardened, a tightening around the eyes. "It don't make any difference what I think. What I told you is some-body thinks you did."

"But I didn't."

Kelly dismissed this. "You or one of your pals. Look, McNulty. You had this scrape with Eliot. Against my better judgment, I let you try to work it out. The whole fucking thing blows up. I'm asked, 'What went on here? You told us no problems.' I don't got time to waste on one big-mouth bartender."

I believed Kelly was being straight with me. The workers who voted him into office each time weren't stupid. Kelly was a player in the city's power structures, the ones on top and the ones underneath. His track record said he was on the side of the workers—at least, more on our side than the other big shots—but I'd learned from Pop.

"With all due respect, Pete," I said. "The world isn't necessarily shaped in the boardrooms. You still got to get the workers back into the hotel."

Kelly's voice took on a deep, round timbre; rose a few decibels in volume, and came at me like a foghorn. "You wanna take me on, McNulty? Give it a try. When I'm done, those fucking workers will step on your face as they're walking back in."

This wasn't good. I tried to regroup. "Don't get me wrong, Pete. You said tell you what we want. This is it: the same contract as the other hotels, the fired waitress goes back . . ." I took a deep breath. "We get rid of Eliot."

Kelly took a deep breath himself. "We can get the waitress back. Her problem was MacAlister. We can do something on the contract. Maybe not scale yet, but I'll see what I can do." His gray eyes locked onto mine, and he shook his head. "I can't do Eliot."

Pop had taught me you can't win in negotiations what the other party isn't able to give. I thought this over quickly. Did I believe that Kelly couldn't get rid of Eliot? Yes and no.

"What if we gave you an excuse?"

Interest flickered in those hard eyes.

"If the corporation knows he and MacAlister were stealing, they'd demand you get rid of him, right?"

Kelly shook his head, a slight movement powered by that thick neck.

"What if someone dropped a dime? He got arrested."

Kelly made a slight gesture with his hand, as if he were, without much enthusiasm, chasing off a fly.

"What if he was charged in the murders?"

A spring went off behind his eyelids, but that was it. No comment. Kelly told me to call him before the union meeting that night.

It was after three when I left Kelly, so I went uptown to be home when Kevin got back from school. Part of our agreement was that he take the train out to Brooklyn to school every day and come home right after school unless I told him he could do otherwise. When he showed up around four, I realized I had to either bring him with me to the union meeting or leave him alone in the apartment.

"I don't want to go to your lame meeting," he said when I suggested it. "Why can't I stay here?"

I thought of a number of reasons but didn't have much choice. So after an early dinner of takeout Chinese food, I called around to a couple of bars and tracked down Sam the Hammer, asking him to check a couple of times to make sure Kevin didn't sneak out. I warned and threatened Kevin, left him to do homework, and headed downtown to meet with the Savoy workers.

The first gathering was in the Greeks'. Sam, Francois, Mary, and Betsy sat at a table in the back room while I told them about my talk with Kelly. After assessing our chances, we agreed that if Kelly came up with anything half decent we'd have to take it since the strike was falling apart anyway.

No one was pleased with the outcome, especially with Eliot staying on. Sam and Francois were philosophical; Mary resigned. Betsy, being hounded by the precinct detectives in Brooklyn and given the cold shoulder by the couple of hundred cops, the police wives, and practically everyone else who went to her husband's wake, was preoccupied. She told me she'd talked to my pal Peter the lawyer, who wanted me to call him. No one mentioned Barney, but he hovered over us, like one of those guardian angels my mother told me about when I was a kid.

When I called Kelly, he said he'd gotten most of what we'd asked for. I asked for specifics, but he couldn't be bothered. When I told him I needed the information for the meeting, he decided he could be bothered after all and would come to the meeting and present the settlement himself.

The meeting was a raucous, happy event. Word began circulating even before it began that there was a settlement in the wind. Folks who dragged themselves around the picket line with downcast eyes and heavy hearts were shouting wisecracks across the hall, slapping backs, and laughing out loud. They were even glad to see me. How the news got out was a mystery. I thought only the five of us knew. The word must have been blowing in the wind.

When Kelly arrived, he was alone. No thugs. He wore a blue business suit and carried a manila folder. Climbing out of a cab, a short, squat, thick-necked guy, with a broad, open face and an iron gray crew cut, he looked like a construction boss or a former army colonel, someone who earned his way into a suit by the sweat of his brow and the strength of his back. The hotel workers quieted, respectful if not reverential, when he entered the hall. He didn't stop to talk to me or any of the other strike leaders but went directly to the podium.

He was good on his feet, like one of the labor orators of old, praising the workers for their militancy, talking about their need for decent pay to take care of their families, and saying how without them and those like them the hotels and restaurants of the city would grind to a halt. He brought them to their feet cheering when he said the hotel had agreed to provide the full union health care plan, mumbled through a plan that would bring Savoy wages to near-parity with the other hotels in the city by the end of the five-year contract—and ended with a word of praise for business agent Tom Eliot, who made sure the unjustly fired waitress would return to work, who stuck with the workers through thick and thin, with never a thought of folding under pressure from management. This didn't bring anyone to his feet, but the voice vote was overwhelming to approve the contract, which wouldn't have made a difference anyway since Kelly was doing the counting. He left then, shaking hands and patting backs along the aisle on his way to the door, again with nothing to say to us, the group of also-rans by the door. Slam bam, thank you, ma'am. Just like that it was over. The hotel would begin calling the day shift to come back in the morning.

When I got home, I remembered Betsy telling me Peter Finch the lawyer wanted to talk to me, so I called him.

"We have a reliability problem," he said when I reached him.

"What's that mean?"

"Your friend Betsy hasn't been fully forthcoming."

"Oh?"

"Do you know a person named Barney Saunders?"

Uh-oh, I said to myself.

"Betsy's husband was pursuing an investigation of Barney Saunders when he was killed. She met with Saunders the day before her husband was killed, possibly to tell him her husband had found out something damaging about him."

"How do you know this?"

Peter's tone was cynical. "Not from Betsy."

"So how do you know?"

Peter was evasive. "I can't tell you. But the detectives investigating Tierney's murder know. Does the name Patrick Donohue, a cop, mean anything to you?"

It took a second to click—Mary's husband. "Yes," I said warily.

"There's an Irish organization loosely connected to the NYPD, one of those groups that does benefits and sends kids to summer camp, marches in parades with bagpipes. It's a pretty big deal. Some of the brass belong, but it's run by cops, the rank-and-file guys. This guy Donohue is one of the leaders, a former president, on the board, that sort of thing."

"So?"

"According to cop rumor, the group has a clandestine side that's connected to the IRA in Ireland."

I felt that chill you feel when you're about to hear something bad, that time before the dreaded news is uttered when your heart starts to beat more rapidly and your body temperature plunges, when you're both impatient to hear and wishing you never would.

"Some of the older guys on the force were born in Ireland and have contacts back there. They're men who've never given up the battle; they're more gung ho for the fight than the people back there fighting it—"

"Get to the point."

"They raise money. There are rumors of gun smuggling. Among

the things they're reputed to do is help acculturate fugitives from the battles there."

"Run that by me again."

"Irish fugitives wanted by the police in Northern Ireland for bombings or murders or anything else, they escape, make it to the U.S. These Friendly Sons of Ireland guys help them get new identities, find jobs, blend into the Irish population in the city, and disappear."

I hung up the phone deep in thought. I knew Barney was here in the states illegally. He'd told me so himself, and so had Betsy when he was in the hospital. I'd thought then Barney must have told her. Now I wasn't sure how she knew. It was possible her husband was looking into Barney's background even then, and he told her.

That Mary and her husband hadn't told me about Pat helping Barney slip into the country illegally—if he did—or that Barney was an IRA fugitive—if he was—might surprise a less cynical person than myself, just as Betsy not telling me her husband was hounding Barney might disappoint someone whose view of human nature hadn't been formed during twenty years behind a New York City bar.

chapter seventeen

During my call to Peter, Kevin had been watching TV on my antiquated set that sufficed for old movies and the occasional Knicks game. He'd ignored me when I came in and continued to ignore me when I finished the call, but whatever he was watching ended soon after that, so he found me in the kitchen where I was eating potato chips and dip and drinking a beer.

"That's not healthy," he said. "You're getting fat."

This was true.

"Can I bring my TV from my room at home? It's a lot better than this one."

"We'll see," I stalled. I'd talked to his mother briefly that morning, but she was still mad and wanted him to stay with me for a while, presumably so he could see what it was like living with his bum of a father. I had to wait for her to calm down before we could find a way for him to go back home. Even I knew living with me was not the best thing for him. His mother was a pain in the ass, but she was stable. With her, he ate normal meals, lived near his school and his friends. She was home at night, knew the doctors and dentists—and she provided discipline, something I wasn't very good at.

Teenagers need rules, I'd been told by the counselors and therapists his mother has foisted on me over the years. I was sure this was true, but rules made me nervous. Not that I didn't believe in rules. I did— wholeheartedly. You couldn't play basketball without them. It's the stupid rules that get to me. You dribble the ball and pick it up, you can't dribble again. That's fine with me. You have to wear a tie to the basketball dinner. Why? What happens if you don't wear a fucking tie? You get an unfair advantage over the other diners?

The you-gotta-wear-a-tie kind of rule drives me nuts. Somehow I communicated this phobia to Kevin, so he doesn't like rules, either. He has a larger list of stupid rules than I do, though, and there's the rub. Like why does he have to be home at eleven? Why can't he go out on a school night? Why does he have to tell me where he's going? The easiest way to deal with these questions is to say, "Because I said so." Or threaten to slug him, but this doesn't count because I've never laid a hand on him—except for knocking one of his baby teeth out playing basketball when he was eight. He said I elbowed him under the boards. But I didn't.

The other approach is punishment by deprivation: You can't watch TV, you're grounded, and such things. These are the staples of parenting. Except I'm no good at judging guilt and imposing punishment. Chalk it up to reading Camus about assassins in judges' robes at an impressionable age. So for a host of reasons, it was against my nature to be an enforcer.

"What do you gotta see? It's my TV," he said, interrupting my reverie.

I took the plunge. "We gotta see if you follow the rules before you get your TV."

"That's stupid. You're punishing me before I did anything wrong."

I hated arguing with this kid. He was relentless, like a bulldog. "We'll see," I said finally. "Ask me tomorrow."

This satisfied him for the moment. He headed back to the TV. "Oh, by the way, two guys came by to see you."

"Two guys?"

"Yeah. I never saw them before. They looked like goons from a gangster movie."

My heart stopped. These weren't movie goons; they were the real thing. Sent by whoever it was Kelly had warned me about. I had to get Kevin out of there. I pumped him with questions, but all this did was irritate him and make him clam up. He'd been spending too much time with Sam the Hammer. I gave up the questioning and took up brooding. I called my ex-wife and told her I needed to send Kevin home.

"Sorry," she said in a lilting tone that made clear she wasn't sorry at all. "He's made his bed; he can lie in it. I'm leaving tomorrow on vacation for a week. You can see how it really is to raise a child."

Any more conversation with her would have driven me over the edge, so I hung up and called Pop. He wasn't any help either because he was speaking at some left-wing conference in Atlantic City and would be gone for two days. Kevin would have to stay put until he got back. While I was on the phone with Pop, I told him what had been going on, hoping he might change his mind and stay home. Little chance of that; he hadn't stayed home from the political wars when his own son needed him.

"You've been busy," said Pop.

"Yeah, and I'm gonna be busier unless you can tell me how to get the heat off me and onto where it belongs."

Pop considered this. "Someone knows the truth." He'd long ago cornered the market on truisms.

"Right. And how do I get them to tell me?"

"You'd be surprised what you can find out by asking."

"Right. I just say, 'Excuse me, did you murder the hotel manager?' "

Pop didn't chuckle, nor was he offended. "You ask the staples: Where were you? When? Did you go here? Were you with him or her?—those sorts of questions. Sometimes things don't add up; you recognize efforts at evasion. Someone wasn't where he said he was. Someone gets mad and punches you. You've been through this before. You should have taken notes."

His sarcasm had fermented over decades of quixotic battles against bosses in various guises. Still and all, he was the most perceptive person I knew, so I asked, "Who do you think killed the hotel manager and the cop?"

He took a few seconds to think over his answer. "I'd say that for some person, the consequences of those two men staying alive were so severe that any consequences that might flow from murdering them paled in comparison. Desperation." He paused. "Of course, that's not the only possibility, but it's the one I'd go with."

"Why that one? What are the others?"

"There are many—financial gain, jealousy, hatred, revenge, thrill-seeking, political, probably more. You want to consider these, you need to delve into each man's life. Who knows what you'll find? If you try out my theory, you might eliminate those on strike as possible killers. Or not. But isn't that what you want?"

Getting off the phone after one of these question-and-answer sessions with Pop, I always felt like I'd been to visit an oracle. I didn't know what I wanted. Why did I care who killed MacAlister and Tierney? It wasn't as if I was going to miss them. For one thing, some gangster thought I killed them and was pissed. For another, the cops suspected Betsy and Barney. In both cases, I believed Tom Eliot was feeding information to the gangsters and the cops to get suspicion off of him and onto us. Why he would do that was one question, and how we could turn things around was another question. Thinking along the lines Pop suggested, what would make Eliot—or possibly someone else—desperate enough to kill two men?

It was late, after midnight, but still early for the gathering of the winos at Oscar's. I got Kevin squared away with the TV and the fold-out couch, after giving up my effort to get him to read a book before he went to sleep, and headed down the block to arrange backup for keeping an eye on him. Given the thugs who came to my door—even though they were after me and not him—I didn't want him alone in my apartment.

As I crossed 107th Street, I spied my pal Carl, a doorman on West End Avenue, leaving the all-night deli with his buttered hard roll and Coke and heading for work. I gave him a quick rundown and asked if he'd spend some time in my apartment in the evenings when I couldn't be there. I didn't go into detail because Carl, who was having some success getting his poems published in small magazines of late, was a Nero Wolfe fan and got excited about mysteries just as the portly detective might. If I told him there was a murder involved, he'd ask me questions all night.

At Oscar's, I found Sam the Hammer with the *Daily News* again. I was hoping for the Boss, but you never knew when he was going to be there since he had so many other joints he stopped into on his appointed rounds—half the bars on Broadway, Amsterdam, and Columbus above 79th Street. I went into a little more detail with Sam the Hammer than I did with Carl since Sam knew the terrain better than most people.

"They were lookin' for you, right?" Sam said, without any visible sign that he was concerned. "I'd make it hard for them to find me." He went back to reading his paper without telling me whether he'd look in on Kevin or not. Next was Eric the Red, whose enthusiasm for the task was exceeded only by his unfailing unreliability.

I had a couple of pops and began to notice that wisps of the waitress's long black hair had slipped out of the bun she'd tied it into and flickered around her dark eyes quite becomingly. She smiled in a cute, shy way when she found me watching her. I'd seen her a couple of times before, but this night she became pretty right before my eyes. A tiny ember of hope flickered in the burned-out wreck of my heart, but it had been a long day, Kevin was alone in my apartment, and the odds of romance were long, so I packed it in.

The worst thing about Kevin living with me was getting up to see him off for school. He had to leave the house by six in the morning, a time I was more used to getting home at than getting up at. When the alarm went off, I staggered around, poured him a bowl of cereal, gave him lunch money, and sent him on his way. I fought off the temptation to go back to sleep and instead put in a call to my pal Ntango, who lately had been working a seven-to-seven shift and should be getting off about then. I wanted to go to the Bronx to talk to Barney. I hadn't talked to him since the strike ended, for one thing, and Peter had asked me to find out what went on between Betsy and Barney and why she hadn't told Peter about it.

The night I saw him at the Donohues', Barney told me he was working at an Irish butcher shop, whatever the hell that was. We were

swilling down Guinness, and in truth I wasn't paying attention. I did
remember where Mary and Pat lived—or thought I did—so I figured
one of them could point me toward him. If I was lucky, Pat might be
home and I could find out more about the Friendly Sons of Ireland
and what it meant that Dennis Tierney was snooping around trying to
find out about Barney.

. I asked Ntango's dispatcher to have him meet me at La Rosita, the
neighborhood Cuban restaurant, hoping that, for the price of gas,
lunch, a couple of beers, and a joint or two, he'd check out the Irish
Bronx with me. I bought some coffee for the French-Canadian Christmas tree guys on the corner and chatted with them while I waited.
They came down right after Thanksgiving with a truckload of trees
and lived in their van in shifts until Christmas, selling them. Since
they were there all the time, I asked if they'd keep an eye on my
apartment and call the cops if they saw any linebackers wearing suits
approach it. They were nice guys but didn't speak a lot of English, so
I don't know if they got the message or not.

Ntango got to La Rosita around eight, having got the message
when he was picking up a fare at LaGuardia that was coming to the
Upper West Side anyway.

"Why not?" he said when I asked him about the Bronx trip. "We
haven't had an adventure in a long time, Mr. Brian."

"Don't remind me."

I told him about the demise of the strike. We also talked about the
murders.

"I read about them in the paper," he said. "The story mentioned
the police questioning the wife. I never thought of that nice blond
waitress at the hotel. They didn't connect the policeman being killed
with the strike, though I read in a different story about the hotel manager's death—an unusual combination of events. You lead an exciting
life."

This struck a nerve. I'd been thinking about why I found myself in
the middle of evil doings again. "You can't spend your life in bars
without a lot of trouble finding you," I told Ntango. "Especially if
you have a disposition like mine that leads you to go where you

shouldn't go and get involved with folks you shouldn't because you think they're more interesting than everyday folks. I see a person that's practically bent double with the troubles they've brought on themselves or had foisted onto them, and I know damn well I should turn and run. Give them cab fare to the next borough and go home and sit by the fireside bright. But no, I get curious. I have to find out what's going on with them, then I need to find out one more thing. I find out that one thing and I get curiouser and curiouser until I'm ass-deep in trouble myself."

"It's good to know your own nature," said Ntango.

There was more to the story, too, but I didn't bend Ntango's ear with any more of my thinking. What happened when you spent a long time in bars was that you got a heightened sense of what makes people tick, as folks tend to loosen up when they've had a few drinks and talk about the things that weigh most heavily on them. Working the stick, you saw the winos at their best and at their worst, and in having bests and worsts winos aren't so different from other people. You learn there's a lot of suffering going on that only sometimes slips out. You learn there's goodness that sometimes makes its way out, too. But there's another side—the friend-of-mine-that-hits-you-from-behind side. You see the good in people that's trying to get out, but you're not surprised when the goodness doesn't quite make it. Bartenders develop a great sympathy for suffering humanity and faith in our fellow man, but we still want to cut the cards.

I found the street Pat and Mary lived on more easily than I thought I would. The house was more difficult. There were two or three distinct possibilities.

"Knock on a door," Ntango suggested.

I didn't have to. A door opened a few houses down from us, and Pat Donohue came through it, dressed in his NYPD windbreaker and wearing a matching baseball cap. I called to him from the cab as he walked past. He went into a crouch almost as deep as Sam had when we were leaving Eliot's office, turning his head toward the sound of my voice, reaching toward his ankle as he turned. The movement was graceful, not panicked, a just-making-sure movement, so that he was relaxed and smiling when he recognized me a second later.

"Hello, Brian McNulty, and what brings you to this neck of the woods?"

"I'm looking for Barney."

"So you are," said Pat.

He was on his way to the butcher for some sausage and Irish bacon, he told us—this being his day off, he wanted an Irish breakfast—and he'd ask when Barney would be in.

"Do you know where he's staying? I'd like to find him this morning if I could."

Pat shook his head, his brow wrinkled with worry. "I don't know. I hope there's nothing wrong."

"You got a couple of minutes? There's something I'd like to ask you about."

He looked about him uncomfortably. "I do," he said, with what sounded like regret for his delayed breakfast, and opened the cab door and ushered me out.

He listened with interest as I related what Peter Finch told me about Dennis Tierney trying to get information about Barney from the Friendly Sons of Ireland, while the worry lines in his brow deepened. I realized I was treading on dangerous ground since admitting to the activities Peter attributed to the Friendly Sons would be admitting to a crime, if not treason. He didn't know me well enough to let me in on political secrets, so I told him I was interested in what Tierney was doing, not the activities of the organization.

We'd walked as far as Bainbridge Avenue, bustling at that time of the day, with double-parked delivery trucks and deliverymen crossing the sidewalk with hand trucks, and women in kerchiefs and woolen coats pulling along shopping carts.

"Brian, you know the troubles in Ireland all these many years. I came from near the border, from Cavan. Your man Barney was reared in South Armagh in terrible poverty—"

I must have looked surprised.

"He's from Cavan now; he is. The way he could get out of Ireland on an Irish passport. South Armagh is down to the north. He and his brothers and sisters and cousins lived in fierce poverty there, the poorest of the poor. Not long before I came to America in the 1960s, a cease-fire was declared. The IRA disbanded itself, and the prisoners were released in a general amnesty. That was the first time Barney ever met his da."

Pat stopped me by placing his hand gently on my arm and steering me into an old-fashioned butcher shop straight out of my childhood, with sawdust on the floor and giants of men in white aprons with hearty laughs behind the white-enamel-and-glass meat cases. There were three of them, loud and cheerful, with gruff voices and thick arms and thicker brogues, each a decade older or younger than the next. They knew Pat and everyone else who came into the shop.

Pat ordered his bacon and sausage and turned down a roast that he was told would melt in his mouth. I was the butt of a couple of jokes, with the men behind the counter assuming I was a cop also and Pat in need of protection to get his bacon and sausage home and not be stopping off for an eye-opener at the Old Shillelagh next door.

Pat asked when Barney might be in, and this started another round of joking about Barney trying to sweep the floor wearing his mitten. "We keep him in the window as an ornament for all the use he is," one of them said. They didn't know where he was staying but said he'd be in around three.

On the walk back, Pat continued his story. "The conditions of the Catholics in the North were terrible. The poor were treated like an old dog you'd throw scraps to if you had a mind to or leave to himself if you didn't, a half-dozen families trying to make a go of it on a wee piece of land that would barely support one family. That's the world Barney was born into, as well as his sisters and his cousins."

He stopped and put his hand gently on my arm again to get my full attention. "The whole family, Barney and his sisters, and his father, and his father before him, was IRA. Sure, isn't nearly every Catholic family in South Armagh? But if they fought for a dream to free Ireland, they fought for their own survival as well, to put food on the table, a roof over their heads, to get back for their families the land the

British stole from them years before. Make no mistake about it, Brian McNulty, it's a war there in the North, a war to regain land that by all rights belongs to the Irish, that our grandfathers' grandfathers made into farms and had stolen away from them, and let no man tell you otherwise."

We walked the next block in silence, until he began again. "Barney grew up into the IRA. His father was imprisoned again when he was a teenager. His cousins—and his sister, begod—were jailed, whether they did anything at all or not to deserve it. Barney was younger than the crowd that first went to jail. He was just a lad when I left Ireland. I don't know if he was an IRA man later on, but he got in trouble whether of his own doing or not. He was wanted by the British, but he was fortunate enough to get to Cavan before they got their hands on him, and then to America. By rights, he's a political refugee who'd be subjected to jail and torture without even a bloody trial if he returned home. The poor man's been forced into exile. But the American government won't help him, so, begod, someone has to."

Pat was silent then, his expression fierce, as if he expected an argument and was damn well ready for it. He wasn't going to get one from me. If he and the friendly sons of whoever it was wanted to smuggle in fugitives, it was no business of mine. I already had my hands full with a cat, a teenager, a woman with a baby, and two unsolved murders.

Now Pat Donohue insisted Ntango and I come in for a real Irish breakfast. The fact that we'd eaten a real Latin breakfast a couple of hours before made no nevermind to Pat. "Aragh, what do the Cubans know about breakfast?" he asked.

So we gave in and had breakfast: two eggs, bacon, sausage, a little pile of black mush that he called blood pudding, and tea with milk and sugar. Ntango, who has a good appetite, despite being skinny as a rail, gobbled up everything in sight, while I tried to figure out how to get rid of the pile of black mush without actually eating it.

As we were finishing, I asked Pat what it meant that Tierney was trying to uncover information about Barney through the police department and what he might find out.

"He would know of the organization, I'm sure," Pat said, "and he's a Tierney, so he wouldn't find it difficult getting in with some of the boys. And there's those who after a couple of drinks start to blather. He might well find out we gave Barney a hand getting settled."

"Do you think he would expose Barney as an illegal alien?"

"If he betrayed the man, he'd never live it down. Cops don't abide informers. Tierney bloody well knew—" Pat caught himself, then started again. "He knew what would happen to my pension if it was known officially that I had a hand in bringing a fugitive into the country. He couldn't show his face in a precinct house again if he were known to have betrayed me."

"Why did he want to know, then?"

Pat shook his head.

"What did other cops think about Tierney?"

"I hardly knew the man, but I'd say he wasn't well liked, too eager. You wouldn't want him for a partner."

"Did he have enemies?"

Pat shook his head. "I wouldn't know."

"Could his looking into this situation with Barney have been an official investigation?"

Pat shook his head. "We would have known."

When I got home, I called Betsy, who was still at her mother's. "She's out," her mother told me, and hung up.

When Kevin got home from school, we talked over his day at school for about twenty seconds before he ran out of things to say and told me to stop bugging him. Next, I told him to do his homework, and he said he didn't have any. After that, I asked him how he liked living with me instead of his mother, and he said it was great. I said it would end pretty quickly if he didn't find some homework to do. He said he would and to leave him alone. So much for fathering.

I put the Christmas tree guys on alert and flagged down a northbound gypsy cab on Broadway. Barney was behind the meat counter when I got to the butcher shop on Bainbridge Avenue. Cheerful as ever in his white apron and white shirt, he looked like he belonged there, though he got shooed out from behind the counter a few minutes later. When he put on his coat and picked up a bag filled with hunks of meat of varied shapes and sizes wrapped in butcher paper, I realized he'd hired on as a deliveryman.

I walked along with him on his errand, despite the chill and my not having dressed for the out-of-doors.

"So, Brian, a lot has happened since last we met. The strike is settled?"

"We had to," I said defensively. "We were going to lose it—and we would have had to take on Kelly."

"No harm," said Barney. "We'll live to fight another day. And you, Brian?" His dancing blue eyes searched mine. "Are you doing well?"

"I'm okay." It's hard not to go soft under Barney's concern for you.

"And poor Betsy, are you looking after her?"

"She's holding up," I said. "She's got a lot to worry about." He knew now, by virtue of the *Daily News* if not otherwise, about her coming for Katie the night I found her and about both of them spending the night at my apartment. But he didn't seem to share everyone else's—including now a couple of million New Yorkers after the tabloid stories—suspicion that we were shacked up together. Barney patted me on the back and turned to walk up the steps of an apartment building.

I paced the sidewalk in front of the building while he went up in the elevator with his delivery. Barney was disarming. He came at you with such openness, it was difficult to keep anything from him. Pop said to ask where-and-when questions, so the culprits might trip themselves up. I suppose what I really wanted was for Barney to explain things that needed explaining, like when he saw Betsy last, how much he knew about her dead husband's campaign against him, whether he left a baby on my doorstep.

In the worst of worlds, Barney and Betsy conspired to kill her husband. No denying that this thought snuck into the back of my mind, even though the consequences of it being true were unimaginable to me. The reverberations of a murder are devastating. Of course, I hoped they didn't kill anyone, that someone else did. Just because they had reason to kill Tierney didn't mean they did kill him. And why would they kill MacAlister? I could come up with reasons for many of us, including me, to kill MacAlister, but not for anyone to kill Tierney. Betsy, and perhaps Barney, was the only person I knew better off with Tierney dead—unless I had overlooked something that connected Eliot, MacAlister, and Tierney. What could it be? For everyone's sake, including my own, I hoped I could find out.

chapter eighteen

When Barney finished his chore, he suggested we stop at the Old Shillelagh for a quick one. I asked if he wasn't worried about getting back to work, but he laughed. "The McNamara brothers are from near me at home. They've only taken me under their wing until I get on me feet. I'm little use to them. They'll hardly notice if I'm not there."

We took our pints of Guinness to a booth across from the bar. The Shillelagh was a no-frills affair, bearing little resemblance to newly minted, trendy Manhattan Irish pubs. On tap there was Guinness, Harp, and Budweiser; the house specialty cocktail was a shot and a beer.

I went straight to the heart of the matter with Barney. "They knew you at home? Where exactly was that?"

He could tell by my directness that I was on to something, so he considered his answer through a long swallow of stout. "What are you asking me, Brian?"

I shook my head. I didn't want to play games with him, so I told him what Pat Donohue told me.

He took it like a man, but I'd certainly deflated his cheerfulness. "It's a poor man will lie to his friends," he said, "but it wasn't only myself I had to protect. I don't know that you're much the wiser knowing."

"That's not what I'm worried about." I went over the police questioning Betsy again, my hooking her up with a lawyer, and the lawyer finding out things from the police he should have found out from her. "How much did you know about Betsy's husband?"

"I knew enough of him."

"What did Betsy tell you about him?"

"She was a very unhappy girl, Brian, as you well know. It wasn't right for me to be talking to a married woman, but I did. The girl married young not knowing what she was getting into. He was a hard man. The pity of it was they had a child."

"Did she plan on leaving him?"

"She gave it a thought," said Barney, "but it was a Catholic marriage. The families are close. She had a mind to persuade him it would be well for both of them to part, but she hadn't the nerve. She was afraid of him."

"Did she plan on leaving him for you?"

Barney's face colored. "She was a married woman, Brian. We talked about no such thing. No such thing at all."

I was confronted by the alien morality of my forefathers. The idea that marriage and propriety could be so honored seemed foreign to my godless secular soul. Humbled now myself, I laid my cards on the table. "What I'm getting at, Barney, is for how long did this guy Tierney have it in for you."

Barney's eyes danced once more, the irrepressible mischievous smile flittering around his lips. "I know what you're getting at, Brian. The Lord knows it looks like I've murdered Betsy's husband. Here I'm a firebrand rebel from Ireland, leading a strike and threatening the hotel manager, making up to a man's wife, and the both of them found dead later. But Brian, me lad, I didn't kill anyone.

"Your man Eliot is the likely murderer. Didn't he have enough to fear from MacAlister to want him safely underground, where he'd be silenced forever and not be talking about the affairs that went on between them? MacAlister was the kind of man would turn on you in a second, not a man to share a secret with, not a man to be trusted. He would easily be holding out on him, or worse, holding something over his head."

"Why would the gangsters be after us if Eliot did the killings?"

"Sure, Eliot could have taken the killings upon himself without telling his superiors a thing about it," answered Barney. "He wouldn't want them to know he's the responsible one. So why not put the blame on us poor blokes? Bejaysus, we might have played right into his hands, with going out on strike and setting up a reason for one of us to kill MacAlister."

"Maybe. How would Betsy's husband fit into this?"

Barney eyes darkened. "I can't tell you for sure, Brian, but I'll tell you this. Dennis Tierney was an evil man, with no conscience. Some men serve in the garda with honor. You know yourself, there are bad ones. In the North, the RUC was rife with bullies and blackguards, a bad lot who used their badges and their uniforms to steal from Protestant and Catholic alike. Uniformed hoodlums was all they were. Couldn't this happen in New York as well—a hoodlum with a uniform? God forgive me for speaking evil of the dead, but who knows if Tierney might not have been in league with Eliot and MacAlister, with none of us the wiser?"

"But doing what, Barney? We don't know that any of this is true."

His eyes were clear and penetrating, his jaw set, the picture of determination. He held up his damaged paw. "I've a score to settle, Brian McNulty. We'll go after Tom Eliot yet. First is to let your man know we're on to him and then watch him like a hawk. At home, I more than once haunted the killers of Irishmen until they gave themselves away."

I was willing to buy the possibility that Eliot was the killer and that if we put pressure on him he'd panic and reveal himself. As much as I liked Barney, though, I had to admit he hadn't told me much when I asked what he knew about Betsy's husband and when he knew it. I'd still have to find out from Betsy, for her own sake, if she could tell a straighter story than Barney did. But right now, I needed to go to work. I'd called in and found out I was on the schedule.

When I went home to shower and change, I found a note from

Kevin telling me he'd gone to try out for a basketball team in Brooklyn. That was it. Brooklyn, reputed to be the nation's fourth largest city, with a couple of dozen teen basketball leagues, and I'm supposed to know where he is. What was I going to do? I couldn't go looking for him, so I left him a note asking him to call me at work as soon as he got home. I wrote the note politely, while I secretly planned to break his neck as soon as he was safely home. The cat was in, so I closed the window. At least I could hold on to him. He was sitting beneath the window meowing when I left.

It was strange walking through the door of the hotel again, like testing out a leg that had been in a cast for a while. I walked gingerly across the lobby rug, not recognizing anyone behind the front desk, and entered the lounge as if it were someone else's house. Ducking under the flap at the end of the service bar and coming up on the other side, I felt, as I often did, like a boxer entering the ring. I barely kept myself from dancing in place and shadowboxing. Sam was putting the bar in order after the day shift and gathering up fruits and juices for a banquet bar he was working that evening. Betsy was the night cocktail waitress. I was glad to see both of them. I can't say I ever loved my job, but I felt a real contentment being behind the stick again—a sure thing in a life of chaos.

It was slow at the bar, but busy enough to keep me occupied. Betsy had only a couple of tables after an early flurry. Since the hotel hadn't yet recovered from the strike, there was only one bartender, one waitress, and no entertainment.

"I saw Barney," I told her during a lull.

"Oh, good," she gushed, as she leaned across the service bar. "I'm glad you thought of him. How is he?"

"He's okay. When did you see him last?"

Betsy shifted her glance away from me. When she turned toward me again, her smile had lost some of its radiance. "Not since all this began. The night on the picket line when—" She looked away again.

"The night your husband attacked him?"

She nodded.

"Did your husband know MacAlister?"

Betsy looked perplexed. "From in here, I guess . . . knew him a little bit."

"No dealings with him?"

"Not that I know of. Why?"

"Who do you think killed your husband?"

She started to answer, but lost her composure and stopped. Her glowing, cheerful expression drooped into that of a beleaguered, worried young woman. "I don't know," she said softly enough to be a whisper.

"No one you can think of?"

"Someone from his past. Someone he arrested who wanted revenge. That's what I thought in the beginning."

"Did you ever think it might have been Barney?"

"Barney?" She shook her head violently from side to side, as if to physically ward off the idea. "Why would you say that?" Her nostrils flared; her eyes flamed. I thought she'd go for my throat.

"Because other people are saying it, so you and Barney need to do a better job answering questions than you've done so far."

"Oh, Brian." She opened those deep blue pools of helplessness. "I'm so confused. I don't know what to do or who to trust." Those big sad eyes tugged at my heart. "What should I do?"

I held myself in check. "The funny thing is, I don't know who to trust, either. I don't know if I can trust you."

Oh, the pitiable smile, the guilt and the sadness. "Oh, Brian, I'm afraid."

"What are you afraid of?"

"Could I have caused all this?" She stood back from the bar now, stoop-shouldered, a tear trickling down her cheek, waiting for me, as if I were the last person on earth who could help her, waiting for me to comfort her—something I knew was no good for either of us. She called to me anyway. I could feel her pulling me toward her, feel it in my heart, so I went under the flap of the bar, went to her passionately, not to comfort her but to pull her body to mine, wrap my arms around her back and her hips and pull her body into mine so her pelvis ground against me and her breasts flattened against my chest. I yanked her head back by the hair and crushed my mouth against hers—and that's where we were when I heard someone clear his throat and opened my eyes to see Detective Sergeant Sheehan watching us from the lobby doorway.

Talk about getting caught in the sack! Betsy and I both jumped about a foot up and three feet back. This drove me right into the bar, where I smacked my spine and my elbow. We stared at Sheehan. He looked calmly back at us.

"If you can tear yourself away, McNulty, I'd like a word with you. You, too, Mrs. Tierney, when I finish with the bartender here."

I went back behind the bar, rubbing my elbow with one hand and my spine with the hand that was connected to the sore elbow. Sheehan sat on a stool at the far corner, away from the service bar. Betsy hurried off to the kitchen.

"We're looking for a friend of yours. I don't suppose you've seen him."

"Who's that?"

"The Wild Colonial Boy."

"Barney? Why are you still looking for him?"

Sheehan blinked a couple of times and pursed his lips. "I thought I'd be asking the questions."

"You want something to drink?"

"Coffee?"

Poor Betsy had to bring it. Her face was red, her movements jittery; she looked as harried as if all the tables in the lounge were full, instead of just one.

Sheehan watched her walk away. I wouldn't say she slunk, but she had that crouch people have when they expect they might get hit from behind.

"Pretty girl," Sheehan said. "I hope you take this the right way. What you do with her is none of my business, but the police business is that she's connected to this guy Barney Saunders. Been seeing him for a while on the q.t."

I'm sure I stiffened, that my jaw went square, but I kept quiet.

"There's not much of a record on this Saunders guy. Usually people have a past. He materialized in Manhattan one day about three years ago—makes you wonder."

"If I see him, I'll tell him you're looking for him. Is he wanted? Do you have a warrant?"

Sheehan shook his head. "Just to talk."

"Why are you involved in this, anyway? I thought the investigation was out in Brooklyn."

"There was a murder here, too. Remember?"

"Did you check on the guy I told you about, Eliot?"

Sheehan nodded. "We know him. I'm sure he'd swindle his mother. But we don't have anything to tie him to MacAlister, just contact in the line of work."

"MacAlister was paying him off."

"Says you." Sheehan relented before I could say anything. "I wouldn't put it past him. Matter of fact, I'd be surprised if he wasn't doing something like that, but we'd have to have more than you saying it, McNulty." Was that a twinkle in his eye? "Even if you are an upstanding citizen." He finished his coffee. "Would you ask Mrs. Tierney if I could have a word with her?"

I got Betsy and told her I'd watch her table. "You've got a lawyer now. You don't have to answer any questions." She gripped my arm, her fingers digging in. It felt like Kevin clutching me when he was a kid and didn't want to get in the dentist's chair. "Remember James Cagney," I said. "Don't tell him nothin'!" It was interesting, I thought as I went to check on her table, that I assumed she had something to hide.

Later that night, Betsy and I clung to each other in the back of a cab for the ride uptown. To someone looking in at us, I'm sure we looked like two terrified children on a roller coaster. After Sheehan left, Betsy had fallen apart, crying, angry. When I asked what was wrong, she wouldn't tell me.

"I shouldn't be here," Betsy said when we got to my apartment. "I should be home with Katie. Everything is so horrible. I wish I'd never been born." She flopped onto the couch Kevin had vacated when I shooed him off to bed in my room.

Things were getting out of hand. I didn't know what Betsy was doing in my apartment, either, when she should be home with her baby. She was in too many places at the same time. I couldn't figure her out. The thought kept creeping in that she was playing games with me, setting me up to do something for her, the way she might have set Barney up to kill her husband. It felt like she'd cast a spell on me. I never intended to get tied up romantically with her. All she did was bat her eyes and I went crashing through the bar like it was rutting season. Now, she sat on the couch patting the space next to her. I held back this time, and the cat took my place. She petted the cat.

"Look, Betsy, I understand you gotta watch out for yourself, and you should go ahead and do that, whatever it takes. But I gotta take care of myself, too, and Kevin." I paced around my not so large living room while Betsy and the cat followed me with their eyes. Every time I looked at Betsy, her wide-eyed innocence, I lost my nerve. People should be hard in the city. They couldn't be as gentle and guileless as Betsy seemed. So maybe she wasn't. It might be an act.

"Somebody killed your husband," I said. "That's a big fucking problem. It's not like the fucking wicked witch is dead and everyone's going to live happily ever after. No. Someone's going to get royally fucked over this—" I realized I was shouting and then realized that Betsy was sobbing.

"Great," I said to myself. I wanted to kick her but tried to comfort her instead. She wasn't having any of it, just waved me away and kept sobbing while I stood helplessly over her. After a while, I began pacing again, trying to explain myself. Finally, I blurted out, "Betsy, God damn it, you haven't told me the truth."

She stopped crying.

For a moment, I was overcome with doubt. She, too, might be better off with her secrets. Besides, if I didn't trust her based on her keeping things from me in the past, why would I believe what she told me now? But it was too late.

"I don't know why I thought I could do this," she said. "Something's wrong with me." She spoke as if she were in a trance, speaking with her eyes as much as her voice, which was cold and lifeless. "I thought once Dennis was gone I would be free. I never would have wished for it to happen this way, but once it did, I felt relief. Isn't that terrible, to feel relief when someone is dead, someone I loved once, or thought I did, who was the father of my baby?" Her eyes opened wide, as if something horrible were happening right in front of her—and she was looking at me. That helpless look, those sad searching eyes, she was pulling me to her again.

My expression must have been something to see, because despite everything she laughed. "You should see yourself," she said, and patted the couch beside her again. This time I did sit, pushing the cat aside, though he hissed and took a swat at me, a quick right cross with his claws out. "I do know what it is about you, Brian," she said. "You're easy. You don't ask anything. You don't judge . . . You're kind."

"I'm confused," I owned up. By then, I'd given up any caginess I thought I might use to trap her into the truth. If what was unfolding in front of me wasn't the truth, she had me so completely befuddled I wouldn't know true from false, up from down, or in from out anyway. "I have no idea what to make of you at all," I told her with all sincerity. "Tell me whatever you want."

"I'm afraid to tell you and afraid not to."

"That's a start."

She tried a smile. "It's not terrible that I lied to you, is it?"

"I don't know. Why don't you try some bits and pieces of the truth to start with and see how it turns out?"

She stiffened and then relaxed. "I lied about seeing Barney," she said, clutching my arm and pulling on it slightly so that I faced her. "That afternoon, before he came to the picket line, Dennis grabbed me when I was leaving for work. He said he'd told MacAlister that Barney was in the country illegally and that he was a fugitive from Northern Ireland." She faltered for a moment, took a deep breath, and went on. "He said Barney was done for. He would be deported and put in prison if he wasn't killed by the Protestants." She waited for me to say something, and when I didn't, she went on. "I went back to the picket line and told Mary Donohue to tell Barney what Dennis had said. When I found Dennis was dead, I was afraid to tell anyone what had happened."

"Because you were afraid Barney had killed your husband?"

"No. Not that. Because I was afraid people would think he had."

"You were afraid to leave your husband, afraid of what he might do?"

"Yes," she said tentatively.

"Were you romantically involved with Barney?"

She slumped back into the couch away from me. "I honestly don't know. I talked to him a lot. I felt close to him. I was attracted to him. He was chivalrous—and so shy; he is very Catholic, you know, so he was respectful and never let on what he felt. I don't know if he was interested in me or not. I think he was. I went out with him for drinks after work a few times. We talked. He told me about Ireland—he really misses it. He was very careful because I was married to not step over the line. He called me at home, and we met a couple of times when we were off. Dennis found out about that somehow. He thought I was having an affair."

"Did you ask Barney to help you get away from Dennis?"

Now the flashing eyes and flaring nostrils; I thought she was going to slap me. Instead, she choked a couple of times, snorted once, and began bawling. "How"—she hiccupped—"how could"—hiccup—"how could you . . . could you . . . think that?"

I stumbled around for a couple of minutes trying to apologize. Finally, I said, "If the cops didn't ask you that already, they will. They suspect Barney killed your husband, and you helped him or told him to. Part of the reason is that you're not being straight with them."

The tears stopped. She pulled herself up straight, her chin jutting out, "Well, I won't tell them, and you better not, either." The fire was back.

"Not even to save you from jail?"

"Jail?" She was horrified. "They wouldn't send me to jail." Her eyes opened wide. "Would they?"

chapter nineteen

I called and arranged for Ntango to come by and take Betsy to her mother's in Gerritsen Beach—the end of the earth in New York City cab-ride terms. I also had to ask him to put it on my tab, spending more money that I didn't have.

Betsy's latest admission didn't just alter the landscape, it took a bulldozer to it. I already suspected she'd told Barney about her husband's investigation, but this didn't mean Barney killed him. What it meant was he had a reason to kill him. So did other people. Now Barney had a good reason to kill MacAlister, too—and while Eliot might have had a reason to kill MacAlister, I didn't know of any reason for him to kill Tierney, Barney's theory notwithstanding.

The phone woke me up the next morning not long after I'd gone back to bed after getting up to see Kevin off to school. It was Pete Kelly's secretary. "Mr. Kelly would like to see you this morning at ten in his office," she said in a tone that sounded like she was used to giving commands.

"What time is it now?"

"Nine A.M., hon." Then, in a more confidential tone, "He wanted to meet you earlier, but I reminded him you were a bartender. He thinks everyone can start work at seven thirty like he does."

"Thanks." I meant it. Someone should sympathize with bartenders.

Before I left to meet Kelly, I called Peter Finch and laid Barney's theory of a connection between MacAlister and Tierney on him, asking if he could do a cursory background check on MacAlister to see if Tierney somehow turned up. He grumbled but said he would.

I showered and took the train to Times Square. It was early enough for the car to be full of rush-hour straphangers. The only good thing about the rush-hour train is getting squashed up against one of the pretty office-worker girls. This morning, I was fortunate to get squashed between two of them so tightly that if I'd picked my feet up off the floor I would have been held up by the back end of one and the front of the other. It was a cold morning with everyone bundled up in thick coats, so there wasn't anything indecent going on, just being squashed, and everyone smiled. Fortunately, one young woman got off at 59th Street and the other at Times Square, or I would have stayed on past my stop.

Kelly, as usual, was ready for me. His desk was clear, as it had been the last time. I wondered what he did all day. Nothing mundane, probably; he had hirelings for that. He was by himself, none of the goons around. Not that I was such a fearsome person that he needed them. I also wondered what they did. I could ask, it occurred to me; after all, my dues money paid their salaries—except for the extra bucks they might pick up shaking down bar owners.

"A guy I know wants to have a sit-down with you," Kelly said, before I'd gotten all the way into his office.

"A what?"

Kelly grimaced. "Don't be a smart-ass. This is an important guy; he's talking to you on my say-so." With his thick head and neck and sour expression, he looked like a bulldog about to bite. "Don't think you don't owe me."

We went by cab the few blocks to a small Italian restaurant off Seventh Avenue in the garment district. Tucked in among the textile shops, it was a surprise—a well-worn gentility, white tablecloths, red rug, dim lights, candles on the tables, two waiters in tuxedos acting like foreign dignitaries. An elderly, gracious man with a thick Italian accent greeted Kelly as "Mr. Kelly," paid little attention to me, and led us to a booth against the far wall, where another elderly, almost frail man in an expensive pinstriped suit sat drinking out of a small espresso cup. He didn't stand up but greeted Kelly, who, to my surprise, kissed him on both cheeks. This wasn't the usual greeting in the circles I traveled in. Kelly indicated I should sit down on the inside part of the booth across from the old man, not bothering to introduce me this time, either.

"So, Peter?"

Kelly nudged me. I didn't know what he wanted me to do, so I didn't do anything.

The old man looked at me. He had those rheumy eyes old people get that are unpleasant to look at, and you wonder whether they can see out of them. He seemed content to wait until I thought of something.

"McNulty's the bartender with that strike I told you about," Kelly said. "He says he wasn't involved in any of the other unfortunate events."

The old man shrugged his shoulders.

I wondered if I was supposed to plead for my life. I was willing, but this guy didn't seem the type you impressed by pleading. I understood from Kelly's careful choice of words that I should speak in euphemisms, too.

"I'm a bartender," I began. "No big deal. I'm sorry about the unfortunate events, but I wasn't involved."

"You know who?" the old man asked.

"Sorry. I'd like to help you out. I don't know."

"The girl? The Irishman?"

The guy had done his homework. This was now a ticklish situation. Was I going to save my own ass by throwing Barney to the sharks? I had to answer quickly or the guy would know I was hiding something.

"Not them," I said. "If you ask me, it was Tom Eliot, the business agent." I told him Barney's theory as if it were my own—and as if there were some reason to believe it was true. MacAlister was tapping the till and sharing with Eliot, I told him. MacAlister used Tierney as a private cop, a muscle to lean on Eliot until Eliot had enough of it.

"You know this?" The old man didn't open his eyes any wider or show any other sign of interest. Kelly, on the other hand, showed a lot of interest, more like astonishment.

"I don't know it for sure, but—"

The old man interrupted me. "You say but you don't know?" He indicated by shifting his glance that he expected Kelly to take over.

"He don't know shit," Kelly said. "He's got a bug up his ass about Eliot. I thought he knew something."

Sipping his coffee, the old man took stock of me again. In repose like this, he seemed kindly. "You give me a problem," he said. "Or someone give me a problem. You are a nice man, a gentleman. I don't dislike you. You have a boy. I don't want to give you trouble. But how can I believe you?"

So far so good, I told myself, without shaking the feeling this wasn't going to end well.

He spread out his hands in front of him. "Peter, my good friend, says I should hear you out. But you don't have anything to tell me."

Fear began creeping up my back. "I'm telling you I didn't kill anyone. I promise you that's true."

This time when he shrugged his shoulders he held his hands, palms up, out in front of him. "If not you, who?"

On the cab ride back to his office, Kelly was deep in thought. He didn't say anything until we were out of the cab, standing on the sidewalk. It was cold, more for him in his suit jacket than for me in my pea coat, but he didn't seem to notice.

"You gotta have some reason to think this Eliot thing." This wasn't a question, and it didn't allow for the fact that I didn't.

"It makes sense," was what I said. "The dead cop was a muscle for MacAlister. Something went wrong, so Eliot got rid of them both."

"What went wrong?"

"I don't know. Maybe the strike stirred something up. They were gonna be found out, so they were willing to give each other up."

Kelly was thinking again, putting more credence in the crap I was peddling than I did. "You gotta come up with somethin' more than that. I'll see what I can find out." He looked at me steadily, and I didn't know what to do: Shake his hand? Pat him on the back? Why had he become my guardian? No use asking him. He was heading back into the union building without even a "see you later."

Since it was nearing lunchtime and I was in the neighborhood, more or less, I walked over to the hotel to check in with Downtown Sam. It was still too early for the lunch crowd; he was setting up the bar when I got there.

"What's up, McNulty."

Little did he know. I told him about my morning coffee klatsch and Barney's theory about the murders.

Sam wasn't impressed by Barney's theory, but my conversation with the godfather made him sit up and take notice. I moped over the bar with a cup of coffee, watching him work. He was good, moving effortlessly, pouring juices without spilling, cutting fruit without a mess, nothing hurried, no wasted effort.

"So you think you can give him Eliot? Don't look like that to me."

"I don't know what to do. You used to be a cop. Maybe you could catch the bad guy. Isn't that what you used to do?"

"Damn right." He flashed me the evil eye. "But what if it's you?"

"Me?"

"How do I know it ain't you? I ain't begun to investigate yet."

I must have looked worried, because he laughed, real enjoyment in the sound.

A man in a suit, who looked too young to be wearing one, walked into the lounge then, circled the bar, looked everything over, nodded to Sam, and walked away.

"New food and beverage manager?"

"Yeah," said Sam dismissively.

"What's he like?"

"An asshole," said Sam. He paused. "Aren't they all?"

I moped some more, ordered another coffee.

"Don't be takin' up space when lunch starts," Sam said when he delivered it, joking and not joking. Not joking because the bar stool was money to him, joking because he knew I wouldn't take up space and cost him money.

After another few minutes, Sam took pity and came over again. "Look, McNulty, you been a bartender long enough to know some things. You get me? You know when someone's puttin' you on. You know when someone's for real. Like you know that cat you saw this mornin' wasn't puttin' you on. You hear what I'm sayin'? He could put some hurtin' on you. You gotta get that guy off your back, man." He made a couple of drinks at the service bar for one of the dining room waitresses and came back. "Bartenders know how to listen. You know a lot of people; you know your way around; you gotta use that stuff. Be the invisible man."

"The what?"

Sam rolled his eyes. "C'mon, man—"

"You could help."

Sam gave a start. So did I. Asking for help wasn't something I did very well. Still the words were out.

"Come in early for your shift," he said. "Maybe we can do somethin'."

A brief sense of well-being lifted me up for a moment. The idea that I had friends, that folks helped me out when I needed it, led me to think, at least for the moment, that something might be right with the world, after all.

Before I left the hotel, I stopped in the kitchen to see Francois. We hadn't talked after the strike ended, and since he more or less started the whole commotion, I wanted to make sure he was okay with the outcome. What I found out instead was that Francois was a suspect.

"Idiots," he said. "Where was I? What was I doing? Who can vouch for me?" He waved his arms, puffing like an old locomotive. "No one must vouch for Francois DeLouge. *Fou!* Cretins!"

"Did they ask about anyone else?"

Francois shook his head. "He asked about you, Sam, Barney. He asked about Betsy, about Betsy and MacAlister. *Porc!* A pig!"

"Did he ask about Eliot?"

Francois shook his head.

Since he didn't seem busy in the kitchen—Francois never seemed busy; it was as if he blew a whistle and a dozen or so kitchen slaves started up and the place ran like a clock. Every once in a while, he'd storm into the kitchen from his office, berate the sous chef, rip a sauté pan out of his hand, dump the contents into the garbage can, harangue the entire kitchen crew in a loud and profane mixture of French, Spanish, and English that I doubt anyone understood, and then stomp back into his office. Occasionally, during one of these tirades, an offended cook would quit and walk out, so Francois would have to take over his station for the shift. Otherwise, everything returned to normal and everyone began churning along at the same breakneck speed as before the blow-up.

Since he didn't seem busy, I asked him to come talk to the woman at the front desk who had told him about Mary Donohue's visit to MacAlister. I wanted to find out who else she might have seen coming and going from MacAlister's office, but I hesitated to go by myself. She was an assistant manager, for one thing. For another, she was a French woman, and I'm nervous around French women—especially pretty ones. They seem so sophisticated and aloof that I'm intimidated.

Jeanne was working the desk—and she was busy, but she took enough time to answer my questions, with a good deal of thought and carefully chosen words. She tried to understand as I described, as best I could, various folks from Barney to Eliot to Kelly. Given the language barrier and my inability to come up with anything better than generic descriptions, we didn't get far. She knew Barney but hadn't seen him in the hotel during the strike. Eliot and Kelly were another story.

"If you were to have pictures," she offered helpfully. She was pretty but, as I suspected, very serious, almost severe, dressed in a conservative pantsuit, her hair tied back in a bun. Maybe when she lets her hair down, I thought, while I smiled like an idiot at her.

Pictures, I thought. Plenty of pictures of Kelly in the union newspaper, on every page of every issue; there'd probably be pictures of Eliot, too, if I went through some back issues. I told Jeanne I'd get back to her by the end of her shift or tomorrow morning. A slight smile. Was that a come-hither look in her eyes? It was. She was signaling the next guest in line to step up to the desk.

"Sam the Hammer wants to see you," Kevin told me when I got home.
  "Where is he?"
  "He said he'd be around, you'd find him."
  "What does he want to see me about?"
  "He didn't tell me." Then, after a pause, offhandedly, "I made the team."
  The team? My God, the basketball tryout, and I hadn't even asked him about it. I tried to make up for my mistake with an excess of enthusiasm, but he saw right through me. "I have practice three nights a week now and games or practice almost every night once the season starts in January."
  I understood he was preparing me for his return to Brooklyn. Getting to school in the morning was tough enough. Going back at night for basketball was impossible. I told him this, and that I liked having him with me—and I did—but if he wanted to play basketball he had to go back to his mother's.
  He nodded. "We might need an assistant coach."
  Kevin knew I loved basketball, so he was trying to arrange more time for the father to be with the son—a job I should be doing, and should have been doing all his life. I almost cried. "I'll talk to your coach and see what I can do."
  We had things pretty much settled when the doorbell rang. I didn't like the doorbell ringing in the middle of the day. It might be a delivery, but usually the super handled those. Before I pushed the buzzer for the outside door, the apartment doorbell rang. Two burly guys, both young, one white, one black, both wearing suits, stood in the doorway when I opened the door.
  "Mr. McNulty?" the white guy asked.
  When I didn't answer, he came into the apartment. He didn't push through me, but I sensed he would have if I hadn't stepped back.
  Kevin came up behind me. "These are the guys I told you about."

"Take a hike, kid," the white guy said to Kevin.

"No," Kevin said.

I was scared, trembling scared, and jumped at the chance to get Kevin out of there. "Go," I told him.

"No," he said again, his voice shaking, fear in his eyes.

The black guy moved toward him, but I grabbed Kevin's arm first. "He's going," I said, my tone more forceful than I thought it could be. The black guy hesitated. "It's better for you to go," I said gently to Kevin. "I can take care of this. Nothing's going to happen to me."

Kevin sized up the two guys. No way were we going to do anything against them if it came to a fight. Then something changed in his face; the tension drained, as if he'd found something he'd lost. The black guy began to move toward him again, so I moved between them.

"He'll go," I said.

"I'll go," Kevin said this time, to my great relief. In a flash, he squeezed between the two guys and out the door.

"Don't talk to no one and you can come back in ten minutes," the black guy said as he was going.

"You know what we want," the white guy said when he was gone.

"I could probably guess."

"You know where a certain person is. A gentleman you spoke to thought you might tell us."

The guy had shoulders as wide across as the M104 bus, but he didn't come across as a tough guy. He didn't have to. Clean-shaven, well-groomed, soft-spoken, polite, he was like one of those good-natured giants constantly reassuring folks he isn't going to squash them—the black guy, too, except he seemed bored and impatient. I didn't want to think about what he was impatient for. If I remembered my gangster movies correctly, the two gentlemen in my foyer intended to put a hurtin' on me, as Sam had suggested they might. The alternative was to tell them what they wanted to know.

Here goes nothin', I thought. I considered blessing myself. "You gotta give me a hint here, guys. I'm not hiding anything. I told the other guy—gentleman, I mean—what I knew. I'll tell you, too. Just tell me what you're lookin' for."

"Where's the Irish guy?"

"The Irish guy?"

The black guy took a step toward me. His expression didn't change, but when he took the step he became menacing.

"Oh, you mean Barney," I said quickly before he could get to me. "He's hiding out. No one knows where he is."

They waited, neither speaking.

"Look, if this is about those unfortunate happenings, Barney didn't have anything to do with that. This guy Eliot, the business agent for the bartenders, is the guy you want."

"The guy we want is the Irish guy."

The black assassin's expression changed to something like distaste, as if he didn't much like what was going to happen next. He took another step toward me. Reflexively, I took a step back. He took another step, rubbing the knuckles of his right hand with the other hand. Just then the door opened. Both of my guests spun to look. It was Kevin.

"Not yet, kid—" the black guy started to say, but stopped when he saw Sam the Hammer behind Kevin.

chapter twenty

Sam came into the foyer with his right hand in his windbreaker pocket. He was chewing a toothpick, and his eyes were calm. "Beat it," he said.

All of us watched Sam's pocket until the white-guy thug reached for his own.

"Go ahead," said Sam. "We'll all die this afternoon right here in this hallway."

The standoff lasted about ten seconds while I stood frozen to the spot, too shocked to feel. Then my two visitors left, without a word but not without a couple of backward glances. Sam left right behind them, without a word to me, either, and with no backward glance. Kevin and I collapsed in the living room in stunned silence.

"Are you going to call the cops?" Kevin asked finally.

"And tell them what?" I said, shaking now, as my systems began to work again.

"I don't know. I thought cops protected you from people like that."

"I wish they did. But what did those guys do, really? They asked questions. They didn't hurt me or threaten me, at least not directly. Even if the cops did arrest them, there'd be others to take their places."

"You should get a gun."

"What would I do with it? Shoot them and then have them shoot me and we all end up dead on the hallway floor, like Sam said?"

Dumping this despairing view on Kevin was a lousy idea, I decided, so I stood up and tousled his hair. "Time for you to go to Brooklyn. This will blow over. I've got friends. Something will turn up."

He looked as unconvinced as I felt, but I took him to Pop's apartment, after calling Pop in New Jersey to tell him it was an emergency and he had to come home. He said he would.

"Go talk to your friend Barney," said Pop a few hours later when we were seated at his dining room table. "Maybe he can prove he didn't kill anyone and make peace with those gangsters before they kill you. Make your case to Pete Kelly, too. He should have some influence with those people after all the years he's spent in their hip pocket."

"He already set up that meeting. It didn't do any good."

"Tell them what they want to know. Warn Barney, then tell them." Pop seemed genuinely worried.

"They'll take it out on me if I warn him."

Pop pursed his lips and looked me over. "You're in a tough spot."

"I knew that."

I went from Pop's apartment to work that evening, cringing every time the outside door opened and someone came in. Mary Donohue was working a Christmas party with Sam, and Betsy was working the lounge. Both women looked haggard, on edge, and irritated. I was out of sorts myself, expecting two goons to come through the door any minute to pound me into submission like one of Francois's veal cutlets.

We made it through the busy night, with the loud and obstreperous residue from a couple of office Christmas parties at one end of the bar, and also a bunch of regulars back now that the strike was over, full of advice as to what we should have done instead of what we did do, two of them convinced Barney killed MacAlister, the other two looking sideways at Sam each time he came into the bar from the party he was working. The conversation stopped a couple of times I went near them, too, so I wouldn't have been surprised if some of them were betting on me for the kill. It wasn't a great night. Every time I tried to talk to Betsy, she dashed off to one of her tables whether they wanted something or not. Mary and Sam came into the bar when they needed something and dashed out again. So I didn't have anyone to talk to, not that I felt like talking anyway.

Around midnight, everything changed. I heard the door and, fearing the worst, turned to look. Ntango and Sam the Hammer were shaking the cold off themselves in the doorway. I wouldn't have been more surprised if it had been Santa Claus. It was the first time, I was sure, Sam the Hammer had been below 72nd Street, not counting trips to Belmont and Aqueduct, since the 1970s. I set them up with drinks—Sam the Hammer a light beer, Ntango a rum and grapefruit juice—and ran a tab for them.

"What's the occasion?" I asked Ntango, though I knew already why they'd come.

He gestured with his head toward Uptown Sam. "Kevin went back to Brooklyn, so he decided to watch over you."

Once more, I thought about friends. What a strange manner of being we folks are. Sam the Hammer, a convicted killer, an outlaw since childhood, a scourge on respectable society, no family, no visible means of support, no friends, really, except folks he knows from the street, yet he goes to the mat for me, a bartender who slipped him a beer now and again and took the trouble to pay attention when he told me things he considered important. Ntango, another one, a cabdriver from the wretched of the earth, an exile from northeast Africa, stoned more often than he wasn't, who befriended me, saved my life, risked his own to protect my son. What kind of friendship is this that's based on sucking down a couple of cold ones as you watch the Knicks on a barroom TV, sharing a joint in an alley behind a gin mill, or telling tales over drinks late at night after the bar has closed, friendship that happens because folks who don't have much in the way of homes are thrown together in some New York City version of a clean, well-lighted place?

At closing time, we had a confab at the end of the bar—Betsy, Mary, Downtown Sam, Francois, and our new consultants Ntango and Uptown Sam the Hammer. The new manager stuck his head in but decided against intervention, which I took as a good sign. For the hotel, it had been a good night—a good week since the strike ended—so he didn't begrudge us a couple of pops at the end of the shift.

What began things was my pouring what would have been the first mouthful of my beer out onto the floor in memory of Barney, hiding out upriver in the Bronx. We talked about him then, mostly despairing talk about whether things would ever calm down enough for him to come back.

After a bit, and her second Irish whiskey punch, Mary Donohue had enough of our whining. "For the love of God, can't any of you men stand up against the pair of crooks that caused us this trouble in the first place? Isn't it Tom Eliot and Peter Kelly who'll be the ruination of us all, if we don't put a stop to them? Are ye no men at all, that you can't put them in their place?"

"And what place is that, Mary?" I asked quietly.

"Behind bars." She didn't miss a beat.

I remembered then that I'd forgotten to show pictures of Kelly and Eliot to Jeanne, the French desk clerk. Downtown Sam had back copies of the union newspaper in his locker, which he retrieved. Sure enough, there was Kelly on nearly every page, and in the third issue I looked at I found a picture of Eliot and some other business agents at the union's scholarship banquet. I'd have to wait until tomorrow to show the pictures to Jeanne. I didn't even know what good it would do if she did recognize them.

"Okay, so we know all this. I've already told the cops that Eliot is behind the killings, and I told it to the guys who want to pound me. None of them believe me."

"Give them proof," said Betsy.

"That's a good idea. Why didn't I think of that?" I glowered at Betsy. "I don't have any proof—just Barney's half-assed idea about what he thinks happened."

"Sweat it out of him," said Francois.

"Up in the office on the Quai des Orfèvres, I guess?" Francois seemed to have me confused with his countryman *le commissaire* Maigret of the French Police Judiciaire.

Francois was saddling up his Francophile high horse again. "The Police Judiciaire know how to bring about a confession."

Around two, we went our separate ways, with Ntango driving me uptown and Sam the Hammer riding shotgun. Nothing happened on the way home, and Sam spent the night on my couch. It was reassuring to have him there, but I didn't want to adopt him permanently. Before we'd left the hotel, Betsy told me she was off the next day and wanted to stop by so I could see Katie. I said fine.

Saturday morning, I spruced myself up, bought Sam breakfast at Tom's, and went downtown to the hotel to show the pictures of Kelly and Eliot to Jeanne. At first, she didn't remember our conversation the day before, or me at all. I thought I'd have to go get Francois to reestablish my legitimacy, but she came around after a few minutes. When I showed her the pictures, she didn't recognize Kelly but was sure Eliot had been to see MacAlister—more than once.

I found Downtown Sam in the bar and told him about it.

"It don't mean shit," Sam explained.

"Oh?"

"Of course Eliot goes to see MacAlister; he's the union business agent. We want to know *when* the motherfucker went to see him." Sam paused. "You got those pictures?" I gave them to him. "I know Jason, one of the security guards. Maybe he can ask around if somebody seen Eliot when MacAlister was killed."

I went back home to wait for Betsy and Kate. When they arrived, I held Katie for a bit and bounced her on my knee. She giggled a lot and seemed to enjoy being with me. I doubted that she saw me as her rescuer, but she seemed comfortable with me, and I had fun playing with her. It had been a long time since I'd spent time with a tyke. After a bit, Betsy nursed her and put her in her stroller for a nap.

When she finished, she came over and sat beside me on the couch. "I feel like I should do something, but I don't know what," she said. "All this suspicion is making me a nervous wreck. I feel like someone's watching me all the time."

We talked for a while, and as we talked, Barney's name came up enough times and with enough tenderness when Betsy talked about him for me to wonder what the real purpose of her coming to see me was.

"Why don't you go see Barney," I said a bit peevishly after the question of his welfare came up for the third time.

"Oh, can we?" Betsy brightened considerably, bouncing around on the couch to face me. I expected her to squeal. She didn't mean to convey how excited she was. Sometimes people don't know their own hearts.

I was willing to take Betsy to the Bronx to see Barney, but I was spooked by her feeling like someone was watching her. If the cops had a tail on her, we'd lead them to him. Betsy didn't know if she'd been followed to my apartment or not. How do you make sure you're not being followed? I figured Sam the Hammer would know. So we bundled up Katie and went to look for him, finding him, after checking a few places, in the Terrace Café on Broadway.

"Gimme the kid and the key to your apartment, go out the back door. Take a cab to 96th Street, the express downtown to 72nd Street, and a local back uptown. Then you can go on your way." Sam said all this sitting at the bar, reading the *Daily News* and drinking coffee without taking the toothpick out of his mouth.

Betsy looked at me with an expression of horror.

"He'll give Katie back," I told her. I happened to know that Sam had been an emergency babysitter for a couple in my building for years. It wasn't something he talked about in public, so neither did I. With that and all the times he'd watched Kevin for me, I was sure he'd be fine, and after a minute or two I convinced Betsy.

When we finally got to the Bronx, after our circuitous journey, we found Barney in the butcher shop and went to the same bar and sat in the same booth as the last time I spoke to him. He and Betsy were shyly glad to see each other, each more bashful than the other as they first shook hands and then hugged like eight-year-olds at a dance party.

I wasn't angry with Barney, but I was tired of beating around the bush. If he wanted me to put my money on his Eliot story, he had to come clean with his own. For a moment, I considered not telling him about the goons because I knew he wouldn't want me in trouble on account of him. Then I said fuck it; he could worry just like I did.

"Jaysus, the bastards," he said when I finished. "You're a great one for keeping a secret, Brian, but you should have told them where I am. Mind you, I appreciate your watching over me, but you can't take my troubles as your own."

"There's trouble enough for everyone," I said. "You've got the cops to worry about, too. They know Betsy's husband found out you were illegal and was about to blow the whistle and that you knew about it. What they may not know yet is he told MacAlister, and you knew that, too."

"No," said Barney. "I knew no such thing."

"Betsy told me you knew."

He turned toward her, his expression anguished, but he softened immediately. "Aragh, so she did." He patted her hand. "It's all right, now," he said. "It's fine to tell Brian."

Betsy moved her hand from under his to on top of it. I thought they were going to hold hands, but they didn't. Instead, Betsy pulled back and clasped her own hands together. "What are we going to do?" she said in a tone as anguished as Barney's expression had been.

"Maybe you should pick up Katie and the three of you head for the hills," I suggested. Man, what a reaction, both of them blushing furiously, as mortified as if I'd caught them in bed. "Sorry," I said.

After a strained silence, I told Barney things looked bleak for him, unless something turned up that would point the finger at Eliot. "Why are you so sure it was Eliot?" I said.

Barney held up his bandages. "Look at me bloody hands."

"We can't prove he did that either."

"Aye, but it's a court of law where you need proof—the courts where the guilty carry proof of their innocence in their hands. At home, we had our own tribunals." Barney's expression hardened; his lively blue eyes stopped dancing. "When we knew who the guilty

DEATH AT THE OLD HOTEL 173

party was, we didn't wait for the British court to deny our evidence and set him free. If we didn't take care of matters on our own, there would be no justice for the Irish." He paused, and we both saw Betsy's face frozen into a look of revulsion. His eyes on her, he went on more quietly. "Mind you, we'd take every precaution to not harm an innocent man, to give even the likes of Tom Eliot a chance to answer the claims against him."

Once more, I felt the gulf between Barney and me gaping wide. What had Mary's husband Pat said, "born into cruel and harsh conditions, the poorest of the poor." Barney had a ruthlessness at his center that I couldn't conjure up. Neither the streets of Flatbush nor the bars of upper Broadway had toughened me up enough to run my own tribunals.

At this point, I made the mistake of telling Barney about the conversation we'd had the night before, which reminded Betsy of what Francois had said.

"What was that?" asked Barney.

"You'd have to be a Georges Simenon reader to get it," I said. "It has to do with taking off your jacket, maybe opening a window, ordering sandwiches and beer from the Brasserie Dauphine, and questioning the suspect through the night until the wee hours of the morning when he confesses."

Barney looked at me quizzically. "You're a great man for a story, Brian McNulty, but I don't know what the hell you're blathering about."

"Sweat the truth out of him, is what Francois suggested," Betsy said. Barney nodded.

I wished she'd kept her mouth shut. "Francois didn't say we should question Eliot. He said the Police Judiciaire should."

chapter twenty-one

On the way back on the train, Betsy brought it up again. "What else can we do, Brian?"

Since I'd already thought this through a number of times, I knew I didn't have an answer. "Sam and I already talked to Eliot. We didn't find out anything."

"Brian, if we don't do something, they'll arrest me or Barney, or both of us. They'll take Katie away from me." The D train rattled like a bucket of bolts, so she leaned close to me to speak, her chest brushing my elbow and her lips brushing my ear when the train jolted around a corner. Her tone was pleading. "Maybe you and Sam didn't do it right. Barney said in Ireland they were able to get people to admit things."

Taken aback for the moment, I wondered if Betsy understood what she suggested, which was that if we put the fear of God into Eliot, he would tell us who killed MacAlister and Tierney and who chopped off Barney's fingers. What if he didn't? The tribunals Barney was talking about were kangaroo courts, the product of war, where they tortured and executed people. Barney didn't actually say this—and I didn't ask him what his tribunal involved—but my understanding of the ways of the IRA suggested this was not a dog-and-pony show he was talking about.

When we got back to my apartment, Sam the Hammer turned Katie over to her mom and went off about his business such as it was.

Betsy and I and the tyke went to the West Side Market. Walking down the aisles, pushing a cart with Katie in it, handing her a bagel out of a bin to gnaw on, brushing shoulders with Betsy, she putting her arm around me casually to lean across to grab something off a shelf, the twenty minutes in the store, and the walk back, carrying Katie in my arms, then playing on the floor with her and Otto, while Betsy rustled up tuna sandwiches—this hour or so with Betsy and the kid brought me a kind of peace I hadn't experienced in many years, reminding me of when Kevin was a baby, and of my own childhood, a kind of togetherness and belonging to others, I realized with an intense pang of sadness, I must have missed much more than I knew.

Betsy and Katie left after lunch. I kissed them both quickly on the lips, and Betsy hugged me. "We'll talk," she said cutely in Brooklynese as she left.

I went downtown an hour early for work to talk to Downtown Sam and to see how seriously Francois took his own suggestion about questioning Eliot. Francois explained that he meant what he said to be a comment on the ineffectiveness of police interrogation in this country. "Brutality instead of psychological intensity," said Francois. "The criminal, he confess—*il veut admettre—une conscience coupable.*"

"I beg your pardon?"

"He needs *son âme.* His soul."

"The criminal wants to confess because he feels guilty?"

"*Oui!!* Correct!!" said Francois, clapping me on the back.

"That may work for your French criminals. Over here, we've bred the conscience out of most of ours. I'm not sure a stake in the heart would work anymore."

Francois shook his head, his hand on my shoulder, his eyes lined up with mine. "No, *mon ami*—my friend Brian. *C'est l'état humain pour admettre sa culpapabilité*—to be forgiven—*pour avoir besoin de remission.*"

"Maybe. But I doubt it."

"*Crime et châtiment, mon ami.* Crime and punishment."

If you're having an early dinner in a hotel dining room, you'd little suspect that behind that closed kitchen door the chef and bartender are discussing the human condition and the nature of guilt. But in my experience these sorts of discussions often take place among hotel work crews, much like the discussions among the players on Charlie Brown's baseball team. I left the kitchen deep in thought about this idea of the need to confess guilt and went to the bar in search of a Beefeater martini and advice from Sam.

Like Uptown Sam, Downtown Sam wasn't much inclined to give advice. He knew how to make a martini, though: stirred in a mixing glass, not shaken in a metal shaker, made with Beefeater and a dash of vermouth, from a bottle, not a mister, and the vermouth stirred with the gin, not sloshed around the glass and poured out before the gin goes in—it's a mixed drink, for Christ's sake—the stem glass chilling while the drink is stirred for twenty to thirty seconds, then poured into the glass, not left to dilute in the mixing glass, and garnished with an olive. No one born after 1955 knows how to make a martini.

I sipped the drink and told Sam some folks wanted to lean on Eliot to see if he'd tell us anything. "What do you think?" I asked him.

"This ain't your fight, man. Why you wanna get mixed up in the middle of it?"

"The fight more or less came to me when Eliot's bosses decided I killed those guys."

"That and Betsy." There was a wariness around Sam as he talked that he seemed to be trying to pass on to me through force of will. "Why would Eliot rat on himself?"

I tried out Francois's theory on Sam. "It's human nature to want to confess and ask forgiveness."

"Bullshit," said Sam. "What if it ain't Eliot at all?" He waited while I squirmed.

I squirmed long enough to finish the drink. "I don't want to think about that."

Sam shook his head. "We already talked to Eliot."

I thought this over, this time with a cup of coffee. "I'm inclined to think we should have a talk with Eliot on our home court this time."

Sam nodded. "Better than his. It's takin' a chance of everything blowin' up. You know what I mean? If it's just Eliot, we might can handle it. If that guy you had lunch with thinks it's his fight, we got trouble."

"We need to isolate Eliot."

"Ain't that what I just said?"

When I got home that night, Sam the Hammer was still on guard at my apartment. Asking Sam anything is a risky venture, because he's almost never thinking along the same lines you are, but I gave it a try.

"Talk to him. Why not?" said Sam when I finished explaining what I thought were the complex dynamics involved in talking to Eliot without upsetting the underworld powers-that-be.

"That's it? We won't get whacked?"

Sam shrugged.

"We might get whacked?"

Sam shrugged again. "You gotta do what you gotta do."

When I explained the situation again, in case he missed something the first time, he put on his jacket, saying he had something to take care of.

"Does it have to do with what I'm telling you about?"

The glance he cast back over his shoulder made clear it didn't.

After thinking it over for a few minutes, I realized Sam had told me all I needed to know. I might well be fucked if I tried to get information from Eliot, but as things stood, I was fucked anyway. Trouble ahead and trouble behind. I didn't need to talk to anyone else.

I don't know the exact point I decided I was going through with this, but somewhere along the line I did, and if I was going to do it, I needed help. Uptown Sam hadn't offered; this left Downtown Sam and Barney, both of whom, unlike me, had experience with strong-arm stuff. We'd also need a driver—a wheelman, as we said in my new trade.

Late the next afternoon I called Ntango's dispatcher and asked for him to stop by my apartment. He was there in a half hour. As we pulled away from my building and passed the Canadian guys selling

Christmas trees on the corner, I noticed their sign read THREE DAYS TILL CHRISTMAS.

"Where to, Mr. Brian?" Ntango asked in his lazy drawl.

"Don't throw the meter flag."

He flipped on his OFF DUTY sign. "Another one of those, eh?"

I told him what we were up to. "You don't have to do this, you know. It's dangerous and probably foolish."

He slid the cab easily through the light Sunday traffic, relaxed in his seat, his wrist draped over the steering wheel. One of the things I liked about Ntango was that he never got angry or frustrated at the traffic—probably because he was stoned most of the time. "But you ask me, my friend. Who knows, someday I need a favor from you?" Ntango was a tough guy, a veteran of his own country's "troubles," one in the fellowship of the dispossessed.

We headed to the Bronx and caught up with Barney at the butcher shop. No jars of porter at the Old Shillelagh this time. I propelled him out of the store and into the cab. Despite his prominent role in the incubation of this plan—a role he immediately repudiated—he was not enthusiastic for the task at hand.

"Bejaysus, Brian, you've lost your senses. To grab the likes of him? Sure, we'll all be killed."

I explained my thinking to Barney, and he continued to resist, putting the kibosh on every reason I came up with. Barney never out-and-out disagreed with you. Instead, he shook his head sadly and doubted.

"Aragh, I don't see how it will work, Brian." He shook his head. "Mind you, I'm as ready for a fight as the next man. Many's the night I lay awake wishing I'd get me hands on Eliot, but I don't see this is the way."

Ntango headed for the hotel to pick up Downtown Sam when he got off work while Barney and I argued in the backseat. That I was leading the charge into action and Barney was trying to hold us back was a surprise, yet try to hold us back he did. I knew Barney wasn't afraid, although he was extremely agitated. Maybe he was right, and it was a lousy idea. We didn't have any others, though.

Before we got to the hotel, Barney spoke softly, fervor in his tone, almost as if he prayed. "Brian, I don't think you realize what you're embarking on." He paused to consider his words. "The things I've seen done in these situations are things no man should have to do."

I wanted to object, to tell Barney this was easy, just a few questions, no violence, but that was kidding myself, and he wouldn't fall for it. What we were about to do was violent. There was no denying that. I didn't intend to harm Eliot, but violence unleashed takes on a life of its own, a dynamic of unintended consequences.

chapter twenty-two

Once Barney realized he wouldn't change my mind, he took charge of the operation. The first thing he did was have Ntango stop at one of the wholesale/retail dry goods stores along Broadway below Herald Square that happened to be open on Sunday, where he jumped out of the cab and came back with a bag of ski masks.

"It's not so easy to recognize a voice when it's muffled and you don't have a face to put with it," he said. "I'll ask questions. If you want to say something, whisper to me."

When we picked up Sam at the hotel, he told us Eliot would be waiting in front of the Empire Diner on Tenth Avenue. Sam had called and told him he had important information for him that he didn't want McNulty to know about and would meet him Sunday evening but nowhere near the hotel or Eliot's office.

Sure enough, Eliot was standing in front of the diner near the curb when the cab pulled up. I waited in the backseat on the driver's side when Sam got out of the front seat and Barney the back. They jacked him up and shoved him into the backseat before he knew what hit him. Because it was the only thing I could think of to shut him up and keep him from jumping back out of the cab, I grabbed him in a headlock—a hold I'd learned from Kevin when he began wrestling in high school. It worked. Eliot kicked his legs, flailed his arms, and blustered into my pea coat where his face was buried and the sound muffled, until Barney, speaking in a fake cockney accent, told him to sit still and shut up, which he did.

When I let go of his head and he sat up, the terror in his eyes brought me up short. I'd seen that much terror only once in my life, right before a guy I once knew threw himself into the Hudson River to drown.

"You got the wrong guy," Eliot said, talking a mile a minute. "You made a mistake. No one sent you after me. I'm Tom Eliot. Ask Angelo. Call your guys. Tell 'em to ask Angelo about Tom Eliot." He paused for breath, his eyes darting around the cab. Because of the ski masks, all he saw was six eyeballs glaring at him, and another two watching the road if he looked in the rearview mirror.

"Tell us about the killing of the hotel manager," Barney said in his phony accent.

"Da what?" His eyes darted around the cab again. "Who are youse guys?"

"Who killed the hotel manager and the cop? You or who besides you?"

"No. No. You got it wrong. Youse guys are nuts—" He paused. "No offense." He directed what he said to Sam in the front seat, even though Barney asked the questions. I guess he thought Sam was the boss because he wasn't saying anything. "I told Angelo, the guys from the strike did the killing. He knows it wasn't me."

"We know it was."

Ntango had headed downtown on West Street along the Hudson after we picked Eliot up. We'd already made it through the Brooklyn Battery Tunnel and were driving along the Gowanus Expressway through Brooklyn toward the Belt Parkway and the wetlands by Jamaica Bay. This was Ntango's idea, that the desolation of the Jamaica Bay wetlands would strike terror into the hardest heart.

For me, it was tough not talking, especially since Barney was getting nowhere with his questioning and veiled threats. I kept a lid on it because I didn't want Eliot to recognize my voice. As soon as we hit the Belt Parkway, I could see the fear pouring out Eliot's pores and leaking from his eyes. He stunk of it. Still, he told Barney nothing of the murders.

Barney kept his cool. He'd ask Eliot about the murders. Eliot would answer with variations of his first answer. At one point, Barney told Eliot he wasn't going to leave Brooklyn if we didn't get an answer. This one made me sit up and take notice.

Not many people besides truck drivers and cabdrivers know that New York City has a large body of wetlands at the far southern end of Brooklyn. When you're headed toward Long Island and look out the passenger-side window of the car you're in, it seems like you're looking out over these marshes toward eternity. Before this ride, I knew about them by hearsay—the way I knew about the badlands of South Dakota. The folklore of my youth named the swamps and vacant lots of Canarsie as the dumping grounds for the bodies of those who ran afoul of the tough guys of Brooklyn. That the swamps had been renamed wetlands in the modern parlance didn't lessen my apprehension at entering them, picturing dark roads that led to nowhere and would at any moment drop off into the murky deep. I imagined Eliot thought he'd come to his final resting place.

We found a deserted road at the end of Flatbush Avenue near Marine Park after we left the Belt Parkway. After driving alongside a golf course for a bit, we turned into a pull-off that featured pools and gullies of water and fields of gray-brown reeds. The wind off the murky darkness of Jamaica Bay was steady and bone-chilling. Clouds covered the moon and the stars, while the lights in the distance behind us merged into the darkness to become a half-lit gray curtain hanging over Brooklyn. Barney gestured for all of us to get out of the car, which we did, except Ntango, who stayed in the cab with the motor running. He hadn't said anything, but I could tell by his grim expression and the way he was rigidly hunched over the steering wheel that he had a good mind to leave us all there.

By this time, Eliot was a wreck. He stumbled out of the car on my side and would have fallen if I hadn't caught him. Dressed in a gray business suit, with no overcoat, he shook and shivered. The suit was wrinkled, and there was a broad dark stain in the back of the pants where he'd befouled himself. I would have felt sorrier for him if his fear hadn't turned him so repulsive—there wasn't enough of him left to feel sorry for. He'd given up talking in favor of lurching around like a captured animal. If he'd gotten loose from us, I think he'd have run off into the swamp.

Everything we were doing made me sick. I wished we'd never started. I wanted out of there. This had been a mistake—and it was my mistake. I was about to tell Barney and Sam that the deal was off. I didn't have the stomach for any more. But Barney spoke first.

"Talking to the man is useless."

My eyes sprung open. I let go of Eliot and sidled up beside Barney. "Whoa, Barney," I said, barely above a whisper. "We brought this guy out here to ask him about the murders. That's it. We still don't know."

"Look at him," said Barney. "He's that pathetic. What use is he to anyone?"

We argued heatedly in low voices.

"We want him to admit he did it," I said.

"And even if he does, what then?" Barney asked. "It will be only us that knows the truth."

"If he tells us what happened, we'll know what the connections are, the reason he wanted them dead." I was scrambling to get the words out because I was afraid Barney might be right and I didn't want to admit it. What good would it do to tell the cops Eliot confessed to us? We still wouldn't have any evidence.

"And if we know he's guilty, what then?" Barney's gaze was steady, his voice calm, unlike mine.

"Well, we're not going to shoot him or hurt him." This time, my determination shored up my voice.

Barney searched my face. His look was hard, but there was sympathy there also, like you might have for a child learning a painful lesson. "I'll tell him 'talk or I'll shoot you,'" Barney said. "If he doesn't talk and then I don't shoot, he'll know he doesn't have to talk. There'll be no point in asking him anything else."

"Yeah, well, if you pull the trigger, there won't be any point in asking him anything else, either. We didn't come out here to execute the guy."

"We'll have done away with a murderer," said Barney. "Is there harm in that?"

At this point, Sam, who had listened to our exchange, butted in. Shaking his head, he said, "You Irish got some crazy ways about you, man. Bring this guy all the way out here and then the two of you stand around arguing all night. Both of you crazier than a couple of shithouse rats."

This got Barney back on track again. "For the love of God, man, we didn't go through all this for nothing," he said to me. "Give me another chance with him." He looked at Sam. "Let me have your gun, Sam."

Sam hesitated, but I didn't react fast enough, so Barney took the gun from Sam and leaned it against Eliot's head. "If you ever want to get back to your thuggish ways, tell me now that you're the man responsible for the two murders. That's all. Tell me that and you're a free man. If you don't tell me now, I'll pull the trigger."

I was too stunned to move. Eliot shivered as the seconds ticked off, and as the seconds ticked off, I shivered, too, but made myself ready to move. I was going to jump Barney and grab the gun before he could shoot—Wild West heroics to save the sleazy bastard even though I believed he killed two people and chopped off Barney's fingers with a machete. I couldn't have told myself why I would do this, but I was certain I would.

"Tell me the truth, man. It's as simple as this. Confess and you walk away. Keep up your lying and you'll never leave this swamp. I've got the gun now, and if you look me in the eye, you'll know I'm well able to pull the trigger."

"I did," Eliot whispered, a choked sound but loud enough for all of us to hear it.

"You killed them yourself?"

Eliot whimpered, unable to speak. He wobbled as his legs began to give out again. Barney pushed the gun harder against his forehead.

"I did." It was hardly a sound at all.

"And who was it you had chop off me fingers?"

"Not me," said Eliot, his voice stronger than it had been all night. "MacAlister . . . hired guys . . . I never saw them. I swear."

Barney asked a few more questions. Who else knew? Was Tierney working for MacAlister? Why did he kill them? Eliot mumbled his answers, almost incoherent by this time after his brief flurry of clarity, or else Barney provided an answer for him and he only nodded.

After a few questions, something changed in Barney as if whatever had steeled him up until that point for this gruesome task gave out on him. His expression was difficult to read—weariness, sadness, disappointment, despair. "Aragh, what's the use?" he said. "He won't tell us anything more." He weighed the gun in his hand, his eyes meeting mine.

"We have to let him go," I said.

Barney's features softened into the man I'd come to know over our time together, no longer the hardened hangman's expression of the past couple of hours. "We'll let him go, so," he said.

Barney handed the gun back to Sam, walked to the back of Ntango's cab, and vomited. I felt awkward as Sam and I waited, uncertain what to do next, not exactly ashamed of myself—I didn't know if Barney would have killed Eliot, but I knew I wanted no part of killing him—but as if I'd bitten off more than I could chew, tried something I wasn't able for, turned out not to be as tough a guy as I pretended to be. Barney's prophecy would come true, it looked like now. We had Eliot's confession but no evidence to take to the police. I thought about dragging him to the nearest precinct or calling Sheehan, but Sam ixnayed the idea, saying the cops would arrest us when we tried to hand him over. Our only choice was to let him go, now that we'd decided not to play by Barney's IRA rules and take justice into our own hands. By the time Barney pulled himself together and we saw headlights cutting through the dark swamp, all of our nerves were shot, so we panicked and piled back into the cab.

Eliot didn't say anything when I pushed him into the backseat. I asked a couple of questions during the car ride, like what Tierney had to do with MacAlister, but, as Barney had said, Eliot clammed up now that he knew we weren't going to kill him. He just stared at me with a vacant expression. We drove into Canarsie and dropped him at the L train on Rockaway Boulevard. He didn't beg for his life as we drove to the train, or thank us once he realized he'd been spared. At the end, he didn't say anything, nor did we, when we parted company.

In a strange neighborhood that far out in Brooklyn, you might want to be careful where you stopped for a drink, but we all dearly needed one.

"Doesn't Betsy live near here?" Barney asked.

She did. We'd cut across on Avenue U to Sheepshead Bay after we dropped off Eliot and weren't far from Gerritsen Beach, so I called her from a pay phone—the fourth one we tried. She told us she'd meet us at an Italian restaurant right there in Sheepshead Bay.

Roberto's at Avenue R and Nostrand Avenue was the kind of structure that makes Brooklynites proud: a stand-alone, one-story building with bright blue awnings over the windows and walls made from a kind of white stucco and stone that is sold only to build Italian restaurants—or an occasional Moroccan belly dancer joint—and that clues you in from two blocks away that you're coming up on one.

Inside were murals of dark-haired men paddling gondolas, small Italian villages, and Leaning Towers of Pisa, plush carpets, waiters in dinner jackets, a large menu, and a good wine list. The maître d' didn't bat an eye at the arrival of two black guys and two white guys, one an Irishman with a bandaged hand, all of whom ordered double shots of whiskey before they even looked at the menu.

The waiters were gracious and efficient, and there was enough light to read the menu. You can go almost anywhere in New York and find a good restaurant—maybe even Staten Island. The problem with this one would be paying the check, since none of us had been working regularly lately.

When Betsy arrived and half the restaurant staff rushed over to her, I realized we'd made a mistake. She was well known here, most likely as the wife of a dead cop.

"I told them you were friends of my husband," Betsy said when she sat down. "This probably wasn't the best place to come." She redeemed herself by saying she'd pick up the check.

"Is this a cop place?" I asked her.

"Not really. Someone might come for dinner with his family, but not a hangout."

We ate antipasto followed by pasta and drank the house Chianti. I gave Betsy a sanitized version of our adventure with Eliot.

"I'm surprised he told you anything," said Betsy. "Why should he?"

Because we were going to dump him into Jamaica Bay if he didn't, was the answer I might have given. Instead, I said, "Sometimes, people who commit crimes feel a need to admit their guilt, to clear their consciences."

"Whoever told you that?" Betsy asked incredulously.

It was uncomfortable talking about the murders and Eliot. So we talked about the strike and what we accomplished and didn't accomplish, and this brought us back to Eliot anyway.

"What's the matter with everyone?" asked Betsy after the conversation died for the third or fourth time. "All of you look as if you've come from a funeral."

Toward the end of dinner, she told us she was supposed to go and speak with the detectives at the Sixty-first Precinct the next day. I told her to have Peter Finch go with her.

"Why should she do that?" Barney asked. "Won't that make everyone think she's guilty if she goes with a solicitor? Sure, what's the girl to fear? She's innocent of everything."

Sam and I spent the next few minutes persuading Barney that Betsy needed a lawyer. Convinced finally, he switched and began trying to figure out how we were going to hang the crimes on Eliot, now that he'd admitted to them.

Bent over the table in the tradition of gangs of desperadoes throughout the centuries, we listened to Barney's whispered plan. Betsy would drop some information on the detectives questioning her. Innocently, she would mention that her husband had some connection to MacAlister and Eliot. She'd overheard her husband talking to MacAlister on the phone; she'd seen him and Eliot together. The point was to hint at a link between the three of them, and let the cops take it from there.

"He doesn't have to talk, mind you," said Barney. "If the police begin an investigation of Tom Eliot, the Lord knows what they may find."

"Should I tell the lawyer?" Betsy asked.

This was a bit of a sticky wicket, as they say. You're not supposed to lie to your lawyer, but she couldn't tell him what she was doing. The problem was that if she didn't tell him in advance, he'd hear about this new wrinkle at the same time the cops did, and he wasn't going to like that.

"I think you better not tell Peter," I said. "Lawyers aren't supposed to let their clients lie. It violates the Hippocratic Oath, or something."

On the way back, I asked Ntango to drop me off at Pop's apartment. We dropped Sam, who lived in Bedford-Stuyvesant, at the Nostrand Avenue subway stop. Then Barney and Ntango dropped me at Cortelyou Road and headed to the Bronx.

I don't usually keep things from Pop, but I didn't want to tell him about Eliot and the Jamaica Bay standoff. I've done a lot of things in my life I'm not proud of—some I'm downright ashamed of—nothing like this, though, where I felt a kind of revulsion at myself. I'd stopped to talk to Pop because, while I was pretty sure now that Eliot was the killer we were looking for, some things about how he acted and how he'd said things seemed like they could have been made up, and this caused me to wonder if he might have been, despite his abject fear, protecting someone.

"How powerful is Peter Kelly?" I asked, after he'd gotten us a couple of Pilsner Urquells and I'd told him I now thought Eliot was the killer. He asked why I thought this, but I didn't tell him.

"Kelly rose to the top because he's smart. He's an opportunist, and he's tough. He worked with the left; he worked with the politicians; he worked with the gangsters when he needed to. He built a powerful union, and he's got a lot to lose if things go wrong."

"Is he a gangster?"

"I'd say no."

"Do they control him?"

"Not in their pocket. He uses them. They use him."

"Is he afraid of them?"

"If he isn't, he should be. With crooks like your business agent, he lets them be. In exchange, when he needs them—to fight off a rank-and-file challenge like yours, let's say—they support him."

The question I was getting at was whether the mobsters would kill someone if Kelly asked them to. When I finally got around to asking it, Pop said, "I don't know that it works quite like that. It would depend who it was, what was in it for them, things like that."

"Did Kelly ever kill anyone?"

"Some would say yes. I doubt it myself. This thing you're getting at with the hotel manager and the cop doesn't look like anything Kelly would do."

"You think it was Eliot on his own?"

Pop shrugged his shoulders. "You seem to think so. But I don't know why."

chapter twenty-three

Kevin arrived shortly after this. He'd been at Sunday night basketball practice. I was glad to see him, as always, and hoped he'd be glad to see me, but he didn't seem to care that I was there. Then again, I hadn't gone out of my way to be with him much lately. With a pang of regret, I remembered it was only a couple of days until Christmas and we hadn't done anything together. When he was young, I'd taken him Christmas shopping, to the Bronx Zoo to see the lights, after Thanksgiving to the Pete Seeger holiday concert at Carnegie Hall. Christmas had always been a special time for us, and it seemed to be slipping away, as he seemed to be slipping away.

"Pretty late practice," I said.

He mumbled something and headed toward the bedroom, but I intercepted him. I'd noticed the telltale redness and a kind of wildness to the expression in his eyes. I looked at him carefully and let him go, not wanting to confront him when he was stoned.

"I thought you were going to ask about being an assistant coach," he said as he walked away.

I'd forgotten that, too. Anything I said now would be too lame, as he would say, to bother with.

"How's he been?" I asked Pop.

"He watches the TV, does some homework, spends a lot of time on basketball, doesn't communicate."

"He's been smoking pot."

Pop nodded. "I thought as much. I've told him he's not allowed to. I don't know what else to do. I didn't have much success stopping you, either."

This wasn't an I-told-you-so statement. Pop has too much compassion for that. He thought he'd failed bringing me up, that I'd never fulfilled the potential he'd seen in me as a child nor found the happiness he'd hoped I'd find. Seeing his failure passed on through me to his grandson only brought him pain.

"He's a good boy," I said. "We'll get beyond this."

Pop's expression was unyielding. "Not without a great deal of work on your part."

I tossed and turned on the couch for a long time before I slept that night, watching the streetlight patterns on the living room ceiling, as I did when I was Kevin's age, lying on the couch waiting for dinner or for Pop to come home. I wanted so much for Kevin. Since he was a baby, I'd thought him the most perfect person in the world. His sullenness, his aloofness, the contempt he showed me, all of it was probably no more than being a teenager, but I'd never expected it from him. I'd expected him to be perfect, I realized. The same expectation Pop had had for me—that I'd spent my life trying to live up to without ever making it.

Lying awake that night, I came to understand that I needed to get my son back. To do this, I had to get my life back to normal. I thought about Betsy and Katie also. Betsy needed her life back, too. She needed to be with her kid. I thought more about Betsy and the little one, imagining the possibility of this and that, but I let it go pretty quick.

In the morning, despite an almost sleepless night, I got up with Kevin as he prepared for school. He was sleep-logged and sullen, refusing to eat breakfast and answering my offers to pour him cereal or cook him an egg by shouting "Go away" or "Leave me alone." As he headed out the door, I told him I knew he'd been smoking pot the night before. He denied it. I also told him I'd be at his next practice to talk to his coach about helping out.

"We've already got an assistant coach," he said from the elevator.

"That's okay. I'll be second assistant. I wouldn't be much help anyway."

Kevin rolled his eyes as the elevator door closed. But was that the beginning of a slight smile?

Instead of going back to bed, I went home and got there just in time for an angry phone call from Betsy's lawyer. Peter Finch was so mad, he was sputtering.

"I thought you lawyers had secretaries to make your phone calls for you," I said, hoping a bit of humor might calm him down.

"Cut the shit, McNulty," he said, then continued to browbeat me. Betsy, it seemed, had let the cat out of the bag.

"It's pretty clear to me that Eliot is the killer," I said when the sputtering died down.

"It's nice that it's clear to you, but that doesn't help your friend Betsy. Nor does that cock-and-bull story you guys came up with about this guy Eliot and her husband. The cops saw through it before the words were out of her mouth. I don't know when they're going to charge her, but my guess is they're going to. Now, there are two things wrong. First, she's a suspect who's hiding something about another suspect—that Irish guy. Maybe it has nothing to do with the murders, but I need to know what it is. I don't want any more surprises. Now, on top of that, she pretty obviously made up a story attempting to implicate someone else."

"But Eliot is the killer."

"You suspect Eliot." Peter clearly enunciated the word "suspect." "Unless you have proof, it doesn't mean anything. Why are you so sure it was him?"

I certainly didn't want to tell Peter about our adventure at Jamaica Bay, and I didn't know which pieces of Betsy's story about her husband and Eliot he believed or didn't believe, so I was stumped for an answer. "I just know," I said lamely. "You'll see."

"Good. I'll see. Until then, you better find out for me what Betsy is hiding."

I already knew what she was hiding, or thought I did, but I didn't want to tell Peter. There was also the possibility she was hiding something else I didn't know about.

In the middle of the afternoon, I went to the Savoy. It was as if I needed to be at my job in order to find the normalcy in my life. Lots of places I worked, the bartenders or waitresses, after complaining all week about the job, would invariably show up at some point on their nights off. I was guilty, too. Hotels, bars, and restaurants easily become a center for your life, especially when nothing much else is going on in it. On this afternoon, the joint was dead, and I found Downtown Sam sitting at the bar, drinking a cup of coffee and reading the paper. He looked up once and went back to reading the paper.

I got a cup of coffee and joined him. "Suppose you wanted to prove Eliot killed MacAlister and Tierney. What would you do?"

Sam folded up his newspaper and gave me that hard stare of his. "First thing, I'd lock up you and that Irishman to keep you out of the way while I tried to figure it out."

"You know this detective Sheehan?"

"The cop investigating this?"

"Do you think it would do any good if I told him what we found out, that Eliot confessed to us?"

Sam thought this over. "I don't know, man. You ain't much of a diplomat. He already don't like you, right?"

"We have a grudging respect for each other."

"That ain't what I heard."

I asked Sam what the cops would do if they did believe me and began to investigate Eliot.

"They ask him where he was and check if anyone says he was there. Then they check some other places and see if someone say he was there. Can't be in both places. Know what I'm sayin'? There's other things, physical evidence, witnesses, confessions. They'd check the area again. Maybe someone was taking pictures and caught him in the background, maybe a surveillance video picked him up. Mostly, they'd lean on him, like we did, although there's rules they suppose to play by, and he prob'ly be smart enough to make them do it. So even the cops don't have much without witnesses or some physical evidence."

"How do you know all this stuff?"

"I watch those cop shows on TV."

I looked surprised.

Sam laughed. "I took the detective test before I quit in Charleston. Studied up real good. Got the highest mark." He laughed again mirthlessly. "Good thing I knew how to bartend."

He dropped his coffee cup in a bus basket and went behind the bar. "Nobody we know gives a shit these guys are dead, man. Some folks are better off. What do you care if Eliot walks?"

I told him the police might charge Betsy, and Barney, too, and there were still a couple of goons who knew where I lived. "It would be good if we could find a way to end all this, before I get ended."

Before going back uptown, I walked around the Savoy's neighborhood, following up on Sam's idea that the cops might have overlooked something like a video camera or someone with a hot dog cart who was there the morning MacAlister was killed and saw someone who wasn't supposed to be there, but I didn't find anything worth pursuing. When I got back to the hotel, as luck would have it, I ran into Detective Sergeant Pat Sheehan in the lobby. He saw me before I saw him, or I wouldn't have gone in, but I was in the revolving door and I knew he'd seen me.

"Hey, McNulty. I thought you only came out at night." He waited for me to say something. When I didn't, he said, "Glad you settled the strike. Hope it worked out for you. I wish we could strike."

"Me, too. But you should remember it was a police strike in Boston that brought us Calvin Coolidge."

"You don't say."

"You should read about it. Cops haven't always been on the wrong side." Sheehan made me nervous. I was afraid he'd found out about our adventure with Eliot. "What can I do for you, Sergeant?"

"Help me find your Irish friend. Have you seen him?"

I hate to lie. It's the fault of my upbringing. How do you expect to get anywhere in this world if you don't tell lies? So I gave it my best shot, sure Sheehan could see right through me. I said I hadn't.

"What if I told you we'd had a tail on you for the past few days?"

My jaw dropped. The possibility had never come to mind. If the cops had been following me for two days, I'd be headed for jail. Anyone could have followed me. I wasn't paying attention. "Well," I said with a nervous chuckle, "you wouldn't have to ask me where I'd been."

Sheehan didn't chuckle. "We didn't tail you, but someone did follow your girlfriend to Sheepshead Bay last night. She's smarter than she looks, managed to shake off her shadow. We think she was meeting Saunders."

"Oh?"

"Where were you last night?"

I was ready for this one. "At my father's apartment in Brooklyn."

"You didn't see Saunders or the Tierney woman yesterday?"

"No."

"When did you see her last?"

"I don't remember. Not long ago. We work together. You still think she was involved in her husband's murder?"

"What do you think?"

"I told you. It was the business agent, Tom Eliot."

"That's what she says, too. She told the Six-one detectives her husband had dealings with Eliot. You know anything about that?"

The question came too quickly. I didn't have time to think. "I wish I did," I told him honestly. "Have you questioned Eliot? Where does he say he was when those guys were killed?"

Sheehan took a step back and appraised me carefully. "What do we have here? You really must be thinking about police work as a new career."

I debated telling Sheehan about the goons, which would explain my interest, but I didn't see what he could do about it, and I didn't want cops hanging around my apartment. Instead, I said, "I want you guys to leave Betsy alone. She didn't do anything."

"No protecting the guilty this time around?"

"This may surprise you, Sergeant. I don't like trouble, mine or anyone else's. You made a mistake with Betsy. She has a baby to take care of. Just because her husband was an asshole and she knew it doesn't mean she killed him. Why do you want to pin this on her or someone from the hotel when you got guys out there like Eliot whose lives are based on killing people or scaring them into believing they'll be killed? When someone gets killed, you should look at those assholes who do it for a living and not pick on working people."

Sheehan nodded. "We're working stiffs like you, McNulty. Wearing badges doesn't make us different."

"Something does," I said when I should have kept my mouth shut. "You guys are more like Eliot than you are like us."

What I said registered on Sheehan's face in a way I'd never have expected. For a split second, he looked surprised and hurt, like someone might whose offer of help had been rudely rejected, but he hardened up right away. "Yeah, we take care of all the shit this city has, so good citizens like you don't have to. Maybe some of it rubs off."

"Sorry. I didn't mean anything personal," I said. He didn't care.

I was embarrassed and wanted to get out of there, so I asked if he wanted anything else.

"No. I wasn't looking for you anyway. I came for the French chef."

"Is he still a suspect?"

Sheehan almost smiled, but it came out as something closer to a sneer. "Nope. Everything he told us checked out. He's in the clear. The problem we have is with the bartenders and the waitresses getting their stories mixed up."

"You don't have a problem with Eliot or Pete Kelly?"

Sheehan's eyebrows went up. "The union boss. That's a new one. Maybe we should check the mayor out, too."

It was a mistake bringing up Kelly, and when I tried to fix it I made things worse. "Tierney was working for MacAlister. Eliot took them both out before they got him."

Sheehan reached into his inside pocket for his notebook. He licked the tip of the pen and pretended to begin writing. "Could you give me some times and dates here? Places they were seen together? Names of witnesses? The nature of their business together? A few details to tie up some loose ends?"

"I don't know the details. Maybe you could find out."

Sheehan threw his arms open in front of him. "I get it. You come up with the theories and I do the legwork. Sorry, McNulty, I already got one of those in my life, the captain. What I want from you is a straight answer someday."

I called Ntango's dispatcher to ask for him to come by to drive me to the North Bronx. I didn't know if he'd have anything to do with me after the Jamaica Bay fiasco. He was my conscience about many things, and lately I needed one as much as Pinocchio. Yet show up he did, and he had his OFF DUTY light on.

"Hey, no. That's okay," I said after I climbed aboard. "I'll pay you this time."

"I'm taking the day off, my friend. I enjoy your company—on me."

On the way up, we talked about the night before. Ntango had been in the cab for the argument I'd had with Barney but had caught the drift of it anyway.

"What went on out there in the swamp troubled the Irishman as much as it did you," Ntango said. "He's a man of compassion. I knew men like him in Eritrea. Men like my father and his friends. Loving men caught up in violence, whose hearts and minds are in conflict."

The surprise in the North Bronx was that Barney was no longer employed at the butcher shop and no one in the shop had any idea why he left or where we could find him, no idea they would pass along to me, anyway. No one answered the door at the Donohues' when I knocked, either. I knew Mary wasn't on the schedule, so I figured to wait to see if she might have gone to the store or a neighbor's. Instead, after a few minutes, Barney came out through the door I'd knocked on. He looked around himself carefully—like Otto the cat did each time he went out the window—stepped quickly off the stoop, and headed down the street. When I rolled down the cab window and called his name, he sprang about half a foot off the ground and turned to face me—again reminding me of Otto when he was startled. I half expected him to hiss.

"Nerves wound a little tight, eh, pal?" I said.

Relief spread across Barney's ruddy face, forming itself into wrinkles, smiles, and twinkles. "Bejaysus, you're a hard man, Brian McNulty. You scared the wits out of me."

"If you're in hiding, you're doing a lousy job."

"Aye, 'tis true. A poor job indeed."

It turned out Barney had left his job at the butcher shop when two men in suits showed up looking for him. He didn't know if they were the police or goons, but he didn't take any chances.

" 'Twas you lads knocking on the door then earlier," said Barney. "I'd stopped by for a shave and a shower." Looking around him again, Barney said, "I'd feel a bit safer in a different neighborhood."

Ntango drove us across Gun Hill Road to Kingsbridge, where we found a diner on Broadway under the el across from Van Cortlandt Park. The diner, a true outer-borough greasy spoon, had 150 items on the menu, and all the waitresses were over sixty, limping, hoarse-voiced, and able to carry eleven plates at a time. I ate breakfast again, as did Ntango and Barney.

We speculated on who might have been looking for Barney in the butcher shop, then talked, in hushed voices, about our adventure with Eliot.

"It's as simple as that," said Barney. "We let up on him too soon."

On our fourth or fifth coffees, Barney said we should go back to the hotel and to Betsy's house to search for anything the cops might have missed. I didn't think too highly of the idea, since the cops were professionals and knew where to look for evidence and what evidence looked like when they found it. None of us knew our asses from our elbows about where to look or what to look for.

Surprisingly, Ntango agreed with Barney. "It happens that the police overlook things. They comb an area, find nothing, then a week later or a month or a year later a person stumbles across the missing gun. Snow might have melted, a tree fallen, part of a building was knocked down. It's worth looking."

The police hadn't found the gun. So where was it? Thrown in a garbage can, into the river, down a sewer?

"The police would search the sewers and garbage cans in the area," Ntango said.

"What did Eliot tell you about the gun?" I asked Barney. "Did you ask him?"

Barney shrugged. "He said he threw it away, but he didn't know where. Sure, by then he didn't know what he was saying, he had so many lies mixed up with his truths." He was quiet a moment. "Now, when I think back on it, I believe he was lying. It was nothing resembling a straight answer he gave me, saying one thing and then another. Now, suppose the eejit didn't throw the gun away." His expression was mischievous, almost diabolical. "There's no help for it, lads, we'll have to find out."

This was why that night, a day short of the night before Christmas, two men, one with a bandaged hand, approached the garment-district building that housed the office of the United Barmen and Hotel Workers Local 909, while a third accomplice parked a few doors past the building and kept the motor of a Yellow horse-hire cab running. Barney had borrowed a mailman's uniform from an IRA crony in the Bronx, including the bag, in which he carried gloves for both of us, an assortment of pry bars, screwdrivers, hammers, chisels, a glass-cutting contraption, and God knows what else.

We'd argued a bit, but Barney convinced me that Eliot might very well be dumb enough to have held on to the murder weapon. If I hadn't learned much in my years behind the bar, I did learn that folks are forever doing unbelievably dumb things. Pop told me once that if you took the stupid mistakes of criminals out of the equation, the cops would never arrest anyone.

So there we were, standing in front of the building, trying to look inconspicuous, until we got our chance. Barney waited until he saw someone approaching the door from inside, pretended to ring a bell, and grabbed the door when the other person came out. He waited a few minutes, then opened the door for his partner in crime—me.

The problem would come if there was an alarm to go off when we cut a hole through the frosted glass of the outside door of Eliot's office. Because Barney couldn't use his hands so well, cutting through the glass was my job. The contraption Barney handed me had a suction cup, which, following his directions, I stuck to the window. Then I set a marking on something resembling a ruler and turned a cutting wheel that, after what seemed like a couple of hundred turns, cut a six-inch circle that I was able to punch out of the window while holding on to the suction cup. I took out the circle of glass, reached through the hole, felt around for the lock, and unlocked the door. My heart was pounding like rain beating on a tin roof. I figured someone could hear it from across the street. I knew you could get caught doing a B&E because I had been, and I was up shit's creek if I got caught again. Barney, who would probably face a firing squad for impersonating a mailman, obviously had experience in this line of work and was more confident than I was and more determined to carry it out. Pop always said I was too easily led.

Once we were inside the outer office, the thumping of my heart slowed, but I was still excited. I wouldn't say it was fun, but the rush was there. Barney handed me a pair of fake leather gloves and a flashlight from his mailbag. I was impressed. I wouldn't have thought of all these things—but then I'm not a burglar, am I?

The door to the inner office loomed in front of us. I couldn't wait to see what was in there. Twice I'd been to this office. Both times, Eliot met us in the outer office. Now was my chance to enter the forbidden chamber. I knew how Eve felt when she finally got a shot at that apple. I was about to attach Barney's glass-cutting contraption when I thought to try the doorknob. It turned and the door opened. The place was backlit from windows in the far wall, so I could make out what was in the room. That is, I could have made out what was in the room if there had been anything in it. It was stark empty: four walls, including the one with a couple of windows, a ceiling, and a floor. After gaping for a minute or so, I returned to the job at hand. Barney had already whipped through the place.

It wasn't as if there were a lot of hiding places in the office. Barney rifled through the desk, and I checked out an empty file cabinet and a closet with an overcoat, a suit jacket, and some boxes in it. I was beginning to think we'd screwed up again, and that the next thing would be Barney telling me we had to find Eliot's house and search there.

Instead, he said, "We'd not want to be here any longer than we have to, Brian. I'm afraid we've wasted our time." He straightened his back from where he had stooped to look under the desk and gave the room a once-over. "Did you look over there?" He nodded toward a large rubbery-looking plant in a flowerpot. I went over. It was a three-foot-tall plastic plant in a large black flowerpot. The top of the pot, where the soil would be in a real plant, had a loose, brown plastic covering that was a poor imitation of dirt. When I moved the covering, I felt something hard, so I lifted the covering, and beneath it was a gun—a black revolver with a brown grip and about a four-inch-long barrel.

"Don't touch it," Barney shouted, as he ran toward me.

I cringed. "What kind of gun is it?"

Barney shrugged his shoulders. "It looks enough like a .38 for me to believe it is."

I bent down to look more closely. There were file markings on the barrel and on the grip. "It's a gun all right," I said when I stood up. "Now what?"

"Tip the plant on its side, as if it has been knocked over," said Barney, "and leave the gun fall out on the floor beside it."

I did this, and Barney headed for the door. Before we got into Ntango's cab, Barney had me call 911 from a corner pay phone to say a burglary was in progress at Eliot's office. We waited until a couple of Manhattan South squad cars headed into 31st Street from both directions, no sirens or flashing lights, hoping to grab the crooks in the act.

We hotfooted it back uptown and went to Oscar's for a drink. I wasn't quite sure what we'd accomplished, so Barney explained it to me. The police investigating the robbery would find the gun.

"And then?"

Barney looked perplexed.

Now Ntango began to explain. "When the cops find a gun like that with the serial numbers filed off—that's what you said, right?"

"Something was filed off. I don't know what it was because it wasn't there anymore."

"Nonetheless, the cops look to see if the gun was used in any unsolved murders."

"And if they do that," said Barney, "they'll find that Eliot's gun was used in the murders of MacAlister and Betsy's husband."

I had my doubts, suspecting, as I did, that, for the three of us, our knowledge of police procedures came mainly from reading the *Daily News*.

chapter twenty-four

Barney and I stayed long at the bar that night, as the tension drained off into whiskey glasses. It had been a long time since we really talked, so I was glad for the time together after Ntango left. He was right about Barney. As hardened as he'd seemed the other night, Barney was a sentimental and gentle soul. After a few drinks, memories of his childhood in Ireland began to flow. Usually, it was a specific incident he talked about—fishing in Lough Gowna, a football match, or drinking a few jars of porter in the town of Armagh. This night, remembering what Pat Donohue had told me about the poverty where Barney spent his youth, I asked him about growing up.

"Aragh, it was hard, Brian. Many's the night we had only a pot of potatoes for dinner. My mother died when I was two, so my oldest sister took over the rearing of me and my brothers and sisters. When my father was on the run, she was the only one. Try as hard as she would, we all ran wild. But she was very good to us."

I listened to Barney, with the sense that he was trying in his own way to explain to me the person he was the other night in the wetlands.

"Those were troubled times. Internment began, and the women took to the streets. My sister Maura, the one who was like a mother to me, was one of the first women to join the IRA. She was grand, though a young girl, the fiercest of the brigade and a terror to the British soldiers."

He told me about an incident when he was twelve or thirteen and had been caught with another boy throwing rocks at a passing army jeep. His sister came and took him away from the soldiers who held him at gunpoint.

"She walked up, grabbed me hand, and whisked me away, daring the soldiers to shoot. During the Troubles, she was interned, and from then she was different." His eyes that had grown hard again met mine. "What they did to the women in the prison were unspeakable things, Brian. Maura never spoke a word about what was done to her. It was only years later, after the hunger strikers, when I heard from the other women who'd been interned what had been done to her. She left for America after that, so I was on me own by the time I was fourteen. It was a shame her leaving so, and our family breaking up. But those were the times over there. She had to leave, mind you. She would have been jailed again or murdered had she stayed."

"Where is she now?"

Barney was lost in his memories. "Now?" he said, coming from far away in the past. "Aragh, she's in Chicago with another sister of mine."

"So if things got really bad here, you could go to them."

Barney came back to the present, refocusing his eyes, gazing into mine. "Sure, you're not giving up on us now, Brian?"

I didn't ask Barney about his life during the years after the age of fourteen until he left Ireland himself. In a way, I wanted to know, but in another way, I didn't. Deprivation, misery growing up, tossed out on your own when you're too young to handle it—these things didn't excuse the hardness in him, but they did explain where the hardness came from. They explained, too, what it was that brought him to vomit convulsively on the Jamaica Bay marsh when he thought he might have to kill Eliot.

We heard the next day through Pat Donohue that the cops had picked Eliot up, but that he'd made bail and was back on the street. Then Christmas Day, while I was having turkey dinner with Pop and Kevin at Pop's apartment in Brooklyn, cops from the Sixty-ninth

Precinct found Tom Eliot's body in the trunk of a car parked on a dead-end street in Canarsie, not more than a couple of miles from Pop's apartment and even closer to the spot near Jamaica Bay where Barney, Sam, Ntango, and I had taken him a few nights before. Eliot was identified in the next day's *Daily News* as a labor leader with ties to organized crime.

I was sick when I read about Eliot, knowing, without knowing, that his blood was on my hands. His death cast a pall over my Christmas, which was a low-key affair to begin with—a few hours with Kevin in the morning and early afternoon, until he went to his mother's, then watching the Knicks game on TV with Pop. I couldn't get Eliot out of my mind. What I figured was that my rheumy-eyed benefactor found out Eliot killed the cop and MacAlister without getting the okay. Whatever he'd been going to do to Barney or me, he did to Eliot. Since I'd saved my own hide and probably Barney's, too, I shouldn't feel bad, but I did. Eliot's pasty, gaunt face, the terror in his eyes, and the shit-stained suit pants haunted me. I felt like I'd murdered him, and if Francois's theory of guilt eating away at you until you felt an irresistible need to confess applied to no one else in the world, it applied to me.

At work, the night after Christmas, I imagined the lounge was a funeral parlor, with its understated colors, subdued lighting, and the hushed sounds of the almost empty room. Betsy in her thigh-high cocktail skirt—well, Betsy in her cocktail skirt was a different matter. She'd done something to herself again, and my homing devices picked it up immediately.

"Something's different about you," I said, as she leaned against the service bar tugging at my heart with those sparkling eyes and heaving breasts.

"Something good?" she asked fetchingly, pushing her chest forward against the bar so the curve of the top of her breasts pushed further over the lacy top of her outfit. That was it. Betsy was coyly and innocently flirting with me, something she hadn't done since this nightmare began.

"I'm relieved," Betsy said. "Maybe that's what's different. It's terrible about Mr. Eliot's murder, but the detectives in Gerritsen Beach say he killed Dennis and Mr. MacAlister, that they were wrong to think I had anything to do with Dennis being killed."

The thought of the killings brought back my memory of Eliot and the Jamaica Bay swamp. I wanted to tell Betsy what we'd done, but I couldn't. I couldn't tell her about that or about Barney and me breaking into Eliot's office. I hoped it was over now, that the dead would settle down now into their graves and leave us alone.

"Something's bothering you," Betsy said later that night. She had a few tables, and I'd had a party of five or six at the bar for a couple of hours, then a handful of solitary drinkers as the night progressed. At the end of the night, she sat at the bar watching me clean up and restock. "Do you want to tell me?"

I puttered around, searching my mind for words to say, but couldn't find any. She patted my hand when she handed me my tip and smiled sadly before she left.

Late the next morning, as I headed out to Tom's for breakfast, I found Detective Sergeant Pat Sheehan on my doorstep.

"Just the man I wanted to see," said Sheehan.

"I was afraid of that. I thought you guys solved this one."

"Word travels fast. Who told you?"

"Betsy."

"A load off her mind, I guess."

"So? I was going to breakfast. I'm hungry."

"I'll walk with you," said Sheehan, falling into step beside me. It was warm again. I noticed the Christmas tree guys on the corner had packed up and left without a trace—neat Canadians. "You turn out to be a pretty good detective after all. Maybe I can put in a word for you with the department."

"No thanks. Is the case closed now?"

"One case closes, another one opens. A pretty sleazy guy, this Eliot. I don't think a lot of people will miss him. Still, I wouldn't want to end up in the trunk of a car. Usually no one finds you for a few weeks until the smell leaks out, sometimes not even then. We got a tip. Got a tip about a break-in the other night in his office, too. That's how we found the murder weapon. Turns out the gun the officers find in this guy Eliot's office when they go there on a robbery in progress is a cop gun, and ballistics says it's the gun that killed Tierney and MacAlister."

"How do you know it was a cop's gun?"

"The serial number's filed off. On service revolvers, the badge number is stamped on the stock. On this gun, that's filed off, too. So you wonder where the guy gets a cop gun. There's some around because the department's been switching over to nine-millimeters. So maybe Eliot can find one. But it's easier for your girlfriend to find one in her hubby's arsenal, except there don't seem to be any missing. Still, it makes me wonder that someone leads us right to the murderer and the gun. It doesn't happen like that very often." Sheehan managed, by some power of his will over mine, to make me look at him. His gaze was steady into mine.

I dropped the ball and looked away but caught myself pretty quick. "I've never done much in the way of gangland killings."

Sheehan shook his head. "You seem to like the mean streets, though. How's an almost normal guy like you get mixed up with so many shady characters?"

"Mean streets? Shady characters? You sound like a cheap detective novel."

"Nothin's cheap anymore," said Sheehan. "The thing is, when they picked Eliot up, he said someone planted the gun. The calls make me wonder maybe someone did."

"Planted?" The word caromed through my brain. "What do you mean planted?" I don't know if the color drained from my face or my eyes spun in my head. It felt like it. Someone pulled the plug and my world slipped off its axis. I was sure Sheehan clocked my reaction, even as I tried to recover. "Who would do that?" I got my feet under me again. "After all this, you still don't think it's Eliot?" I let myself get angry, my voice rising. "Even when you got the guy, you want to keep hounding us?" Shouting now, "You know fucking well what happened. That asshole went off on his own and killed a cop and the fucking gangsters killed him because he didn't follow their fucking rules. Case closed. Leave me the fuck alone!" I was shaking, but I stood my ground and glared at Sheehan.

He took it in stride, but he did wax philosophical. "Your nerves are shot, McNulty. Pretty soon, you'll be hiding behind lampposts. No one's after you. As concerns the murders, greater minds than mine will decide if the case is closed. You been a cop as long as I have, sometimes you're not satisfied the way something ends. But you get buried in paperwork. Another case comes along. You put it in the basket with all the other things that gnaw at you. After a while, you don't remember the case. You just get a headache or indigestion, or an ulcer. Then it all ends with a big fucking bang when your heart blows up."

He didn't look to me for sympathy, but I sympathized anyway, despite neither him nor me especially wanting it. I couldn't count the ways I thought he was wrong in how he saw people and how he saw life, with this idea that some people were scum and that explained crime. Somewhere in his blackened heart he knew he was wrong, that pretty much everyone who got themselves in terrible trouble traveled a hard road to get themselves there. Still, at the moment, I felt he was the better man, that he had seen weakness and shame in me and had let it go. But he'd seen it, and I couldn't look him in the eye.

Eliot told us he was the killer, I reminded myself. I found the gun in his office. I didn't put it there. Neither did Barney. Right? How would Barney have a gun to plant?

I might know the answer to that, too, so in the afternoon I went once more to the North Bronx. I wanted to talk to Pat Donohue. I don't know why I needed to find out, why I wouldn't be content to let it gnaw at me, like Sheehan. I guess I was beginning to think I might have been part of something I didn't know I was part of and wouldn't have chosen to be if I had known—that I might have been a sucker.

I didn't know if Pat or Mary would be home, but I figured one of them would be. It turned out they both were. Whatever propelled me forward to find out the truth took away any sense of diplomacy I had. When Pat opened the door, before he'd gotten halfway through his warm Irish welcome, I asked him about his gun.

"A Glock," he said, surprised but still smiling, his hand lightly on my shoulder to usher me into the living room.

"Where's your old one, the .38?"

He stopped smiling. At this moment, Mary came hustling around the corner from the kitchen.

"Brian," she said. "What brings you here? Isn't it grand that the crimes are solved, though it was a terrible end for poor Tom Eliot, God rest his soul?" She didn't give me time to speak. "Is it Barney you're looking for?"

I shook my head. "Maybe it is Barney I need to talk to. I don't know. Some things about what happened trouble me. The gun the cops found in Eliot's office, the gun that killed MacAlister and Tierney, once belonged to a cop because it had the badge number filed off. That's why I want to know where your .38 is."

"It's long gone now, isn't it, Pat? Sure, you don't think Eliot used Pat's gun to do his killing?"

"I don't know what I think. Let me get this straight about the gun. You had a .38. Did you turn it in when they issued you a nine-millimeter?"

Pat looked uncomfortably from his wife to me. "No, I didn't turn it in." He squirmed some more. "For the love of God, Brian, what're you asking me? I sold the gun to some fellows from the Friendly Sons of Ireland to use for target practice."

"Who?"

"Aragh, Brian. Do you know what you're asking?"

The light went on. Both of them nodded, as I caught up to their thinking. What no one would say was that the gun had made its way back to Erin's green isle, into the hands of a rebel lad, who would use it for purposes we'd all be better off not knowing about, certainly a New York City peace officer waiting out the time until his retirement.

I left the Donohues' not much wiser than before I got there and headed for the Old Shillelagh, where Mary said I might find Barney.

Sure enough, he was perched on a bar stool with a pint of Guinness in front of him and a phalanx of pals gathered around him. His bartender radar turned on, he spied me as soon as I came through the door.

"You have the look of a troubled man, Brian McNulty," said Barney. "A jar of stout will have you right in no time." He waved the bartender over, and I ordered a Guinness.

"Can we talk?" I asked after I'd taken a few slugs of my drink and Barney had introduced me to the half-dozen men around him.

We took our pints to a booth against the wall. Beams of sunlight filtered through the smoke-filled space between us and the bar. The odor of stale beer replaced any healthy oxygen the smoke hadn't soaked up. Straight out, I told Barney what troubled me.

"I knew it would, Brian," he said solemnly. "It will eat away at your heart. And God forgive you, if you ever can rest easy when you may have had a hand in what led to another man's death." After a moment to let this sink in, he went to the bar for another round. When he came back, he asked if I thought Sheehan suspected him of planting the gun. I told him I didn't know. He shook his head. "I'd like to go back to work, but I can't risk him inquiring about me papers. Why can't the bugger take Eliot at his word?"

"He didn't hear him. No one did but us. Too bad we couldn't convince Sheehan that you couldn't have done the killing because you were somewhere else."

Barney threw up his hands. "Sure, I was somewhere else. I can prove I didn't kill either of the blackguards. I could have the authority of fifty witnesses as innocent as the saints and angels. But what good would it do? I don't have me papers." His expression was that peculiarly Irish mixture of wistfulness and humor, as when the joke's on us, after all.

"Well, maybe you could try it out on me. Where were you when those guys were killed?"

"Not with a host of angels, but close, Brian, me lad. When I left downtown, I hid out at the Passionist Fathers' retreat house in Riverdale. The Cardinal Spellman Retreat House, Brian. There's dozens who don't even know me would vouch for me being there. I'd have to have been an angel myself to get out and kill those men without being missed. But what good does it do me? Once the coppers begin wondering who I am, me voyage to America is over."

"What would happen if you were sent back to Ireland?"

Barney's face became a mask. "You'd never see me again."

No longer willing to accept anything on faith, I went with Ntango the next morning to the Passionists' Spiritual Center in Riverdale, which also fronts for the Cardinal Spellman Retreat House. Riverdale is not what most folks think of when they picture the Bronx, which as long as we're at it is actually Bronx, like Brooklyn, Manhattan, Queens. It's not the Manhattan or the Brooklyn, and officially it's not the Bronx, either—actually, it's da Bronx. Riverdale is hilly, has lots of old trees with thick trunks, single-family houses among the tony apartment buildings, and its share of mansions.

Ntango found the place with no trouble. "You been here before?" I asked him.

"This is where I brought your friend Barney the night I brought him from Brooklyn."

The retreat house was on a hilly estate with grassy lawns that rolled down to cliffs overlooking the Hudson and the palisades on the Jersey side of the river. The main structure was a three-story redbrick building that looked like a dormitory on the campus of a second-tier public university, but the grounds and view were breathtaking. A plaque on the doorway claimed the establishment provided "retreat programs, spiritual services, hospitality, and welcoming to all God's people, especially the hurting and wounded." You'd have to say Barney knew how to pick 'em.

The priest who answered the door was disappointing, with much more of a businesslike air about him than anything Friar Tuckish. He had the accent of a Bronx native and was initially as distrustful as any native New Yorker and as protective as any Irishman when the long arm of the Crown might be about. I showed him a Polaroid picture of Barney that one of the regulars had given me some time back and asked if he'd ever seen him. After a couple of rounds about who was who and who wanted to know, he owned up that Barney had stayed there, going so far as to find his name in the register and tell me the dates. Thus the door closed on my unfounded suspicions that Barney was a killer. I have to say my weary heart leapt.

chapter twenty-five

My joy, however—as has been my lifelong experience with joy—was short-lived. We went from the retreat house to the Donohues'. Figuring there might be a cop-to-cop thing here, I wanted to see if it might be better if Pat approached Sheehan with this new information on Barney's whereabouts the day MacAlister and Tierney were killed. I hoped if we told Sheehan the truth about Barney's immigration status and the retreat house he would let the illegal immigrant thing go and lay off Barney since he wasn't a murderer.

When we got there, I saw Barney leave the Donohue house and jump into a car-service Lincoln. I didn't know if it was his IRA buddy or not; they were gone before we got close. I wouldn't have thought anything of Barney being there, either, and no bells would have rung later if it hadn't been for one thing.

It took Ntango nearly ten minutes to find a parking space, so by the time we knocked on the door, Mary was leaving herself. She said Pat was working days and would be home around four. Then she asked if I'd seen Barney and how was he. It didn't seem right to tell her I'd just seen him leaving her house, so I didn't. What she said struck me as strange, but I didn't dwell on it, at least not then.

The picture got cloudier that night when I got to work and came upon Sam Jones. His demeanor was more serious than I'd ever seen it. "I got some news you ain't gonna like."

I stopped in my tracks, my coat half on and half off. It was as if I knew what was coming. Not that I knew the facts of anything Sam might tell me, just that I knew some truth was missing from my understanding of things and knew now that that truth was about to come at me.

"You see those Christmas decorations gone from the lobby and the front of the hotel?"

Perplexed for a second by the syntax of Sam's question, I didn't answer.

"You 'member when they got here?"

I didn't.

"The mornin' MacAlister got offed."

"So?" My brain didn't know what was coming, but my body heard danger knocking on the door.

"Jason, the security guy I told you about, remembered they were here. He jacked them up when they came back this morning to take the stuff down. They told him they saw a wild-looking woman come steaming out of the hotel through the service door off the lobby that morning."

My thoughts tumbled over one another, as I tried to catch up with what this meant. I must have known on one level and not known on another—but I felt an intense sense of loss, without knowing what for, just that something was gone for good.

"Those guys didn't know about no murder," Sam said. "They don't want no problems." He looked at me with that practiced look poker players have when they figure out you're bluffing—a not unkind superiority. "Everyone don't read the *Daily News,* you know." I could read sympathy in Sam's eyes, "Jason don't know that it means much, either. It's you and me know it means somethin'."

I stared at him. "You're telling me a woman killed MacAlister?"

"I'm tellin' you what I told you. Those guys ain't lying. What they got to be lyin' for?" Sam watched me stare at him for another minute or so. "You comin' to work or what?"

In a daze, I went to the liquor room, hung up my coat, got on my bar jacket. Sam was ready to leave when I got back to the bar.

"What does it mean?" I asked him, hoping for an explanation other than what was running through my mind.

"What you think it means, brother?" said Sam, cocking his head to one side, his expression somewhere between sympathy and rebuke.

In a daze, I went through the motions of tending bar that night. Neither Mary nor Betsy was on the schedule. I don't remember who was, or whether it was busy or slow. In my mind, I kept replaying all that had happened since the fateful night Mary slapped MacAlister with her cocktail tray and Francois threw his apron on the bar.

The woman coming out of MacAlister's office could have been anyone, I told myself. For sure, it wasn't Betsy, since she was with me. That was the bright side. The dark side, I didn't want to think about. I told myself again it could have been anyone: a jilted lover, an ex-wife, a disgruntled former employee. It didn't have to be someone from the strike—we were disgruntled current employees—but I had a foreboding, and I needed to run down a hunch that I had if I was to have any peace of mind, if I was to get rid of the picture of Eliot and his shit-stained slacks. One thing was clear: If it was a woman who killed MacAlister, it wasn't Eliot who did. His last ride in the trunk of his shiny Cadillac was looking like a case of mistaken identity—another spaldeen down the sewer grate.

The next afternoon, I went up to the North Bronx, the last stop on the D train, and began my trek. New Yorkers say New York is a small town, and that's true, though more accurately it's a series of small towns; that is, we New Yorkers each have our own small town. Bainbridge was Barney's, as it was Pat and Mary Donohue's. In a small town, if you talk to enough neighbors for long enough, you often find out most of what there is to know about somebody. In this case, it wouldn't be the neighbors. It would be the bars I visited and the bartenders and barflies who could tell me what I wanted to know.

I stopped in a few places the first afternoon and picked up a couple of tidbits of information. The most interesting was that Pat Donohue was from Cavan but not Mary. The bartender in the Old Shillelagh himself was from Cavan and knew Pat from home and would have known of Mary had she been from Cavan, too. Asking questions, finding out things, is a slow process. You need to be around when someone has something to tell you. The Irish are a garrulous lot, and if there's one thing the Irish know, as my mother often told me, it's who's related to whom, going back generations and extending outwards to second and third cousins.

If these same charming and talkative folks sense you're prying, or think you might do harm to one of their own, they become closed-mouthed. If, on the other hand, you're a narrowback like myself trying to track down your relations in the auld country, they'll leave no gravestone unturned to help you out. Armed with this knowledge of the ways of the Irish, I wended me way through the exiles in the Bronx, under the guise of tracking down, in preparation for my trip to Ireland, my Cavan relations on me mother's side and me da's relations—forgive me, Pop—from Armagh on the other side.

The bartender at the pub across the street from the Old Shillelagh told me the best source for genealogy for Armagh would be the seamstress at the Irish gift shop on Bainbridge near 204th Street. From her, I found out that Mary Donohue's maiden name was Hughes and that she hailed from Armagh.

"As did Barney," I said.

"Aye," she said. "Barney, of course." She paused to look at me suspiciously.

"And did Mary Hughes sponsor Barney's coming over to America?"

"Aye, she did." But something clicked in her now. I could see the distrust rising. "And your father's people, from where in Armagh were they?"

"I don't know," I said. I hadn't thought that far ahead, and she saw through that.

"You'll have a divil of a time finding yer relations if you don't know the town or a townland or the name of a village." She smelled a rat. I could tell by the way her tone had sharpened and her eyes tried to bore deeper into mine. "And what's your interest in Mary Donohue, now? As generous and kind a woman as you're ever likely to meet."

No answer here was going to be good enough. This lady had figured out I was snooping, and nothing I said was going to dissuade her. I gave it a halfhearted try anyway. "Nothing really. I heard she might be from Armagh and might tell me something about it."

"Sure, and couldn't I tell you all you'd need to know about Armagh?"

"Yep, you sure could. But I'm going to be late for work if I don't get going," said I, backing toward the door.

There may be something about smiling Irish eyes stealing your heart away, but these angry and glaring ones, they'd rip it bloody and shattered right out of your chest. I beat it back to Manhattan with my tail between my legs.

Despite my misstep with the lady from Armagh, I believed I was closing in on what had happened. Mary Donohue called in sick for work that night, and Betsy covered for her. Betsy looked gorgeous as usual, watching me most of the night with those doe eyes of hers. It should have melted my heart, but life had toughened me up again. I wanted to tell her what I was thinking but couldn't bring myself to, not only because I thought it would shock her and cause her unhappiness, but because it would do those things to me, too.

Late in the evening, near closing time, Betsy put her hand on top of mine when I reached across the service bar for a glass. She gathered me up with that sweetness of hers, drawing me in until she had me all wrapped up.

"All this has been so terrible, Brian." Her eyes searched mine. "Last night I woke up before dawn terrified because I felt like I was being strangled."

I patted her hand, remembering our trip to the West Side Market, pushing the stroller along Broadway, the feeling I had then of wanting to be part of something again, and how Betsy, as young as she was, seemed to effortlessly fit herself into my life. Yet I didn't know that I would be right for her, or for anyone. After what had happened, what

I had done, I didn't like myself. I felt damaged, that there was something wrong with me and I would infect her with it.

In the end, after closing, sitting in the dark, we held hands for a moment. We didn't talk much, and nothing felt as sweet as it was supposed to feel. So I sent her home in a car-service cab with a plan to see her and Katie on Sunday. When she left, I walked all the way home up Broadway, watching the cabs streaming back downtown with their dome lights on.

The next afternoon, I sat in the Old Shillelagh with a feeling of dread, waiting for Barney to show up. Earlier, I'd spoken to the bartender, whom I'd met a few times with Barney. We talked about old times, under the guise of my trying to get straight with him when exactly it was that Barney arrived in America and wasn't it that he came over to Mary Donohue's when he arrived.

"I believe you're right," said the bartender.

"From home together, I imagine," I said.

"Home together?" he said. "Sure, I thought they were brother and sister."

The face of the Donohues' younger son, a spitting image of his uncle, rose up in front of me. Sometimes, you don't see the simplest things right in front of your nose.

It wasn't Barney who slid onto the bar stool next to mine. It was Pat Donohue, wearing his uniform. He ordered a Jameson and, without asking, one for me also.

"You've become the talk of the neighborhood," he said after pouring a splash of water into his whiskey, taking a sip, and smacking his lips, "the narrowback with all the questions."

I took a sip of my own whiskey straight. I'd found out and been found out, it seemed. I was nervous.

"More than twenty years a cop," he said, "and it will be soon over. In that time, I never once pulled my gun."

I wondered, without feeling any panic, if he would pull it now and shoot me.

He took another drink of whiskey. "So, and what did you discover with all your questioning, anything strange?" He turned to face me for the first time.

I told him the truth. "I was wrong to think Tom Eliot killed MacAlister and Tierney. Not only was I wrong. I was led astray by folks I trusted."

Pat nodded. "And so you were," he said, and finished off his whiskey.

"Your wife is Barney's oldest sister, watching out for him still, I guess."

"So you know the truth, Brian. My wife murdered two men in cold blood. Still fighting the bloody war in Ireland, still watching over her younger brother. That's all there is to it, as simple as that. The both of them born into a war, not knowing there was another kind of life. Here in America, too. She never let go of it for a minute. Except, thank God, not for the kids. She spared them the hate that was their birthright."

There wasn't much Pat needed to tell me. Everything had fallen into place as soon as I realized that Mary Hughes Donohue was the sister who reared Barney Hughes aka Saunders—one of the first of the Irish women to join the IRA, a fierce protector of her own, not one who would let an unholy alliance of MacAlister and Tierney turn her brother over to the immigration authorities and have him sent back to Northern Ireland to face prison or death.

Pat had the good sense not to ask me what I was going to do now that I knew the truth. We sat together for a couple more shots, the spirits firing my anger and bitterness. He talked of his wife's hard life when she was young, her time in prison, the fear she had for her brother if he was caught. I only half listened. I wanted to be alone. I thought about our torturing Eliot until he was scared for his life, reduced to blubbering, admitting to anything we wanted him to say, not an iota of dignity left. I was disgusted with myself for letting it happen, more than I was ashamed of being fool enough to help Barney plant the gun in his office.

Later that day, I stopped to see Pop on my way to Kevin's basketball practice and told him everything.

"She killed MacAlister because he knew about whatever it was in Barney's past that drove him from Ireland. She killed Tierney because it was he who told MacAlister and was out to get Barney. Knowing this, though I don't know when he came to know it, Barney set up Eliot to protect his sister. He arranged things for me to believe it was Eliot and planted the gun to make sure there was no doubt about it.

"I should have known it was Mary or Barney because of the baby. Mary would know to leave the baby with me. The diapers and new clothes and all of that suggested a mother had taken the baby under her wing."

Pop had seen a lot in his time. Nothing much shocked him. "So that's how it ends," he said. "What's there to do now? You want this Donohue woman arrested. What for? Whatever's eating away at you is probably much worse for her."

"And Barney?"

"What about Barney?"

"He was my friend. He tricked me."

"To protect his sister. You'll have to decide about him yourself down the road."

Basketball practice was great. The coach did need me after all. A cheerful, lighthearted guy, tough as nails with the kids but generous in his dealings with a dad who wanted to coach his son. Once practice got going, I lost my inhibitions. I even made eight of ten of my foul shots teaching shooting drills. The good thing was that in the intensity of the practice I could forget everything else.

Afterward, Kevin told me he'd read about Eliot's murder in the paper. "That was those two guys who were after you who done it. Right?"

"I don't know. It's possible."

"That guy had it coming. Right?"

"I don't know if anyone has it coming. Dying's too final for me to wish it on anyone."

"Better him than you," said Kevin philosophically.

"I'm glad you think so."

———

Betsy and Katie came to visit the next day. Being with them brought me a measure of peace. I could feel Katie's little arms wrapped around my neck long after she let go, and an almost embarrassing rush of joy when she'd reach from her mother's arms toward me and come grab me around the neck again. Betsy turned my kitchen from a place to store beer bottles into a place where meals were made at least for the day. What with Kevin's practice and Betsy's visit, I didn't set foot in a bar for two days, probably the longest stretch since I was sixteen. When I was left alone for any length of time, I did go over in my mind what had happened and what I might have done differently, but something was stirring in me, a kind of contentment I hardly recognized.

When Betsy was making ready to leave, I tried to say something about that contentment and what it might mean. "You can stay, you know," I said finally. "You and Katie, as long as you like." As soon as I saw Betsy's confused and then sympathetic expression I wanted to kick myself.

"Oh, Brian," she said. "That's so sweet of you to take me and Katie in. I should have known you would. But you have your life here. You're so set in your ways, and it would spoil things to change you from what you are. Katie and I are going to be fine, and we'll always be your friends." She must have seen something in my expression, something that slipped through—the reason I never made any money at poker. "You'll be all right, Brian, won't you? You're not sad, are you?" Her lip trembled; her eyes got misty. "You're not going to be lonely without us?"

I caught up with myself then. Shook my head. "I'm fine. You guys are great. You don't need me. I just wanted to offer. You know? I'm fine. I've got my hands full with Kevin." Just then Otto hopped through the window and streaked across the floor. "And the cat."

McNulty's Old Favorites

Have a drink with McNulty.

MARTINI

(A true martini is made with gin [maybe vodka] and vermouth. Those other things with apples or chocolate are cocktails, not martinis.)

> 3 oz. Beefeater gin
> dash of dry vermouth (French)
> olive

Fill a mixing glass with ice cubes, add gin and dash (8–10 drops) of vermouth; stir for 20 to 30 seconds. Pour into a chilled stem glass. Add the olive and a couple of drops of olive juice.

MANHATTAN

> 2 oz. blended whiskey or bourbon
> ¾ oz. red (sweet) vermouth
> dash of bitters (optional)
> maraschino cherry

Combine ingredients with ice in a mixing glass; stir until chilled. Strain into a stem cocktail glass. Garnish with a cherry.

STINGER

1 oz. brandy

1 oz. white crème de menthe

Fill a mixing glass with ice; add liquors. Stir for 20 or 30 seconds. Strain into a cocktail glass.

GIMLET

2 oz. gin (or vodka)

½ oz. Rose's Lime Juice

Fill a mixing glass with ice cubes, add gin and Rose's Lime Juice; stir for 20 to 30 seconds. Pour into a chilled stem glass.

OLD-FASHIONED

2 oz. bourbon or whiskey

cube (or teaspoon) of sugar

dash of Angostura bitters

orange slice

maraschino cherry

Muddle the sugar and bitter in a rocks glass (or old-fashioned glass, if you can find one), add bourbon and ice. Stir. Garnish with a slice of orange and a maraschino cherry.

BLOODY MARY

4 oz. tomato juice

1.5 oz. vodka

2 dashes Worcestershire sauce

1–3 dashes Tabasco

juice of ¼ lemon or lime

dash celery salt

dash salt, pepper

celery stalk

Combine all ingredients in a shaker with ice. (You have to juggle the proportions of ingredients until you find the mixture that suits you.) Shake until chilled.

Strain into a rocks glass or pour over ice in a highball glass (It's a toss-up). Garnish with a celery stalk.

MARGARITA

2 oz. white tequila (gold if you want to show off)
1 oz. Cointreau (triple sec if you're on a tight budget)
1 oz. fresh lime juice
lime wedge

Combine ingredients in a shaker. Shake vigorously for 20 to 30 seconds. Strain into a cocktail glass with a salted rim. (To salt glass, run a lime wedge around the rim of the glass, dip the rim in a bowl of salt.) Garnish with the aforementioned lime wedge.

SHOT OF TEQUILA
(ONE OF MCNULTY'S FAVORITES)

1.5 oz of tequila in shot glass
wedge of lime
salt shaker

Rub the wedge of lime between your thumb and forefinger on the back of either hand. Shake the salt on your lime-flavored hand. Take the lime wedge in your salted hand, and the shot of Tequila in the other. Lick the salt off the back of your hand, and throw down shot. Suck on the lime wedge.

COSMOPOLITAN
(NOT ONE OF MCNULTY'S FAVORITES)

2 oz. vodka
1 oz. Cointreau
½ oz. cranberry juice
½ oz. lemon juice
lemon twist

Combine all liquids in a mixing glass. Add ice and shake until chilled. Strain into a stem glass. Add twist.

DAIQUIRI

1.5 oz. light rum

1 oz. fresh lime juice

1 teaspoon extra fine sugar

Combine ingredients with ice in a shaker. Shake vigorously 20 to 30 seconds. Strain into a cocktail glass.

WHISKEY SOUR

1.5 oz. blended whiskey

juice of ½ lemon

1 teaspoon extra fine sugar

Combine ingredients with ice in a shaker. Shake vigorously 20 to 30 seconds. Pour into a sour glass. Garnish with a slice of orange and a maraschino cherry. (Add ½ oz. of grenadine to make it Ward Eight.)

JACK ROSE

2 oz. applejack

1 oz. lime juice

½ oz. grenadine

Shake with ice and strain into a cocktail glass.

SIDECAR

2 oz. Cognac (or brandy)

1 oz. Cointreau (or triple sec)

1 oz. lemon juice

Coat the rim of a chilled cocktail glass with sugar. Shake the ingredients with cracked ice and strain into the cocktail glass.

BALTIMORE BRACER

1 oz. brandy

1 oz. anisette

1 egg white

Combine ingredients in a shaker with ice. Shake vigorously until chilled. Pour into a cocktail glass.

IRISH DRINKS

IRISH WHISKEY PUNCH
   1.5 oz Irish whiskey
   1 teaspoon of sugar
   2 slices of lemon
   3 or 4 cloves
   6 oz. boiling water

Combine whiskey, sugar, lemon, and cloves in glass with a metal spoon to conduct heat. Pour in boiling water.

IRISH COFFEE
   1 teaspoon sugar
   6 oz. hot black coffee
   1.5 oz. Irish whiskey
   2 tablespoons whipped cream

Combine sugar and enough hot coffee to dissolve the sugar. Add Irish whiskey and stir. Fill the glass to within an inch of the rim, using a metal spoon to conduct heat. Float the whipped cream on top of the coffee. Do not stir. Sip the whiskey-laced coffee through the whipped cream.

SOME BASIC HIGHBALLS (STIRRED DRINKS)

SCOTCH AND SODA (THE CROWN PRINCE OF STIRRED DRINKS)
   1.5 oz. scotch
   6 oz. club soda

Stir with ice in a highball glass.

MRS. MCNULTY'S STANDARD HIGHBALL

1.5 oz blended whiskey
6 oz. ginger ale

Stir with ice in a highball glass.

PRESBYTERIAN

1.5 oz. blended whiskey
3 oz. ginger ale
3 oz. club soda

Stir with ice in a highball glass.

BRANDY AND SODA

1.5 oz. brandy
6 oz. club soda

Stir with ice in a highball glass.

GIN AND TONIC

1.5 oz. gin
6 oz. tonic water

Stir with ice in a highball glass; garnish with a lime wedge.

RUM AND COKE

1.5 oz. rum
6 oz. Coke

Stir with ice in a highball glass.

CUBE LIBRE

Add a wedge of lime to a rum and Coke.

SCREWDRIVER

1.5 oz. vodka
6 oz. orange juice

Stir with ice in a highball glass.

CAPE CODDER
1.5 oz. vodka

6 oz. cranberry juice

Stir with ice in a highball glass.

MADRAS
1.5 oz. vodka

4 oz. cranberry juice

2 oz. orange juice

Stir with ice in a highball glass.

SEA BREEZE
1.5 oz. vodka

4 oz. cranberry juice

2 oz. grapefruit juice

Stir with ice in a highball glass.

SALTY DOG
1.5 oz. gin

5 oz. grapefruit juice.

Salt the rim of a highball glass by rubbing the rim with a wedge of lime and dipping it in bowl of salt. Pour gin and grapefruit juice over ice in the highball glass.

FANCY CREAM DRINKS

PINK LADY
1 oz. gin

1 teaspoon grenadine

1 teaspoon light cream

1 whole egg white

Shake with ice and strain into a cocktail glass.

PINK SQUIRREL

1 oz. crème de noyeaux
1 tablespoon White Creme de Cacao
1 tablespoon Light Cream

Shake with ice and strain into a cocktail glass.

BRANDY ALEXANDER

1 oz. brandy
1 oz. white crème de cacao
1 oz. heavy cream
dash nutmeg

In a shaker half-filled with ice cubes, combine the brandy, crème de cacao, and cream. Shake well. Strain into a cocktail glass and garnish with the nutmeg.

GRASSHOPPER

1 oz. green crème de menthe
1 oz. white crème de cacao
1 oz. light cream

Shake with ice and strain into a cocktail glass.